Discover the gripping thriller that has readers' heads in a spin . . .

'A clever and emotionally charged debut'   Lesley Kara

'Instantly gripping . . . a psychological thriller with real heart and depth'   Lisa Ballantyne

'Bloody hell this book is powerful, tense and a bit terrifying. It had my head spinning'   Laura Pearson

'Gripping and emotionally devastating'   Emma Curtis

'A modern, clever, daring story that grips from the thrilling opening scene to the final page'   Amanda Reynolds

'What a stunning debut this is – chilling, emotional and full of surprises, impossible to put down'   Clare Empson

'An intense psychological thriller full of twists and turns, yet at the same time a convincing and emotional portrait of mother-hood'   Jenny Quintana

'Such a clever, thought-provoking and topical debut. Smith really messes with your head'   Louise Beech

'Gripping and moving and I suggest you order it now!'   Laura Marshall

'A confident exploration of the darkest reaches of motherhood . . . Elegantly written, thoughtful and suspenseful'   Sarah Vaughan

D0995109

Nikki Smith studied English Literature at Birmingham University, before pursuing a career in finance. Following a 'now or never' moment, she applied for a Curtis Brown Creative course where she started writing this book. She lives near Guildford with her family and a cat who thinks she's a dog.

All In Her Head is her debut novel.

ALL IN HER HEAD

Nikki Smith

ORION

An Orion paperback

First published in Great Britain in 2020
by Orion Fiction,
This paperback edition published in 2020
by Orion Fiction,
an imprint of The Orion Publishing Group Ltd.,
Carmelite House, 50 Victoria Embankment
London EC4Y 0DZ

An Hachette UK Company

1 3 5 7 9 10 8 6 4 2

A CIP catalogue record for this book is
available from the British Library.

ISBN (Paperback) 978 1 4091 9299 2

Typeset by Input Data Services Ltd, Somerset

Printed and bound in Great Britain by Clays Ltd, Elcograf S.p.A.

MIX
Paper from
responsible sources
FSC
www.fsc.org   FSC® C104740

www.orionbooks.co.uk

For my daughters, Charlotte and Liberty

With what price we pay for the glory of motherhood.

Isadora Duncan

Prologue

It's much harder to grip the railing than I had expected. The cold metal bites into my hand until I can't tell if it's attached to my body, the last brittle anchor holding me in place. A crowd gathers a short distance away from me on the bridge; some watching through their car windows, others standing with their vehicle doors wide open. A woman points in my direction, her shouts muffled by the noise of the wind. The strands of hair that whip across my face sting my eyes, and I reach up to tuck them behind my ear. A sudden gust nudges me off balance and my stomach lurches, momentarily suspended, before I scrabble to retrieve the iron bar beneath my fingers.

Ripples appear as tiny white flecks on the muddy surface of the river far below me. The two giant towers guarding each end of the bridge look on in anticipation and I draw strength from their solidity. I glance back at the ensemble whose numbers swell as their sense of urgency escalates. I wonder what Jack would say if he was here. What he would do.

I'd watched him this morning as he'd pulled on his trousers

and T-shirt, and had realised I was staring at a complete
stranger. The urge to get up and unpeel his skin to see if I
could reveal something familiar underneath, some evidence
that would prove we were once connected, had been almost
irresistible. He'd walked out of the bedroom without speaking, whilst I'd feigned sleep, my breath trapped under the
edge of the duvet, warm against my chin.

He's been observing my every move, waiting for an opportunity to vent the anger that flows just beneath the surface of
our daily lives. I know he's hiding something from me. He
denies it, but his eyes say he's lying every time we look at
each other. As soon as he left the room, I knew I would do
it. Now I'm standing on the narrow girder, there is no fear.

Someone in the crowd breaks away from the group and
walks slowly towards me, his hands held up in a gesture of
surrender. The noise of wailing sirens grows louder. The
stranger keeps coming, his confidence and pace increasing
as he makes eye contact and smiles nervously. I turn my face
back towards the river and look down. He sees the movement
of my head and cries out. I hear his footsteps speed up as he
tries to reach the barrier that separates us. He won't make it.

I let go of the railing, feeling the pressure of the wind
against my face that offers up a final moment of contemplation. Then the breeze tapers off, as if acknowledging the
decision has already been made, and I step forward into the
silence.

2

Part One

NOW

Alison

The queue edges along the counter at the back of the canteen. Behind it stand the kitchen staff, wiping off beads of sweat with their stained oven gloves as they ladle out spoonfuls of gelatinous food. Everyone rushes to get here early as the choices are limited, even though there are officially two hours for lunch. I want to eat at my desk, but Mrs Painter made it clear that wasn't an option. She doesn't allow food to be consumed in the library. I sit in my usual seat, hoping not to be disturbed, rearranging my spoon so it's exactly equidistant between my pot of yoghurt and my apple.

A shadow falls across my line of vision and I sense someone is staring at me from the other side of the table.

'Mind if I sit here?' I look up but say nothing. 'No objections?' She's persistent. 'I'll take that as a no then.' She pulls the chair out and steps neatly into the gap. 'It's a nightmare trying to find a space today. Looks like the whole building is down here.' My shoulders tense as her tray clatters onto the table. 'You'd think they'd set specific times for different floors so that this wouldn't happen. It's the third time this week I've had problems finding somewhere to sit.' She smiles. 'I'm Sarah.'

I chew on a mouthful as the silence wraps itself slowly round my throat, then swallow, forcing myself to respond. 'I'm Alison.'

'Right.' She pulls her chair tightly underneath her whilst tucking a wayward strand of dark hair behind her ear. 'How's the sandwich, Alison? Normally I go for the salad, but there wasn't any left.'

I glance at the dry pieces of white bread, spread with the thinnest layer of tuna mayonnaise. 'It's OK.' Her face is familiar. 'Have we met before?' I ask the question, watching as she bites into the bread and tears off a mouthful, leaving smears of grease shining on the skin around her red lipstick. I reach for a napkin, then change my mind as she takes a tissue out of her pocket.

'I get that a lot. I must have one of those faces.' She grins and gestures at the packaging on her tray, adding, 'These are really grim.'

I smile briefly in tacit agreement. 'D'you work here?' I'm sure I recognise her, but I know that doesn't mean anything; I'm often sure of things that turn out to be wrong. I'd been sure about Jack.

She nods and points at the ceiling with one finger. 'Upstairs. You?'

'First floor. In the library. Have you been in recently?' I'm trying to remember where I've seen her before.

She takes a large gulp of coffee and makes a face. 'Ouch. Too hot. Not recently. My office is up on the fourth. I don't get much time for reading. At the moment I barely get enough time to eat lunch.' She checks her watch. 'I need to go. I'll take this with me. It'll take forever to cool down.' As she grips the cup, I notice her nails are perfectly manicured, painted in a dark red colour. I move my hands off the table onto my lap. I've tried to stop biting mine, but the tips are barely visible, tiny slivers of white on top of raw skin. She stands up and attempts to grab the crumpled tissue as it floats off her tray onto the floor. 'Maybe see you here tomorrow?' She bends down to retrieve it and walks off.

I glance at the clock, wondering why she'd sat down at all. Officially, I have ten more minutes of my lunch break, but Mrs Painter doesn't tolerate lateness. It's one of the many things that irritate her. She's always punctual and she insists on everyone else living up to the same standard. I need to get back.

Edging past the tables full of diners, I tip the remnants of my sandwich in the bin and walk towards the heavy doors leading out of the canteen. The air in the corridor is cooler, untainted by the smell of fried food, and the reception area is empty apart from the few staff who stand chatting behind the main entrance desk. They glance at me, but I hurry past them, ignoring the lift, through the doors that lead into the stairwell. Sliding my hand over the polished wooden hand-rail, I head up the stairs to the rear entrance of the library.

There are a few of us who work here, but most days we're on different shifts, apart from Mrs Painter, who's here all the time. I sometimes wonder if she's ever done anything else, or whether she's dedicated her entire life to keeping the books she looks after in some kind of order.

'You finished already, Alison?' She emerges from underneath her desk, pulling out a small bag. I nod. We're pleasant enough to each other during the day, but there's an unspoken boundary in our relationship. She's Mrs Painter to me, never Julia, although she always insists on calling me Alison. 'I'll take my break now then.' She doesn't mind if I go down to the canteen first as she always brings in her own packed lunch.

She heads towards the lift and I wait until the doors close before walking across the library floor to watch through the windows as she appears outside. She sits alone on one of the wooden benches, carefully opening her cling-film-wrapped sandwiches before brushing the errant crumbs off her skirt. She can't see me, but I recognise the loneliness she tries to hide beneath a familiar routine; taking the same Tupperware box out of her bag each day, nodding briefly at other staff who walk past, allowing herself to hope they might stop to chat.

I've never met her husband – I wonder whether he sees a side of her that she doesn't show when she's here. Or perhaps she's one of those people who always looks ill at ease wherever she is, as if she's constantly expecting the worst to happen. Even when she's sitting at her desk, she's always clicking her biro or twisting her glasses chain to keep her hands occupied. I remember being like that after I found out what Jack had done. Picking at the fringe of the blanket on our sofa until I'd made small holes along the edge. And then he'd tried to pretend that everything was normal, and the holes had got bigger, spreading out from the material into our lives in the questions I hadn't wanted to ask.

I walk over to Mrs Painter's office while she's out. She likes to call it an office, but it's really a desk and chair near the counter that forms the main entrance to the library. Sitting in her seat, I can see straight down the rows of bookshelves, past the cluster of tables where visitors are allowed to sit, all the way through to the double-glazed windows that are always shut at the back of the building. As the library is air-conditioned, there's no reason for them to actually open, but I suspect they might be fake, like those decorative drapes that resemble proper curtains until you try to draw them.

Someone presses the bell on the counter to get my attention and I wander over, recognising the man from the canteen. He'd been sitting on the table behind me, his green top a splash of colour amongst all the black and grey. He stares at me with a blank expression, his fingers tapping impatiently on the plastic cover of a book. I reach out to take it and Mrs Painter appears at my shoulder, slightly out of breath, still holding her bag, her Tupperware lunch box poking out of the top. She puts her hand on my arm.

'I'll deal with this, Alison.' She glances at the book cover, then back at the man standing in front of me, before taking the paperback and asking him to follow her. His gaze doesn't leave my face as she walks towards her office. Checking to see that I'm still watching him, he opens his mouth to reveal a chipped front tooth and runs his tongue over his lips in a slow circle before reaching down and stroking his crotch. My cheeks burn. He grins, revelling in my evident discomfort, and strolls after her. I don't respond as the next person in the queue smiles and holds out their book to be scanned, fearful of encouraging a similar reaction. My face is hot and I'm worried everyone can see my embarrassment. I want to rewind the last five minutes and replay them slowly so I can turn away at an appropriate moment, walking off before he has a chance to see my reaction. I hate the fact I've let his pathetic gesture disturb me, but the crudeness of it has lodged under my skin, like a stone in the bottom of my shoe that I can't get rid of.

Mrs Painter stares over the top of her glasses as the man heads empty-handed out of the library. 'There's always one, isn't there?' she says.

I nod, unsure whether she witnessed his gesture, or whether she's referring to something completely different. She runs her hands over the front of her skirt, smoothing out the imaginary creases to help hide her anxiety. I wish that trick worked for me. We've got more in common than she realises, despite her authoritarian manner that makes it impossible to cultivate a proper friendship.

Last month she'd called round uninvited to my flat one evening after I hadn't been to work for a week. I'd opened the door a couple of inches and had glanced at her through the crack until she'd been forced to ask if she could come in. I hadn't felt that I could refuse and had watched as she'd stared a little too long at the blank white walls and spotless surfaces.

'I don't like mess,' I'd told her, wiping a mark off the counter with a tea towel.

'I can see that.' Mrs Painter had stepped forward awkwardly and for a moment I'd thought she was going to hug me, but at the last second she'd hesitated and instead handed me a small bunch of pink carnations tied with an elastic band. My dad had used to buy me the same flowers on my birthday; they seemed to appeal to people of a certain age. I'd always found the fragility of their small feathery petals disturbing.

They reminded me of scrunched-up tissues with an unpleasant peppery scent, but I'd never had the heart to tell him as I'd loved the fact that he had made the effort to remember. I hadn't told Mrs Painter either. She'd sat on a chair in my kitchen and sipped the water I had given her.

'I was worried about you,' she'd said, 'but you seem to be a bit better. There's been a few nasty bugs going around at work. I'm sure I'm coming down with something.' She'd reached for a handkerchief out of her bag and dabbed her nose. I'd been sure she had only been visiting me so that she could pry into the life I didn't share with her at work. 'When do you think you'll be back in?' I'd known she wouldn't be able to resist asking the question.

'Hopefully in a couple of days.'

She had pushed her glasses down her nose and I'd waited for her to vocalise her disapproval, but she'd leaned across, patted my hand and had begun to tell me something about the library scanner playing up. I hadn't focused on the exact details; I'd been too busy resisting the urge to get some kitchen roll to mop up the ring of water her cup had left on the table.

A buzzer sounds in the library to mark the end of my shift which interrupts my thoughts and I pick up my bag. 'I'm off now,' I tell her.

She glances up from some paperwork. 'OK. See you tomorrow, Alison.'

It's a short walk home to my flat and I spot the letter lying on the floor as soon as I step over the threshold. It's a piece of paper which I drop in alarm as soon as I turn it over and see his familiar scrawl twisting its way across the page. The floor swims in and out of focus. I'm not sure how long I stand there, not daring to move. I half expect him to appear, but the corridor remains deserted and the silence echoes around me, waiting in expectation. It can't be from him. He wouldn't write to me. Not after what he's done.

I pull at a loose thread on the cuff of my cardigan, watching it unravel as I wait for the wave of panic to recede. I glance at the floor. It's still lying there, one corner curled over as if it's already been read. I was hoping I'd imagined it. I force myself to breathe more slowly, winding the blue thread round my fingers as I count to ten, pulling it tight until the tips bulge dark purple and the thin white line below the cotton matches the colour of the paper on the floor. I wait until the tingling is unbearable before I loosen it.

Bending down to touch the carpet, the stiff fibres reassuringly unyielding beneath my hands, I pick up the letter, pushing the door shut behind me.

> *Ali,*
> *I'm not sure I should be writing to you. I know I'm not allowed to see you, and apparently, I have to respect that decision.*
> *Twelve years has got to be worth something, hasn't it? You were such a big part of my life, I need to see if we can find some sort of closure. I'm sorry for hurting you and wish I could turn the clock back.*
> *Jack*

I read it twice, then crumple the paper up into a small ball and drop it in the bin. My hands are ice-cold as I trace over the scar on my wrist, still livid after a year. How has he found me? I shiver. Anyone searching for me would find that Alison Reynolds has disappeared. The library pass hanging round my neck confirms it: Alison Reid. It's typed in bold black letters underneath my photo. Jack wouldn't recognise me now; I've changed so much since I last saw him. I'm at least a stone heavier and the lines between my eyebrows at the top of my nose have deepened into furrows. My blonde hair has been cut into a short bob and without any of its former highlights, has morphed into a dull brown colour.

I retrieve the letter from the bin and smooth it out. He said he's sorry. Is he? Jack is never sorry. He doesn't do regret. Even when he'd torn us apart, he'd pretended he had nothing to apologise for. That everything could continue as normal. I stare at the piece of paper before ripping it into narrow strips. I shred the strips into smaller squares until the pieces are too tiny and damp to get hold of properly. When I'm done, I throw everything down the toilet, the white fragments floating on the surface like tiny islands. I press the flush again and again, twisting a piece of my hair round and round into ringlets whilst waiting for the cistern to refill, until the water is finally clear. I'm not sure what to do with the clump of brown strands I find myself holding, so I wrap them in toilet roll and stick them in the bin. I crawl into the safety of my bed, not bothering to undress, and pull the duvet around me in an effort to thaw the chill in my stomach that feels like I've swallowed a mouthful of ice cubes.

The occasional noise from a neighbouring flat makes me jump as I lie awake in the dark. I tell myself that he wouldn't break in, he's not that stupid, but there's a nagging uncertainty that keeps me awake long after any sound has ceased, a suspicion that I'm not alone in the silence.

I'd been sitting next to him in the back of a taxi as he'd slid his hand over mine, his fingers between my own, looking as if they'd been tailored specially to fit. He had been sticky with sweat from the cheap plastic upholstery, heated to an almost painful temperature by the glare of the sun. The car had stopped and I'd moved to open the door, peeling the back of my legs slowly off the seat, but he hadn't let me go.

'You know how much I love you, don't you?' he'd whispered, his brown eyes searching for reciprocation.

I'd kissed him and then turned away, pulling on the door handle. He hadn't taken his eyes off me as he'd leaned forward to pay the driver and my skin had burned beneath his gaze.

I don't want to remember and turn the television on to try and drown out my thoughts, finally nodding off as the canned laughter of a late-night comedy programme distorts itself into whispers that skitter in and out of my dreams.

In the morning, I ignore the one tiny piece of paper that circles round the toilet bowl and take a different route to work to vary my usual routine. There's still no sign of him, and apart from a barely noticeable bald patch in the hair by my ear, everything seems completely normal.

'Ah, there you are. I thought you'd be here earlier.' Mrs Painter catches me as I head towards the library counter. 'Take these, please.' She hands me a sheaf of papers. 'You know the code to open the door. And here's the key card for the copier. I need twenty-five copies. Stapled.' She peers over her glasses to remind me of the last time I'd forgotten this important instruction. The implied accusation makes me

blush with embarrassment. I know she thinks I'm incompetent. I hadn't forgotten the task – I just hadn't known how to
get the copier to do what I wanted and had been too scared
to go back to reception to ask her. She'd made me finish the
job by hand and I'd struggled to staple the thick wodges of
paper together, my palm aching by the time I reached the
bottom of the pile.

I let myself into the small room at the rear of the library and
watch as the warm light of the copier beams in front of me;
searching from left to right like an extra-terrestrial spaceship.
The monotony of the task makes me tired, my eyes growing
heavier until I'm startled by the door slamming shut. I gather
up the stapled piles of paper the machine has neatly spat out
and edge around in the tiny space to reach the door handle.
It doesn't move. I try again. The silver knob doesn't budge.
Resting the stack of copies on the lid of the machine, I turn
it with both hands. Still nothing.

My heart rate begins to quicken and I take a deep breath.
The handle won't turn because the code needs to be punched
into the keypad on the outside of the door to open it. Not
everyone here has the code to get in; Mrs Painter has re-
stricted access to a privileged few. The photocopier is, as we
have been informed on more than one occasion, *expensive
equipment, and should not be used in a frivolous manner.* I reassure
myself the handle isn't broken. I need to stay calm and someone will get me out. I knock hesitantly on the door. Mrs
Painter may be just outside. She may have even heard it shut.

But then the room plunges into darkness. I step backwards,
knocking my elbow on the copier. Any self-consciousness
vanishes into the blackness. My back presses against the

machine and I look behind me to where I can make out the faint lights of the control panel. This time, I bang the door in a frenzied panic. The lights come back on. They respond to movement. Thank God.

A couple of drops of perspiration slide down my face and I wipe them off with the sleeve of my jumper and bang again. Both fists this time. Hard thumps. 'Mrs Painter?' My voice is high-pitched. I clear my throat and shout. 'Mrs Painter?' My knuckles smart from the impact against the hard wood. 'Mrs Painter? It's Alison. Can you hear me?' I pause, listening for any sound outside. The lights go off again. They must be on a sensor. I wave my hands around until the bulbs flash back on. This time I kick the door and it jolts with the force. 'MISS-ES-PAIN-TER?' I shout her name, pressing my ear to the wood, but all I can hear is the sound of my ragged breathing. I cough. There's a smell of chemicals that reminds me of petrol. It must be the toner. It makes me feel dizzy as I listen in vain for any sound of her footsteps.

She sent me to do a job, and she's fastidious with time-keeping. I need to be logical. She'll notice I'm not back in ten . . . fifteen minutes at the most, and come looking for me. It's the only copier in the library, so she knows where I am. I shut my eyes, trying to imagine the room is bigger than it actually is. That the walls aren't closing in around me, pushing out all the air until there's no oxygen left. Panic wraps itself round my throat. I'm trapped. In this tiny space. My desperation bubbles up into a scream, but no sound comes out when I open my mouth. I force myself to breathe slowly, counting in for four and out for six, focusing on the out breath until my thoughts separate into something coherent, rather than a blast of noise that's so painful I realise I've been pressing both sides of my head to keep it from splitting apart.

The lights go off again and I feel something warm against my ear. Someone's breath. My skin prickles, as if someone has run their fingers down the back of my neck.

'Relax, Ali, I'm here.' His voice. He's sitting next to me.

I gasp and scrabble backwards away from him until I'm pushed up against the opposite wall of the cupboard. I kick out in a futile effort to stop him getting hold of me, but despite my flailing, I don't encounter anything solid other than the side of the copier. Where's he gone? Why haven't the lights come back on?

'Jack?' I reach out into the blackness, clutching at shadows. Brightness illuminates the room and extinguishes the visions. There is nothing there. No Jack. Nobody. I pull desperately at the silver door handle. 'Can someone help me? Please?' I twist my hair with one hand as I sink to the floor, pressing my palm against the door with the other in a futile attempt to reach what's on the other side. I have to get out.

There's a sharp click. The door swings open, knocking against my foot on its arc, followed by a rush of cool air that cuts straight through the sticky atmosphere.

'Alison?' Mrs Painter's face appears. 'What are you doing on the floor? Get up, dear. Give me those.' She points at the stack of copies lying on the machine. I pick up the ones that have fallen by my feet.

'I think . . . I must . . . the door . . . locked myself in by mistake.' The words come out garbled, my ability to speak coherently wiped out by my overwhelming relief.

'Yes, I can see that.' She's annoyed. 'You know I always

say to make sure you put the wedge under the door before you start copying. Firstly, so you *don't* lock yourself in and, secondly, so you don't get overwhelmed by the fumes. That toner can be quite potent in a small space.' She chivvies me to my feet and out of the tiny room. 'I have told you about that before. Do try to listen more carefully.' She pauses as she notices I'm finding it difficult to catch my breath. 'Are you all right?' she asks in a kinder tone. I nod. 'Have you got the copier card?' I hand it to her with sweaty fingers. 'Good.' She attempts to wipe it discreetly on her jacket before shuffling the papers into a neat pile, sniffing in what sounds like disapproval, as she thumbs through them. 'At least you managed to finish.' She checks her watch. 'We're supposed to be in a meeting in a minute. We need to get a move on.'

I follow her back to the counter, the heat of my humiliation failing to melt her frosty demeanour that's still evident despite her brief attempt to be sympathetic. She'll make a note of this to use against me in the future. She already thinks I can't do this job.

I run my hand over the spines of the books, their solidness acting as a comfort to give me something to hold onto as we walk past the shelves and try to ignore the feeling that someone is walking beside me, their invisible fingers tapping my arm in an effort to get my attention.

THEN

Jack

I wash down a couple of ibuprofen with a large glass of water as I read through the letter again, then fold it up carefully and put it in the bag with my laptop. I can't remember how many times I've pored over the words since it arrived three days ago, but each time it's been harder to swallow the resentment that sits like a stone in the bottom of my stomach. The legal jargon has been written deliberately to provoke me. I'd been tempted to rip it up in disgust, but after a weekend of thinking about little else, I'm calmer. I've planned what I'm going to do and it only requires a few adjustments to my usual routine.

Before I went to bed, I'd packed a change of clothes in my sports holdall and put it in the hall, ready. Picking it up with my bag and travel mug full of coffee, I shut the front door of the flat and walk down the communal corridor to let myself out of the block. Throwing the holdall in the boot of my car that I've parked next to the black iron railings surrounding the front of the building, I slot my coffee into the cup holder. Normally I catch the bus, but if I'm going to make it from my office to where she works before she finishes for the day, I need to drive.

The rush-hour traffic slows the car to a crawl as soon as I pull out onto the main road and it takes longer than I expect before the symmetry of red-and-cream-brick Georgian buildings gives way to modern high-rise office blocks with their smooth, stark concrete and anonymous entrances. I'm worried that I haven't left enough time and the constant stop-start motion makes me feel nauseous. The caffeine kicks in after a few mouthfuls and stops my hands trembling as they grip the steering wheel, but in hindsight I wish I hadn't opened that last bottle. I rely on it to get to sleep, but it doesn't stop the nightmares and my hangovers are worse than ever. I should really cut down. Starting today.

I consider whether there's any possibility I've misunderstood what was written in the letter; I'm sure I haven't. The tone was deliberately official, not open to interpretation. I want to read it again but need to concentrate on driving. I've memorised most of it and can't get phrases like 'issues of confidentiality' out of my head. I don't understand how she can do this. I'm still her husband, for God's sake.

I take a deep breath. Stick to the plan. It's futile to waste valuable energy getting angry. I'll save that for when I see her. I flick off the air vents more roughly than necessary, the exhaust fumes from the vehicle in front are making my headache worse.

The traffic doesn't ease for the entire journey and by the time I arrive, my leg aches from constantly pressing the clutch. I've pre-booked a car-parking space in the NCP nearest to where I work at Butler Reynolds as the ones in our company basement are reserved solely for client use. Lowering my window, I pull a ticket out of the machine at the entrance and hold it between my teeth, one hand on the steering wheel, the other fumbling for the button to shut the window as I drive up the ramps to the fifth floor. A woman gets out of her car and I slam on my brakes. It's her. I hold my breath. She flicks her blonde hair out of her face as she opens her boot and, in the elation of seeing her, I stall the engine. I'm about to open my door when she turns and looks at me, smiling, as she shakes her head. She thinks I'm waiting for her space.

It's not Ali. The air in my lungs escapes in a loud rush with the realisation. Her coat is similar to the blue one she used to wear, but her face is completely different. Older. The disappointment hits me as hard as if I'd slammed myself against the windscreen and I restart the car, an acrid taste in my mouth as I drive up to the next floor.

I tell myself that nothing has changed even though it feels like it has. Believing that I've seen her, even for an instant, makes me miss her even more than I did before. I've become accustomed to the dull ache that's replaced her as an ever-constant companion, but the agony of the piercing disappointment that follows brief moments of hope is almost unbearable.

As I park up, my mobile rings and I glance at the number, letting it go to voicemail. My mum. I only spoke to her last night. I shouldn't have told her about the letter. I knew she'd worry.

The lift in the NCP is out of order, so I walk down to the ground floor, taking two concrete steps at a time to avoid a puddle that smells suspiciously of ammonia. Once I'm out onto the street, it's a short walk to my office building. Three minutes at the most. I should be able to do the whole journey later this afternoon in under an hour and that includes stopping to change out of my suit. Of the ones I own, it had been her favourite. We'd bought it together a couple of years ago in John Lewis and I'd taken so long in the changing rooms trying it on that she'd insisted I took her for lunch afterwards. We'd found a space in the corner where we could fit all our carrier bags full of shopping and I'd leant over the table to kiss her, the taste of the coffee she'd drunk at breakfast still on her lips.

I smile at the girl behind reception and hold my pass over the barrier. It beeps and the three metal prongs on the turnstile revolve to let me in. The marble decor and bank of lifts have been designed specifically to impress clients. They don't get to see the floors like mine which don't have any meeting rooms and aren't nearly as lavish.

I shut the door of my office and open up my laptop. Taking the letter out, I unfold it and dial the phone number shown under the address. There's a standard recorded message advising I'm in a queue and I press a variety of buttons in an effort to get through to a real person. Finally, a voice answers.

'Ms Henderson's office, can I help you?'

I clear my throat. 'I hope so. Is she in today?'

There's a pause. 'Yes, she is. Would you like me to put you through?'

I hang up and google her name, along with the one on the letterhead, clicking on the small photo of her next to her contact details. She looks about the same age as me, her dark hair cut sharply in a bob, framing her face. Pretty. Not what I'd expected. I jump as there's a sharp knock on the door and Harry walks in.

'Hi, Jack. Good weekend?'

I nod and minimise the browser on my computer, sliding the letter off my desk onto my lap. 'Not too bad,' I reply.

'I've come to ask if you've got those figures for Marley Brown's?'

I point at the blank screen on my laptop, which he can't see. 'I'm just finishing them off now. I'll bring them through when I'm done.'

'Thanks. They've asked to meet us on Thursday, so it would be good to run through them this morning. I'm sure they're going to need to shut at least one of their branches, but we might be able to suggest options to redeploy some of the staff.' He hesitates before adding, 'And Em wanted me to check we're still on for dinner at yours on Friday? I forgot to ask when we saw you yesterday. Too busy trying to make sure Jessica didn't destroy your flat.'

I'd forgotten I'd invited them. The three of us had kept in touch after we left University but since Harry and Em moved into a flat a few roads away, we've seen each other more regularly. 'Sure. Looking forward to it.' I think quickly. 'Any time after seven?'

'Sounds great.' Harry hesitates. 'Em's been a bit quiet since you came to ours last week.' He glances at the door to check no one's listening. 'Between you and me, I think we got a bit raucous. She was definitely less than impressed the next day.' He grimaces. 'Wasn't happy with me at all.'

My stomach clenches. Most of that night is a blur after we'd sat down to eat, but I have a vague recollection of Em staring at me, a look of confusion on her face. I can't remember what I'd said to her.

Harry continues, oblivious to my anxiety. 'So, to avoid my wife not speaking to me again, I'd better be on my best behaviour. It'll be good to catch up though. We've got a sitter for the kids, so we might be able to have an uninterrupted conversation for once. Providing Jess manages to sleep. She was a nightmare last night. Sometimes makes me wonder . . .' He pauses and his cheeks flush. 'Sorry.'

I cut across him. 'It's fine.' I look back at my screen. 'Once I'm done with this, I'll let you know.'

He pulls the door shut on his way out and I put the letter back into my bag. I promise myself that I won't look at it again until I leave the office. I need to focus.

I push all thoughts of Ali out of my head as I open up the spreadsheet that Harry has been talking about and finish the budget. It takes longer than I'd expected as I can't resist switching screens and enlarging the photo of the woman's face to study her more closely. She's smiling, but it's professional; only for the camera. She must have had it taken at work; the stark white background has drained the colour out of her already pale face. Large diamond studs sit neatly in her ears. I bet they're real. In a few hours I'll be able to ask her in person.

I print off the page of figures and take it into Harry's office, where we discuss each item until the numbers swim into meaningless shapes. My head starts to throb. I could really do with a coffee. Harry notices me stifle a yawn.

'Fancy getting something to eat?' he suggests.

I nod. 'That would be great.'

We head out of the office towards the nearest sandwich shop, past a couple of restaurants and a bar whose sizeable glass frontage reveals several empty tables with wooden stools turned upside down on their polished surfaces, balancing precariously. I deliberately turn my head to look in the opposite direction, a shudder running down my back. We'd met in there. I'm reminded of it every time I walk past. How I'd debated whether to turn up at all. I tell myself that if I could go back to that afternoon, I wouldn't give in so easily, but I know I'm lying. I wouldn't be able to help myself. I'd just be more careful to make sure she didn't find out.

Harry offers to pay as I sit down in a café a couple of doors further along the street with a latte and a bottle of water. I hadn't realised how thirsty I was.

'Heavy night?' Harry raises his eyebrows.

I avoid his gaze. 'Not particularly.'

He tilts his head a fraction, as if disagreeing with me without wanting to say so. I remember that look. He stares as my hand trembles when I lift up the bottle but doesn't comment and looks away as I finish the last few drops. I concentrate as I put it down on the table, gripping it more tightly than necessary. I know what he's thinking, I used to think the same thing when I'd watched one of our old clients as he'd offered us a glass of whisky from the almost empty bottle in the bottom drawer in his office. It's impossible to stop your body betraying itself with tiny tell-tale movements.

'I've got to leave a bit earlier tonight,' I say as he bites into his sandwich. 'I've got a doctor's appointment.'

He looks at me. 'Everything OK?'

I nod. 'Yes, just some routine tests.' I don't elaborate.

★

I glance at the clock on the wall of my office throughout the afternoon, willing the hands to move round more quickly. I break the earlier promise I made to myself and read the letter again, my jaw clenched. Nearest Relative. *I'm* her nearest relative. How is she allowed to disregard that on a whim? I comfort myself with the knowledge that it's impossible for our relationship to be defined in two words. We were so much more than that. I remember her meeting my mother for the first time and how she was able to think of all the right things to say to cover the awkward silences, leaving the conversation to flow, seemingly with no effort. I'd envied the way she'd been able to get my mum to open up and talk about my childhood – snippets of forgotten memories that had lit up like tiny stars amongst the expanse of darkness I remembered. I had felt tearful with gratitude.

When Mum had nipped to the ladies, I'd leaned across the table and taken one of Ali's hands, squeezing it wordlessly between my own, unable to vocalise how much the evening had meant to me. She'd smiled as I'd told her she was mine, repeating the words in my head after I'd said them out loud to make myself believe them. I'd signalled for the bill, wondering whether there was a way I could somehow preserve forever how I felt about her at that moment.

I stuff the letter back into my bag as soon as the alarm I've set on my phone as a reminder goes off. Logging off my laptop, I walk out of the office. I don't tell Harry I'm leaving as I know how much work there is still do on the Marley Brown's account, but if I don't go now, I might miss her.

According to Google Maps, it's ten miles away and should take twenty-three minutes. I'll easily make it by five. I've planned to stop at the Royal Oak, which doesn't take me far off my route and is the kind of pub where it's unlikely I'll bump into anyone I know. Parking isn't a problem as there are plenty of spaces fifty yards away down the road next to an area of grass which has a playground in its centre. Ignoring the squeals of delight coming from small children being pushed on the swings, I open the boot and take out my holdall.

Three stone flowerbeds have been built next to the patch of grass, I presume in an effort to brighten the place up. Two contain nothing but soil and the flowers in the other are dead, their wispy brown stalks hanging stiffly over the edge. I walk towards the pub past a warehouse, its dark metal shutters are pulled down over the windows, all sprayed with the same white graffiti tag. A couple of empty cigarette packets litter the gutter.

Edging past the group of teenagers with their bikes who are leaning against the fence that runs alongside the warehouse, I glance back across the road at the families in the playground. A father grips the roundabout and spins his daughter round, her small hands clinging on for dear life. Another childhood experience that I missed out on to add to my collection. My father never came near a playground. The little girl twists, faster and faster until the rail is just a blur of colour. Her father steps back, laughing, as a woman comes up behind him and circles her hands round his waist. I try unsuccessfully to swallow a pang of envy and push open the heavy door, deliberately letting it swing back and catch my shoulder. The physical pain makes me wince but I embrace it as it helps distract me from thinking about what might have been.

Walking straight through the bar to the Gents, I lock myself in one of the cubicles and take out my jeans, trainers and a hooded sweatshirt. I strip off my work clothes, shoving them into the bag. It's freezing. Pub toilets are like that. No matter how warm it is outside, they always seem to be ten degrees lower. I change as fast as I can and shiver as I pull the hoodie over my head.

Once dressed, I undo the lock and stand in front of one of the chipped mirrors fixed to the wall above the urinals. Dark, puffy circles hang in bags under each eye from a lack of sleep.

I push the nozzle down on the tap and splash some water on my face, pulling a couple of green paper hand towels out of the metal holder on the wall to dry myself. It's like rubbing my skin with sandpaper. I scrunch the paper round my finger to get underneath the gold band that I still haven't taken off and then glance in the mirror again. Not much of an improvement. I still look exhausted. I stare at my reflection, asking myself the same questions I've asked myself all weekend. What do I need to do, Ali? What do I have to say to get through to you?

I look away hurriedly, not wanting to see the guilt in the eyes of the person who gazes back. I throw the damp paper towel into the overflowing pedal bin near the door and head into the pub.

The barman watches me as I walk out, probably trying to decide if I'm the same person who walked in wearing different clothes a few minutes earlier. If I had more time, I'd stop for a drink. I really need one but don't want to ruin my earlier good intentions. Harry's comment at work makes me suspect Em has said something to him. She'd asked about the bottles in my recycling last month.

I follow the satnav as it takes me away from the centre of town, from busy roads which narrow from four lanes to two as the blur outside the windows turns from grey to green. A black and white chequered flag appears on the screen and a voice informs me I've reached my destination as I turn into a large car park and pull into a space that's far enough away from the modern building in front of me to be unobtrusive, but from where I have a clear view of the glass doors at the entrance.

I take out my phone and google her name again. Her photo flashes up on the screen. I had assumed she wouldn't finish work before five, but now I'm worried this could be a wasted journey if it transpires she's already left. I pull the letter she sent me out of my bag, together with the envelope I've brought with me to give her, checking its contents before peeling the thin strip of paper off the flap to seal it, putting them both on the seat beside me.

Half an hour goes by and she still doesn't appear. I can be patient for a bit longer, having waited almost a year. The glass doors open and shut intermittently and several people dressed in office attire come out, but none of the women look like her.

I decide I've had enough of waiting and get out of the car, pulling my hoodie up over my head as I walk towards the entrance. I'm not going inside but sneak round the edge of the building, following the path. Large rectangular windows are set at regular intervals along the brick wall of the ground floor, but they're all heavily tinted, and it's difficult to see anything when I stop and peer inside. I go around the back, but they're identical. I spot the occasional security camera and make a mental note of its position, keeping my head down as I walk.

Back at the car, I sit in the driver's seat whilst staring at her picture on my phone, stretching the image of her face on the screen with my fingers to make it as big as possible. Her green eyes appear serious, focused on the camera. She looks like she's used to getting what she wants, but she's under-estimated us. She doesn't realise the bond we have can't be broken by a few words on a page.

'Come on,' I mutter. 'Where are you?'

My knee twitches and I take a deep breath to calm myself. Don't blow it now. I've practised what I'm going to say. I just need a chance to talk to her. To explain. The letter I've been sent must be a misunderstanding. There's no way Ali would refuse to meet me. I know I've made mistakes, but she doesn't understand how much I love her.

I'd known how special she was when we'd first met at university. Our graduation ball. A dance floor that had been sticky with spilt drinks as The Killers' 'Mr Brightside' had thumped out through the speakers. The tap on my shoul-der as she'd discovered me minesweeping, her half-finished bottle of Smirnoff Ice in my hand. I'd apologised – and had ended up sharing a cab home with her through the deserted streets of Birmingham, watching her face highlighted mo-mentarily in the darkness whenever we'd passed under a street light. I'd moved towards her as the taxi had pulled up next to the kerb, but she'd opened the door to get out and cold air had rushed in, sobering me up as she'd walked away.

She hadn't turned around as I'd called after her then, either.

I spot her as the glass doors slide open. She's alone, walking purposefully across the tarmac, wearing the same red jacket as she'd had on in the photo. I check my phone again. It's definitely her. I pick up her letter and my envelope and slide down in my seat until she passes me, before getting out of my car and following a few feet behind her, my trainers almost silent on the tarmac surface.

She points at a black vehicle nearby that flashes its lights as she presses her keys to unlock it. I begin to run, making up the short distance between us, and overtake her just as she reaches the car, blocking her from getting inside.

'Hi,' I say, smiling.

She steps backwards and stares at me, clutching her car keys defensively. For a split second I'm aware of what my father must have felt when he looked at my mother. The power you can exert over someone physically smaller and weaker than yourself.

'Can I help you?' she asks.

'Yes, I think you can,' I reply. 'I'd like to speak to my wife. I've got something for her.'

NOW

Alison

Sarah's sitting in my seat. She catches me staring at her, wondering why she's deliberately chosen to sit where I normally do, whilst I hold my tray, looking for an empty space amongst the tables of diners. She waves at me. I can't simply turn in the opposite direction, so walk over to her on the far side of the canteen.

'Hi, Alison.' She smiles. 'I thought it was you. We sat here yesterday.'

I frown. 'I know. At lunch.'

There's a scraping noise as I pull out my chair and several people on the table nearest to us turn around.

Sarah leans forward. 'Ignore them,' she mutters as I squirm awkwardly on my seat and struggle to open the plastic wrapper on my sandwich. 'Here, let me have a go.' She holds out her hand. 'It's really tricky unless you've got nails.'

'No, it's fine. I can manage.' My face burns as I fight with the pack, which finally gives way, spilling half its contents onto the table. I pick up the pieces of bread that are still inside the wrapping. I'm not touching the rest of it. There could be any number of germs all over their surface. I read somewhere in the library, there are more germs on a table than a toilet seat.

Sarah continues to munch on some lettuce as she looks at my discarded lunch. 'Those bits are still edible,' she says. I don't like the way she eats and talks at the same time. She puts so much salad on her fork, I'm not sure how she fits it all into her mouth. 'You shouldn't waste them. They won't give you food poisoning. I've only ever had it once after I ate a dodgy curry from a street market in Bangkok. Never had it here – they clean pretty thoroughly.'

'Bangkok?' Something slithers inside my head.

'Yes. Have you been?' Sarah's fork pauses on the way to her mouth.

I don't want to think about it. I don't want to think about him.

'No,' I reply as a memory wriggles its way out from beneath my lie.

He'd laughed as he'd pulled me under the shelter of a plastic awning at the side of the pavement, the black sky lit up by a string of coloured paper lanterns that had swung wildly as the downpour started. The back of my sundress had been soaked and I'd shivered; partly from the cold but more from his touch as his tanned arms had reached around my waist. He'd leaned his face towards mine to kiss me, and I could taste flavours of lemongrass and chilli on his tongue as he'd grazed me with the layer of stubble on his chin. I'd pressed my skin harder against his, wanting him to mark me, evidence to show he was mine.

The aroma of street food had filled the air, of rain evaporating off hot tarmac, of bodies huddling together from the deluge of the monsoon, but all I'd been able to smell was him. His very essence.

I'd buried my head in his T-shirt and breathed him in, forgetting where I was. Who I was.

He'd held onto me as I'd stepped backwards, narrowly missing a passing tuk tuk. I hadn't cared. I'd been as high as a kite, unable to get enough of him.

I swallow.

Sarah stares at me. 'You OK?'

'Yes, fine.'

'It's such an amazing place. Well worth a trip. What about holidays in this country then? Did you grow up round here?' I nod slowly. She smiles. 'Same as me. Bet you used to go to the west coast beaches then. Portishead, Brean, Weston-super-Mare. We visited all of those.' She watches me closely as I shake my head. 'They were great as long as it wasn't raining,' she continues, 'and you didn't have to share the back seat of the car with your brother who was being sick.' She laughs, but I don't find it funny. She's making my head hurt with all her questions. It feels like she's interrogating me.

'Sorry,' I say. 'I need to go. I have to get back.' I pick up the remains of my lunch, lining the items up in a neat square in the middle of the tray.

'But you haven't finished.' She looks concerned.

'I'm not really hungry.' I wince, my hip grazing against the chair as I rush to get away.

I take deep breaths as I walk back up the stairs to the library. I have an urge to run, but I don't, telling myself he's not behind me, his hands aren't reaching out to grab my shoulder so he can look at me with those pleading brown eyes. Even now part of me would find him hard to resist. Until I remember his hands round my wrists. How much

34

he'd hurt me. I'd learnt how to breathe after it happened; slow, smooth breaths. Longer on the outward breath than the inward one to stop me hyperventilating.

I concentrate on doing what I've been told, pausing on each step to focus solely on the movements of my body. That way I can block out everything else. How my hamstrings flex so I can bend my knees and straighten my legs. How my quadriceps ache with the effort of repetition. You spend a lot of time getting to know your body when you have to put it back together.

When I reach the first floor, I stop and allow myself to look behind me. The stairs are empty, but I sense the memories I've tried my hardest to bury are gathering at the outer edges of my consciousness.

'Alison!' Mrs Painter's familiar voice greets me as I walk into the library. 'Can you stack these returns please? I think most people have gone for lunch, so we're not busy. Make sure the autobiographies aren't put back into the fiction section. I discovered a whole load of them in there this morning.' She tuts as though it's my fault and looks at me, adding, 'I don't think it's a good idea to have you photocopying after what happened yesterday.'

I gather up an armful of books, not bothering to tell her I'm not the one who dealt with the returns earlier. It's easier to absorb her disapproval and take it somewhere it can dissipate. I let some of it float away whilst I file *Long Walk to Freedom* and tuck some of it neatly behind *Make the Rules Work for You*. I like to think I'm redistributing negative emotion.

As I reach the end of one of the bookshelves, I glance up to see him sitting at one of the tables. The jolt of recognition is so physical, I let go of the books I'm holding and they slide off my pile one by one, falling like bricks around my feet. He's facing away from me, but I'd recognise him anywhere. The way his dark hair is cut into a V-shape on the back of his neck. His faded blue T-shirt, still covered in paint splashes on one shoulder from where he decorated the hall. He's in one of the library chairs, his right ankle pulled up over his left knee like he used to do in our flat when he was concentrating on something.

For a moment, I can't move. My heart races.

'Jack?' It comes out as little more than a whisper. Half strangled. There's no movement from the figure sitting at the table. 'Jack?'

Nothing. The library is silent. I glance down the bookshelves and can see Mrs Painter bustling around her desk. She isn't looking in my direction, but she shows me normality is less than a hundred feet away.

He sits there. Motionless.

I hold the side of the bookshelf for support and then step forward, avoiding treading on the books round my feet.

'Jack?' I hiss his name, trying to make it louder than the noise of the blood thumping in my ears.

I edge forward towards his chair until I'm close enough to touch him. There's a tear in one knee of his jeans where he caught it on the car door in his haste to get out after we'd argued.

'Jack?' My voice echoes in my head. I can't believe he's here, they told me he wouldn't be able to find me. He doesn't answer. Something tells me to run whilst I have the chance, but my legs don't move.

I stretch out to touch him, to see if I can recognise skin that was once as familiar as my own, and as I do, he reaches over his shoulder and grabs me around the wrist. Hard. My stomach turns to ice as he holds on. I let out a cry and recoil, knocking into the bookshelves behind me, no longer concerned who might hear.

'Alison?' Mrs Painter is at my side. 'Are you OK? I heard you scream. Did you fall? Are you hurt?'

I'm sitting amongst a pile of scattered books. My wrist burns. I remember how that felt. I look for him at the table but he's not there.

'What happened? Did you faint?' Her hand grips my shoulder.

I shake my head, searching the empty tables. 'Did you see—?'

She ignores me. 'Let me help you.' She holds out her hand and I take it, pushing myself up as I glance around the room. The chair he was sitting on is pushed neatly under the table in the same way as all the others. There's no sign of Jack.

Mrs Painter continues to gather the books off the floor and stack them in a pile. She speaks slowly and loudly as if she's talking to a child.

'Let's lay these on the table. You can put them away one at a time. You need to be more careful. I've learned from experience that a nasty fall can take you out for weeks. I went over on my ankle getting off the plane in Madeira last year and it took a good couple of months before I was back on my feet.' She hesitates as she puts down the last of the books. 'Sit here for a minute. Catch your breath.' She pulls out a chair and I lower myself into it, steadying my breathing and

37

rubbing my wrist which throbs heavily. I bet it'll bruise later. 'Better?' she asks. 'I'll get you some water.'

'No.' I shake my head. 'I'm fine.' I don't want her to leave me. Not yet.

'OK. If you're sure.' She pats my shoulder and notices what I'm doing. 'Do you think you've done yourself some damage? I bet you came down hard on it when you fell. We can get it looked at if you think . . .'

'I'm fine.' I won't let myself cry in front of her, but she doesn't look convinced.

'Well, take it easy. Let me know if you need any help putting those away.' She points at the large pile. 'I've got some paperwork to do, but I'll be at my desk. Are you sure you're all right?'

I nod, blinking back tears.

She walks off down the row of bookshelves and I stare after her. She's annoyed; I can see by the way she stops and impatiently shoves a couple of paperbacks that someone has discarded horizontally on top of others back into the already tightly packed shelf. She hates any kind of a scene at work. I don't want to give her another reason to check up on what I'm doing. After the photocopying incident, I know she's been watching me and this is going to make things worse. I can't lose this job. It took me so long to find one after everything that happened. I need to try harder and get myself together. I need to stop inventing things that aren't there.

I pick the first book off the top of the stack on the table and avoid looking at the empty chair, lined up with the others against the side of the table. Nothing appears to be out of place. There's no sign of anyone having been here, but as I glance at the title and open the front cover, I swear I can smell his aftershave on my skin. I tell myself that I'm imagining it and that I'm safe, but there's an ache in my chest as I check the barcode to see where it belongs.

I rub my wrist, but it's really sore. I must have caught it on one of the shelves as I fell.

Mrs Painter is watching me from behind the counter as I bend down to put the book back and I realise it's not my wrist that's bothering me at all; the pain is too deep for that. It's because I miss him. Or part of him. The nice part. The other part of him, the one that hurt me – I don't want to think about that.

I'm restless for the remainder of the afternoon, watching the clock, whose hands slow down as the end of my shift approaches. I stiffen as someone comes up behind me to ask a question, but Jack doesn't reappear. A couple of times, I walk round the tables, staring at people's faces. If I screw up my eyes, I can make them change shape in front of me, blurring their features until they're unrecognisable, but I can't recreate him, or anyone who even resembles him. A man looks up and notices me studying him and glares. I turn away, pretending I'm trying to tidy up a nearby shelf before walking back to the counter.

'So, this is where you hide yourself.'

I look up from the computer to find Sarah standing in front of me, book in hand.

'Great place to work,' she adds. 'You've got so much more space than I have in my office.' My scanner is frozen, mid-air. 'Aren't you going to check this out for me, then?' She pushes the book across the counter until the pages touch my fingers.

I hesitate before I pick it up. 'I thought you said you didn't have time to read.'

'I don't usually. I need this for some research I'm doing, so thought I'd pop in. I remembered you said you worked here; I hoped I'd bump into you.' Her nails tap her library card gently as she speaks. The random pattern of sound is irritating. I wonder if it's some kind of code, whether she's waiting for me to figure out the meaning behind her attempt at polite conversation. She tucks her hair behind her ear and the gesture seems familiar. My brain searches for something just outside its reach and I almost grasp it before it whisks itself away, leaving me empty-handed.

I pass the scanner over the barcode and hand the book to her.

'Thanks. I'll let you know how I get on with it.' She tucks it into her bag and smiles as she walks out.

I'm convinced I know her from somewhere, but I can't recall where. Memories climb over each other in a fight to get to the surface and the struggle makes me dizzy. There are too many to sift through to find her and I don't want to look in case I see something I've tried to forget. My shift is almost over and, as I glance down the aisle, I realise the library is practically empty. Mrs Painter is kneeling down, sticking labels onto books at the far end of the shelves.

I log back into the computer. The last record is still show-ing on the screen. Sarah Henderson. A local address. I run my eyes down the list of books she's borrowed. Eight entries, four in the last five months, the last one returned three weeks ago. She said she hadn't been in here recently. And she's managed to find the time to read four books. I glance up just as Mrs Painter reaches the counter and feel the heat spread across my face as I frantically move the mouse to minimise the record so it disappears.

'Are you all right, Alison?' she asks.

I nod, mutely, not wanting her to hear the tremor in my voice. She looks at the screen and I wait for her to notice my guilt, but she turns away and walks to the end of the shelves. I wipe my sweaty hands on my trousers. I don't understand why Sarah would lie to me; I barely know her. But a niggling voice in my head tells me that perhaps I do and if I tried a bit harder, I'd be able to remember where from.

I try not to think about it as I walk back to my flat after my shift finally finishes, wondering if my subconscious will come up with the solution. I can't stop her face appearing in my head, but it doesn't stay still long enough for me to examine it closely. My brain alters her features, filling them in with familiar details to trick me into believing I've solved the puzzle. I relax for a few seconds until the frustration returns when I realise I'm staring into someone else's eyes and not hers at all.

I push open my front door very slowly, but the mat is empty and it's only as I shut it behind me that I realise I've been holding my breath in anticipation that something unpleasant would be waiting for me. Something designed to cause me more pain.

I press the purple mark on my wrist gently. It hurts and I press harder, pushing my finger into the centre of the colour to remind myself what Jack is capable of, only stopping when my vision blurs with tears. I can't allow myself to forget.

I pull off some toilet paper to dab my eyes and notice the cleaner has been in. She's wiped round the sink, but she never does it properly like I do. Getting deep into the lines of grout along the bathroom tiles and removing any fluff balls from underneath the bed. Scrubbing the kitchen sink with a toothbrush to get the limescale off the bottom of the tap. Taking all the plates out of the cupboard to clean the surface before putting them back. Sometimes I wonder if it's worth her coming once a week.

Dad had done most of the cleaning in our house. At the time, I hadn't thought that was unusual. He'd let me help him wash his car at the weekends. I'd turned the hose on and he'd sponged down his Ford Escort and put on the wax, spreading the liquid over the bonnet, turning the silver paint a dull grey colour. I'd followed behind him with a soft cloth that he'd kept folded in a special bag, rubbing everything off until the metal shone. He had paid me when I'd done it properly and had treated me to one of his speciality hot chocolates after I'd finished, letting me tip hundreds and thousands all over the whipped cream before he'd stuck in a flake, grinning as he'd put his finger up to his lips to let me know it was our secret.

The memory makes me so hungry that I have to refocus on what I'm doing, removing every mark so the surfaces are pristine. It helps clear my brain and for half an hour I don't think about Jack, or Sarah.

After I've wrung out the wet cloths, I make myself a sandwich and sit down to watch television, cold now I'm no longer exerting myself. I pull a cardigan out of my wardrobe and wrap it round me as I curl up on the sofa. The pocket crackles and I reach inside, pulling out a folded note.

Ali,
I'm told that you're doing well and I'm pleased for you. I
wondered if you'd write back and let me know if we could
meet – I'd really like to see you. I wish things could have been
different.
Jack

My first thought is that he's in the flat, but after the initial
surge of adrenaline I realise that's almost impossible. There's
nowhere I know of to hide in the tiny rooms; I would have
seen him. He must have been here when I was at work.
There's no sign of a break-in, but he could have found a way
to get a key. Jack has always been able to find a way to get
what he wants. He'd probably waited until I'd left and then
told the cleaner a sob story about how he'd locked himself
out and asked her to let him back in. And then come to the
library afterwards. To show he's managed to find me. He
knows I'll suffer more if I think he could be watching me
at any time, unaware of his presence until the moment he
decides to confront me.

My heart races. I tell myself he isn't real. That there hadn't
been anyone on that chair when I'd looked up. But something tells me I'm just trying to reassure myself and that I
have to acknowledge, if Jack knows where I live, I'm no
longer safe here.

'Jack is gone,' I say it out loud, forcing a reality I don't feel
into the words.

I fold the piece of paper up and put it inside a notebook on
my kitchen table. I don't want to stare at it, but I don't want

to throw it away either. I want to keep it so I can prove I'm not imagining his letters, even if I'm not sure whether he's real.

I run the tips of my fingers over my eyebrows, searching for hairs that don't follow the neat line of the others. When I find one, I pull it out. There's a sharp prick of pain, followed by a sense of relief that I've restored order. I roll the hair between my fingers, for a few seconds comforted by the sharpness of the end on my skin that I press to make me feel whole. I savour the respite, but it's only temporary. I find another. And another. And after a while it's difficult to follow the line at all.

I glance at myself in the mirror the following morning whilst I'm cleaning my teeth. Something looks odd. I lean in to look more carefully and realise what it is. Part of my eyebrow is missing. There's a large gap in the middle. My left eye now looks slightly higher than my right.

I run my finger under the tap and try to smooth out the existing hairs so they cover the space. It doesn't really work and the gap is still obvious. I resist the desire to pull out any more and hunt around in the bathroom cabinet for something I can use to disguise it. I don't normally wear make-up as no one else at work does, but I find an old eyeshadow lurking at the back of the shelf and dip a damp cotton bud into the brown colour. Carefully, I paint it across the space, creating the illusion of normality that doesn't at all reflect how I feel inside.

THEN

Jack

'I'm sorry, do I know you? I've got no idea what you're talking about.' She clasps her keys firmly in one hand and adjusts the shoulder strap of her handbag with the other, her unconscious movement revealing her concern at the unexpected confrontation.

'I think you do,' I say, still smiling.

'I'm afraid I don't. If you need to speak to someone, you need to ask at reception.' She points towards the glass doors at the entrance to the building. 'Can you move out of the way, please? I want to get to my car.'

I continue to stand in front of the driver's door. 'You sent me a letter.'

She frowns. 'I don't think I did.'

I hold out the piece of paper. 'Read it,' I say. 'It's got your name at the bottom. Sarah Henderson. That's you, isn't it?'

She stares at my face, not taking it out of my hand. 'If you've got something you want to discuss, we can go inside, Mr . . .?' She lets the words hang in the air, waiting for me to answer.

'Reynolds. I'm Alison Reynolds' husband,' I reply.

She says nothing but a muscle in her jaw tenses. I step towards her, but she backs away.

'You do know her, don't you?' I ask quietly. She doesn't answer. 'About five feet five, long blonde hair?' Her green eyes stare into mine, but she stays silent. 'Look, I know you're Sarah Henderson and you work here,' I say. 'You signed this letter and so you must know my wife. It arrived on Friday and says I'm supposed to stay away from her. As her husband, I've got a right to see her.' She's gripping her keys so tightly, her knuckles have turned white. 'Go on,' I add. 'Take it. Tell me what it says.'

'Mr Reynolds, I don't—'

I push the letter into her free hand before she has time to react, bringing my face close to hers. 'I'd really like you to look at it,' I say, my fists clenched. I catch a glimpse of my face in the reflection of the car window and see my father staring at me, which makes me take a step backwards.

'I know what it says.' She speaks calmly, but I can tell she's agitated by the way she's fiddling with the strap on her bag. She scans the page briefly and then hands it back to me. 'I can appreciate you're upset, but I can't give you any information other than what's already been written here.'

I stop smiling. 'You don't understand. I need to give her something.'

'I'm afraid you can't. This letter says you're not allowed near her,' she says. I glance at the entrance to the building. 'There are cameras everywhere,' she adds quickly, 'you'll be spotted straight away. Why don't we go and speak to some-one at reception? They might be able to help you.' She looks over my shoulder to see if anyone else is nearby, but this part of the car park is deserted.

'I'm not here to cause you any trouble,' I say. 'I'm not going to hurt you. Or her. I just want to talk to my wife. I should at least be allowed to talk to her.'

'This isn't the way to do it, Mr Reynolds.'

'It's Jack.'

'This isn't the way, Jack. You need to go through the proper channels. I'm really sorry, but I can't help you.' She tries to walk away, but I stand in front of her.

'Can you at least give her what I've put in here?' I hold out the envelope I've brought with me. 'I know you can get it to her. Please. I need to explain and if she won't see me, I don't have any other way to tell her.'

She hesitates, staring at me, and I catch something that I hope is a flicker of pity in her eyes. She takes it and I notice her hand is trembling. I retreat another couple of steps.

'I just need her to know I'm here. I want her to understand why . . .' I pause, wiping my face on my sleeve, my voice choked. It's a crack in the façade that I can normally keep intact when I talk about Ali.

Keeping her eyes fixed on me, Sarah pulls open her door and gets into the driver's seat. I hear the locks click down before she starts the engine and pulls away, past me and out of the car park. She doesn't look back. I hope she opens what I've given her. All the things that Ali needs to remind her of what we had together, as well as my contact details. Again. Just in case Sarah's lost them. I'll give her a couple of days to follow the instructions I've written down.

As I climb into my car I can't help but think that the way

Sarah had looked at me felt familiar. It reminded me of Ali when I last saw her. Eyes a little too wide.

I jump as the shrill of my ringtone sounds on the seat beside me, and put the call on speaker as the familiar warm tones of my mum's voice fill my car. I tell her I can't talk as I'm on my way back from visiting a client and won't be home until late. I don't like lying to her but don't want her to worry and then turn up at the flat this evening. She'll know something's wrong if she sees me face-to-face. I need to get home and check I've got everything ready for after Sarah does what I've asked.

I drive the short distance through the suburban streets, trying not to look at all the different places that remind me of Ali. Often they're just blurs of colour outside the window that I pretend to ignore despite the bubble of emotion that rises up and then pops inside me as they flash past. But this evening, the crawling traffic doesn't let me escape their presence, reminding me of my guilt.

People ask me why I haven't moved out of the flat, and I can't give them an answer. I wonder if I need to put myself through the continuous pain as a punishment, or whether there's a part of me that doesn't want to forget. That wants to keep her close.

I stop at the local garage to fill up the car and pick up some food; the fridge at home is empty, apart from wine. A woman stands in front of me in the queue, waiting to pay, a small baby – a girl, I think – is fast asleep on her shoulder, her mouth open as she slumbers, oblivious. I glance at her and the mother smiles. I smile back.

'They'll sleep anywhere at this age,' she says, wiping a line of drool off her coat with a tissue.

'I know,' I reply. 'I wish I could do the same.'

She nods. 'Me too. Just a shame she won't do it more at night. But you can't have everything. I don't think I've ever been so knackered, but people keep telling me sleep's overrated.'

The baby opens her eyes and starts to cry. Her blanket's fallen onto the floor and I pick it up. I reach out and touch her hand, stroking her tiny fingers that are squeezed into tight balls. Flawless replicas in miniature, without any of the imperfections that come with age. Her mother frowns and takes the blanket from me, her smile fading as I continue to look at her daughter. I start to speak, but she pretends she can't hear me as she moves towards the cashier, leaving me staring after her.

When I get home, I park outside my flat and hold my key fob up to the panel by the main entrance, struggling to push the door open at the same time as carrying a loaf of bread, a pint of milk and a ready meal. Putting the shopping down onto the kitchen counter, I stick the kettle on and stack the dirty plates on top of each other to clear some space. I glance briefly at the door at one end of the hall, checking it's firmly shut. I can count on one hand the number of times I've opened it in the last year. It's the one place in the flat I avoid going into if I can help it.

As I wait in the kitchen for the kettle to boil, I remember us standing on this spot when we'd first moved in, looking at the many squares of ridiculously named colours I'd painted on the wall. Ali had slid her arms round my waist and rested her head on my shoulder as we'd considered the possible options. I hadn't moved, feeling the warmth of her breath on

49

my skin, until she'd started kissing my neck and I'd turned around, dropping the brush I was holding, and we'd forgotten about having to choose anything at all.

I open a window in the sitting room to let in some air and turn on the television as the doorbell on the intercom buzzes. There's a grainy image on the small video entry screen and I press the button to let Em in.

'I wasn't expecting you,' I say as she comes up the corridor. 'I thought you and Harry were coming on Friday?' I go to hug her, but she pulls away. She looks flustered as she pushes her sunglasses onto her head.

'I know. It's just a flying visit. I think Harry left Jessica's toy dog here yesterday and she's hopeless at sleeping without it. Have you seen it?'

I shake my head. 'The flat's in a bit of a state, but I can't remember coming across it amongst the mess.'

'Do you mind if I come in and have a look?'

I nod and she steps inside.

I wonder if Harry's told her about my fictitious doctor's appointment and she's come to check up on me. She hesitates, seeming unsure of what to say next.

I scan the counter and underneath the table in the kitchen. 'There's nothing here,' I call out.

'He said she was playing with it in the sitting room,' Em says.

I search whilst she leans against the doorway, pretending she hasn't noticed the junk mail and pile of unopened letters that litter the table.

'I should have bought two of the damn things,' she says. 'Always have a spare one as a reserve, that's what all the

super-organised mothers do, according to the magazines.'
She pauses as she glances towards the room at the end of the
hallway. 'Sorry, I don't mean . . .'

'It's OK, Em.' She perches on the arm of the sofa whilst
I lift up envelopes and items of clothing to check there's
nothing hidden underneath.

'Harry said you had a doctor's appointment this afternoon.
Nothing serious I hope?'

I shake my head. So she has been sent to check up on me.
'No, it's fine. Just a routine check. My blood pressure was a
bit high the last time I went in.'

'You need to take better care of yourself, Jack. When
you came over last week, the amount you and Harry drank
was ridiculous.' I can't remember much about that night. I
don't even remember getting home. 'You were hammered.'
Her tone exacerbates my sense of discomfort and I fold up
a sweater that's been flung over the back of a chair whilst I
continue to search to give myself something to do. 'That's
actually the reason I came . . .'

Her phone bleeps and she takes it out of her pocket to
look at the message. I try to think back to that evening, but
everything after we'd sat down to eat is a blur.

I change the subject before she has a chance to start talking
again. 'I can't find it anywhere, Em. Sorry.' The tight feeling in my stomach that I'd had after Harry mentioned how
drunk we'd been resurfaces. I swallow and blink to hide the
memories I don't want her to know about, so she doesn't see
the guilt on my face.

Em stares at me as she puts her phone in her pocket. 'Did
Harry say anything to you?'

I swallow. 'What, about last week?' I shake my head and walk to the doorway. I need to get out of the room. I have a horrible feeling something happened and I have no recollection of what it was. And she does. I wonder if I said something to offend one of my oldest friends and she's waiting for me to apologise. 'I'll have a look in my bedroom for it if you want,' I suggest, hoping she doesn't see how awkward I'm finding this. 'I don't think Jess went in there, but it's tidier, so at least it might be easier to spot.'

She follows me as we walk down the hallway. I catch her as she glances at the door at the other end of the corridor and shivers. I switch on the light in my room and draw the curtains that I haven't bothered to open this morning, hoping she doesn't ask me anything else. Crouching down on my hands and knees, I peer under the bed, waiting for the colour in my cheeks to fade before I get up. There's a mountain of dust and the odd sock, but I can't see any soft toys.

'I'm sorry, Em. There's nothing here. Have you checked your car? It might have fallen under the seat.'

She watches me as I get up. 'I've looked there already,' she says, opening her mouth as if to say something, but then she changes her mind and walks back into the hallway. She pauses as she spots a photo of me tucked into the corner of our pinboard.

I'd been nine or ten, still in my junior school uniform. A smile had turned the edges of my mouth upwards, but the emotion hadn't reached my eyes. I remembered sitting on the small wooden stool whilst they'd adjusted the lighting umbrella. The Headmaster had stood behind the photographer, grinning at me, desperate for the shot to be taken so he could step forwards. As soon as I'd seen him, I'd known something was wrong. His appearance for a quiet chat had always meant bad news. I had prayed that I'd disappear when the flash blinded me, but when the spots had stopped dancing in front of my eyes, I'd still been there.

He'd ushered me to a classroom, where my father was waiting. We'd driven to the hospital in silence. I'd been shocked by the number of stitches down my mother's forehead. I think my father had been too. The way he'd sat on the end of her bed, adjusting the thin blanket and stroking her hand; it had been the most contrite I'd seen him. I knew he'd never actually admit he'd been the one responsible for putting her there in the first place. It seems I have more in common with my father than I want to admit.

'Is this you?' Em asks, pointing at it. I nod. She unpins it and peers at it closely. 'Oh my god, Jack. You're so cute! How old were you here?'

'Not sure. About ten, I think.' I hold out my hand for it. I don't want Em looking at it. I'd forgotten it was there. Ali had wanted to put it up and I hadn't found the courage to tell her why she shouldn't.

Em gives it to me and I slide it into the rear pocket of my jeans. I'll get rid of it later.

Her phone buzzes again and she reads the message. 'I need to go. Harry says the kids are playing up.' I don't try to stop her. I don't want to give her the chance to talk to me about last week before I can remember what happened.

'See you Friday?' I say as I walk towards the front door.

'There it is!' She bends down and extracts a small blue leg out of the wicker basket full of shoes in the hallway. 'Thank

God I found it. We might actually get some sleep tonight.'
She tucks the toy dog into her bag. 'Yes, we'll see you about
seven.' She stares at me, then adds, 'Hopefully we'll have
more time to talk.'

I nod, knowing I need to speak to Harry before they come
over to see if he can remember any more about that night
than I can.

I open the door and she walks straight out. That's unlike
Em. Normally she hugs me, or at least gives me a kiss on the
cheek.

I'm still wondering what I've done to put up a barrier between us as I stick my ready meal in the microwave and then
hesitate for a moment before opening a bottle of Merlot.
Just one glass. Two at the most. That can't hurt. I check my
phone to see if I've had any messages from Sarah, but the
screen is blank. I need to be patient; it's only been a couple
of hours. The timer beeps to tell me the food is cooked and
I rip off the plastic cover, swearing as the hot steam scalds
my hand, spooning out the contents of the black plastic tray
onto a plate. It's an improvement on my usual behaviour.
Yesterday morning I woke up to find I'd eaten straight out
of the container. I run my hand under the cold water tap
until my skin is so numb I can no longer feel it and take my
dinner into the sitting room, picking at it on the sofa whilst
half-watching the television.

One glass of wine doesn't last long, so I generously refill
it before putting the bottle back on the counter. I need the
fuzziness to soften the sharp edges of everything so I can
sleep. Enough to stop me going straight to where I least want
to be, the minute I shut my eyes.

The photo digs into me as I sit back down. I reach into my pocket and pull it out. I barely have any pictures of me when I was young. The few my mother took were mostly too dark, or too out of focus to keep. But here I am, preserved in a single moment of time which in reality has long since faded.

Getting up, I go to my bedroom and lift a small box off the top shelf of my wardrobe and take it into the sitting room, where I put it on the coffee table and open the lid. Different items I've collected over the years lie jumbled together. I take out a suitcase luggage label, an old photo, the tickets from my graduation ball and some tarnished football medals, until there's only a black and white card, a small plastic wristband and one of Ali's T-shirts left in the bottom of the box.

I take a large gulp of wine as I pull out that last item and hold it against my face. The smell is powerful enough to bring her back, releasing memories that explode in front of my eyes like a series of colourful fireworks. It sharpens the tiny details of her face that I've forgotten about. The freckles on her nose. The small scar where she put her tooth through her lip when she was little. I force myself to put it down. As long as Sarah does what I've asked, I won't have to summon up a ghost for much longer.

The medals jangle together as I lift them back inside. I remember how my mother had sat next to me on the sofa, holding one of them by its cheap silk ribbon. I had stayed silent, staring at her whilst the light in her eyes had faded, trying to guess what she had been thinking. Her expression hadn't given anything away, but I'd been sure it had been about my father. And how much she'd been dreading him coming home. I'd wanted to tell her I felt the same way but hadn't wanted to add to her guilt.

I shudder and drop the school photo into the box with the other items, shut the lid and carry it back into my bedroom, where I put it away in the wardrobe. Picking up my glass off the table, I walk into the kitchen, tipping it up to get out the last few drops that take forever to run down the inside before pouring myself another.

The phone buzzes and jolts me awake. Ten fifteen p.m. I've been asleep on the sofa longer than I thought. There's a metallic taste in my mouth and my headache is worse, throbbing each time I move. I squint to read the message. Harry.

I've got client meetings tomorrow and Weds. Don't forget presentation on Thursday – see you at Marley Brown's offices at 9am.

I shut my eyes. Another early start later this week to look forward to.

I let my mind wander, the alcohol swirling my thoughts into incomprehensible patterns until I don't even notice crossing over the boundary into sleep.

I'd had my hands round her wrists as I'd held onto her in our bedroom, my face inches from hers. 'What are you doing? You can't leave. I won't let you.' She hadn't known what she was doing. I'd been trying to protect her.

'Please, get off me,' she'd whispered as she sank down, curling herself into a ball. I'd kicked out at the wall, scuffing the paint.

'You need to listen to me.' I'd crouched down in front of her as she'd tried to pull her pyjama top across her chest and had brushed

away the tear that fell down her cheek with my finger. 'You know how much I love you, don't you?' She hadn't looked at me. 'I'm trying to keep you safe. You don't believe me, do you?'

She'd nodded slowly, but I'd seen she was already slipping away from me and I didn't know how to hold onto her.

I couldn't bear to let her leave.

NOW

Alison

I wake too early, startled by a noise that fades before I have a chance to open my eyes. My senses begin to focus, but I bury my head in the pillow, unwilling to return to consciousness.

Skimming the surface of sleep, I dream of Jack. We're sitting next to each other on a bus, but he leans forward on the seat to talk to the person in front of us and, as they turn around, I can see it's Sarah. She smiles at me. He reaches over to hold her hand, and I try to grab the arm of his coat to pull him away, but he shakes me off. I see how their fingers interlock, hers pale against his, and I want to sink my teeth into her. Rip through her skin until it's a bloody pulp and he doesn't have anything left to grasp at all. He whispers something in her ear, but there's a beeping noise and I can't hear him properly. I'm pleading with him to let go of her, but his coat slips out from between my fingers when I try to hold onto it and the sound gets louder and I wonder why the bus driver is hooting and then I realise my alarm is going off and he was never here at all.

My skin glistens with a layer of sweat and my face is wet. I think I have been crying and have to wipe the dampness off with a towel as I get ready for work. The bruise on my wrist is now purple. In a couple of days, it will turn from blue to green and finally to yellow. I'm familiar with that process. The top of my arm is sore when I touch it. I don't remember hitting it when I fell, but I must have scraped it as there's a tiny scab on it, no bigger than a freckle, which feels rough under my fingers.

Trying to recall how I know Sarah is like having a word on the tip of my tongue, but the harder I try, the further it retreats. I struggle to think back, but I can't get past images of Jack; Jack with a girl who looks like me, but who is so different from the person I am now, I barely recognise her. He's twisted me into a lesser version of myself. Someone who doesn't live in the present. Someone who spends their time watching the past, waiting for it to catch up with them.

I linger in my seat in the canteen at work, taking my time to chew and carefully swallow every mouthful of my sandwich, not taking my eyes off the entrance. Sarah doesn't come in and I can't wait any longer. The large wall clock shows me that Mrs Painter will be starting to wonder where I am. I'll try again tomorrow.

I head back to reception to the stairwell as the lift doors slide open. Sarah stands in front of me, her bright red jacket matching the shade of her lipstick. She's a vision of complete co-ordination. For a moment she looks unsettled, one hand reaches up to adjust her scarf, but then she smiles and any momentary slip in composure vanishes.

'Hi, Alison.'

'Hi.' I don't move.

'I'm just going out for some lunch,' she says. 'Can't face the canteen today.'

'I wondered where you were.' I don't tell her I've been looking for her. Or dreaming about her.

She puts her hand on the side of the lift doors to stop them closing. 'I thought I'd have a change for once. Sorry . . . can I get out?'

'Sure.' I step to one side. 'Perhaps I could come with you?' I blurt out the words, not knowing how to stop her from walking off.

She stares at me and then looks at the floor. 'Maybe another time. Aren't you due back in the library?'

Of course I am. I've already had lunch. What am I thinking? For some reason, I have a lump in my throat.

She smiles kindly at me. 'I can pop in to see you later if you'd like? There's another book I want to borrow.' I shrug, not trusting myself to speak as the lift doors close and it moves off. She pats her pocket, checking she has her keys. 'Well, I'd better go. Need to make the most of the break. It's hardly enough time to get anything useful done.'

I watch as she walks out through the glass doors and across the car park, her red jacket highlighted against the grey tarmac as if someone has deliberately marked her out in felt-tip pen for my benefit.

My mother used to have a whole row of suit jackets in her wardrobe. In a range of appropriate office colours, they'd all been immaculate, hung on identical wooden hangers, sheathed in dry-cleaner's clear plastic bags. She'd told me she hadn't worn them since I'd been born. She'd let me try them on, the shoulder pads sticking out at ridiculous angles as I'd stood in front of a mirror in her bathroom, my small feet stuck into the front of a pair of her black high heels, in which I'd shuffled across the carpet. I'd asked her why she didn't wear them anymore, but she hadn't answered my question, tucking them neatly into their plastic covers before hanging them up. She'd taken a long time smoothing each one out, telling me she wanted to be sure she didn't leave any creases for the next time she needed them, before she'd shut the wardrobe door.

I want to avoid walking past the people who are gathered around the entrance to the stairwell, so I wait in reception for the lift. The doors slide open and I press the button impatiently for the first floor before anyone else can get in. As the lift rises upwards, I wonder if I can find where she works. Maybe something in her office will jog my memory. I push the button for the fourth floor. Sarah's floor. There's a buzzing noise. *'Please present pass'* flashes up in small red letters on the control panel. I hold up my ID card. The letters continue to flash and the lift halts its ascent, the doors opening at the first floor. The entrance to the library is ahead of me. I try holding the button down once more, but the lift remains stationary and the same instruction blinks repetitively on the panel.

I have no choice but to head back into the library, where Mrs Painter is busy ordering new books from the catalogue. She's deep in concentration at her desk; the beaded shell chain that stops her glasses falling off rustles as she twists it through her fingers.

'Mrs Painter?'

'Hmm?' She doesn't look up.

'Have you been up to the fourth floor?'

She pushes her glasses down her nose and raises her head to stare at me.

'The fourth floor?' she repeats my words.

'Yes. Here. Upstairs.' I look down at my shoes. Part of the leather has come away from the sole and I can see my sock through the small gap. I need to get another pair. I try to scrunch up my toes to hide the material that's poking out of the hole; I hope it's not too obvious.

'Not recently.' She pushes her glasses back up and resumes her search through the catalogue, licking her thumb to make turning the pages easier. She doesn't look at me.

'But you have been?'

She takes her time finding one of the codes for a particular book on the ordering sheet. I wait until she's finished, watching her write the numbers in a neat line.

'Yes, I have,' she says, finally.

'What's up there?' I ask.

'Offices.' This time her reply is immediate.

'What kind of offices?'

She shuffles on her chair. 'Alison, do you not have enough to do down here? I can get you some barcodes to stick on if you want. That whole section down there,' she points to one of the bottom rows of shelves, 'needs to have them added into the front of each book.' She pushes her glasses down her nose, reaches into the storage cupboard and pulls out a sheet of labels, which she hands to me before turning back to the catalogue.

I don't understand why I can't go up to the fourth floor if

she's been up there. I don't pay attention to what she's saying to me as I stick on the labels, I'm too busy planning where I'm going to go as soon as I've finished my shift.

As soon as the buzzer sounds at four o'clock, I walk to the rear of the library and let myself out of the door. Flight after flight of stairs twist round on themselves; a black railing encloses the void in the centre that stretches the entire height of the stairwell. When I peer over the edge and look up, I can see all the way to the top of the building. I start walking.

When I get to the fourth floor, I stop and listen. Most people take the lift, but I need to check I'm alone as I don't want to bump into anyone who might ask what I'm doing. There's complete silence. I push the door that leads out of the stairwell. It opens with a click and I step into a tiny entrance hall which has a door on the opposite wall bordered by glass panels on either side which are too narrow to see through properly. All I can make out is a long corridor and large blue carpet tiles. It's deserted. The door to it won't open. I shove it a bit harder, but it stays firmly shut. I notice a small pad on the wall, similar to the one in the lift; a red light on it flashes continuously. I hold up my pass and the pad beeps but the light continues to blink. I try again. It won't open. It's clear I'm not going to be able to get in.

I walk back into the stairwell with a feeling I'm being watched but there's no one around; only a tiny green light in the centre of the ceiling above me that winks as it watches me leave.

I kick the bottom of the railing; I want to find Sarah's office as I'm convinced it might help me remember where I know her from. I walk up the staircase to the top of the building, then down to the first and back up again, counting my steps to keep myself distracted from the aching muscles in my legs. I hope the exercise will help to get rid of the roll of flab that's gathered around my middle over the past few months. The waistband of my jeans presses uncomfortably into my stomach. I never used to have a problem losing weight, but recently the pounds just won't shift. I can't look at myself full-length in the tiny mirror in my bathroom at home, but sometimes when I catch a glimpse of my reflection in the glass doors of the library, I have to wave to check it's actually me. Jack had almost been able to get his fingertips to touch round my waist when we'd first met. Three years of living on a student budget had meant I'd prioritised my social life over food. I'd rounded out in the years since then, my gauntness overtaken by curves, but I don't like the softness that I can feel under my fingers when I touch my stomach.

When I reach the sixth floor for the third time, I stop, out of breath as I lean on the handrail. The silence is interrupted by the sound of footsteps below me and I keep quite still, not wanting to be seen. I've never been told I shouldn't go up to other floors but don't want to explain what I'm doing. Especially to Mrs Painter. She'll ask why I haven't gone straight home after work and I won't be able to give her an answer.

I shrink back against the wall, away from the void in the centre of the stairwell. Perhaps the person I can hear on the stairs beneath me won't come up to where I am. Maybe they'll let themselves out of one of the doors lower down.

The footsteps get closer. I edge forward and peer over the handrail to the stairs below. I can hear the sound of feet moving, but I can't see anyone. The noise seems to be getting louder, but I'm not sure if that's because I'm nearer the void, where it echoes more. A hand appears on the railing a couple of floors below me. I stifle a gasp and step backwards. Would it be better if I began to walk down? Then, if anyone asks me, I could pretend I'd just come out at the sixth floor instead of standing awkwardly at the top of a staircase.

I look over the edge again. The blood is thumping so loudly in my ears, I can't hear anything. I think they've gone. The stairwell is empty. I relax. My legs are shaky and I'm worried they're going to give way. I'm about to start walking when a hand reappears on the railing one level below. The Tag Heuer watch I gave him for his thirtieth birthday is on his wrist. A face stares up at me. His face. Those unmistakable brown eyes.

'I told you I loved you, Ali.' *Jack.*

I stagger back against the stairwell wall. Oh my God. He's real and he's in the building. He must have followed me to work. And I can't get out. I fling open the door that leads into the tiny reception of the sixth floor but am met by the same scenario I'd encountered on the fourth. The control panel flashes red when I press my pass up to it in desperation. There isn't anywhere I can go. My choices are to stay where I am or go down the stairs to meet him. Better to move. At least someone might hear me if I shout for help. *No, they won't. There isn't anyone there.* My subconscious evaluates the options faster than I can. I'm not going to wait in this tiny space, I know that. I'd rather face him in the open.

I push my way out of the door into the stairwell, expecting him to appear at any moment. My hands shake. I stand motionless, every muscle taut, waiting for the inevitable. He doesn't appear. I count to thirty, pressing my back against the wall to keep myself upright. He could have climbed those stairs in under ten. I've seen how fast he can move when he wants to.

I edge to the handrail and look over. Nothing. No faces, no hands. As I stare downwards, I catch a glimpse of a figure heading to the bottom of the building.

'Jack?' I lean over the railing. 'Jack?' I shout his name at the top of my voice, not caring if anyone else can hear me, and sprint down the stairs as fast as I can. As I reach the ground floor there's no sign of him. The stairwell is empty. I fling open the door and run into reception. There's no one there apart from the staff manning the front desk, one of whom gives me an odd look as I stare around helplessly.

The lift doors slide open and I cower, half-expecting him to step out. Instead, Sarah appears and walks straight towards me.

'Alison. Are you OK?' She reaches out to touch my arm, but I back away from her. 'You look worried. Can I help with something?'

I shake my head and adjust my bag on my shoulder.

'No. I'm fine. I . . . I thought I saw someone I knew.' I glance round, convinced he can't have disappeared.

'D'you want me to ask the reception staff if they've seen anyone?' She's trying to be helpful, I can see that. I know how I must look. I rub my forehead and can feel the damp sweat on my fingers. Thank God it's Sarah who's here and not Mrs Painter.

'No . . . it's fine. He must have gone.' I don't resist this time as she puts her hand on my arm. I barely notice her touching me as I try to work out what I'm going to do next. It's so difficult to think clearly, but as I look around, along-side the feeling of panic, a small ball of disappointment rolls across my chest.

'I'll get you some water,' she says as she guides me to a seat.

Moments later, she sits down beside me and hands me a small paper cone. I'm shaking as I swallow the contents, the coldness of the liquid making my head hurt.

'Don't be afraid to talk to someone, Alison. I'm always here to listen.'

I nod briefly, hoping that my face doesn't show the confusion I feel inside. Why would I be afraid to talk to someone? It's just her I don't want to talk to. I don't understand why she's taking such an interest in me and it's making me uncomfortable.

'Thanks. But I think I should go home.'

She smiles, realising I'm not going to volunteer any other information, and stands up and walks towards the lift.

Something had flashed in my head when she'd guided me to the bench. I have met Sarah before. I remember her hand on my arm. Her fingers gripping me tightly as her nails had dug into my bare skin. She'd hurt me and now I'm certain I don't want to see her again.

The blank white walls in my flat normally help me to feel calm, but this evening I'm restless, even though I know I need to sleep. Physically I'm exhausted; I've wrung out every last drop of energy and am left with a shell of a body that I have to drag into my bedroom. As I lie down on my duvet and stare at the ceiling, my mind is still whirling and I have to wait for the carousel of thoughts to slow down.

I don't understand how Jack could have been in the stair-well. Maybe he had followed me when I went to work. I'd only realised after everything happened how good he'd been at watching me without me knowing. But if it was him, it doesn't make any sense that as soon as he'd seen me, he'd run off in the opposite direction. And then vanished. Jack would never have let me get away that easily.

Maybe I'm hallucinating. I've tried so hard to forget about him, perhaps it's making me imagine things that simply aren't there.

THEN

Jack

I'm due to meet Harry at the clients' office at nine and am already running late. I slip on the last clean shirt in my wardrobe without bothering to have a shower, throw two empty wine bottles into the recycling and wash the remaining dregs of the third down the sink. I'm not sure if it's the smell of vinegar or the feeling of guilt that turns my stomach as the dark red liquid circles round the plughole and disappears. I can't face any breakfast. I wonder if I'm subconsciously adopting Ali's old habits in an effort to feel close to her. She was the one who would refuse anything other than a cup of coffee in the mornings, screwing up her nose as she watched me finish three slices of toast and peanut butter before I left. I swallow a couple of paracetamol with a cup of tea, grab my keys from the bowl on the hall shelf and walk out of the flat, slamming the door behind me.

My mum phones as I'm walking to the bus stop. I don't want to answer as I'm in a rush, but I doubt I'll get another chance to speak to her today and she'll worry if she can't get hold of me.

'You all right, love?' She can hear I'm out of breath.

'Fine, Mum. I'm just walking to the bus. I can't talk for long.'

'I wanted to check how you were. I had a missed call from Ali's dad last night so wondered if you'd heard from him. If he's coping OK . . .'

I interrupt her. 'He was fine when I spoke to him. You shouldn't worry.' I haven't talked to him, but I know he'd call me if it was anything really important. 'How are you?' I ask her.

'I'm good. And work's not too stressful?' She changes the subject. She never likes talking about herself.

I spot a gap in the traffic and dart across the road. 'Work's always stressful. That's the nature of management consultancy, but it's no worse than usual. I've got to go, Mum.'

'And you haven't heard anything else since you got that letter?' I know this is what I didn't give her a chance to ask on Monday, and she's been waiting for an opportunity to say it from the start of the conversation but has only just gathered up the courage. She's almost left it too late.

I hesitate. 'Nothing, Mum. Look, I've really got to go, I'm about to miss my bus.' I'm not sure whether she believes me, but I hang up and check my messages before putting the phone back in my pocket. I wonder why Edward called Mum rather than me. He's got my mobile number for anything important. I'll ring him back later. If I have time.

I half walk, half run the rest of the way to the bus stop, my armpits damp with perspiration. The orange letters on the electronic timetable display in the shelter show that there are three minutes until the next bus. Three minutes during which the sweat seeps through my shirt, leaving dark patches

under my arms on the surface of the light blue cotton. I'm
going to have to wear my jacket for the meeting and hope
the room has air conditioning. Ali would have made sure we
left on time.

My phone vibrates. A message from Harry.

I'm here. You?

I text back.

Almost.

It isn't a complete lie as once the bus arrives it won't take
long. I pray we don't get stuck in traffic. He doesn't trust me
not to be late; I've let him down once too often lately.

The bus pulls up and I squeeze against the people packed
into the narrow aisle, pushing my laptop bag into the man
in front of me in an attempt to get him to step forward and
make some space. I haven't got time to wait for the next
one. I've got nothing to hold onto, but it doesn't matter,
I'm glued in place by those around me, unable to move until
someone gets out. We lurch forward as the bus sets off and
I take a deep breath. I should have brought a bottle of water
with me.

The woman behind me steps on my shoe and I turn my
head towards her, trying to pull my foot away. She shuffles
to adjust her position, one hand tucking her dark bob behind
her ear as she looks down at her feet. Her hair reminds me of
Sarah's. Three days, if you count Monday, and I still haven't
heard anything from her. I don't think she's done what I

asked and she's had plenty of time. I think I need to remind her just in case she's forgotten. A phone call should be enough to jog her memory. For now. If that doesn't work, I'll have to pay her another visit.

I stare out of the small area of the bus window that's still visible through the mass of commuters as we travel through an underpass, the grey concrete casting us into shadow before we emerge into daylight on the other side. I wonder what Ali's doing. How her day's started. I wonder if she realises this journey seems to take double the time without her. Even when the bus had been packed like this she'd always smiled, putting her fingers over mine on one of the handrails, her touch more intimate than a whispered conversation. I'd never tired of looking at her in all the years we'd travelled this route together. I'd used to stare at her standing amongst the other commuters and feel how lucky I was, thinking I could read her mind. But if I had been able to, I remind myself as the bus comes to a halt, I'd have known what was going to happen.

The pneumatic door mechanism opens with a gasp and everyone spills out on the pavement. I glance at my watch as I step off. I'm late.

My phone vibrates again.

Where are you? Client wants to start.

Give me a chance, Harry. I text back:

Be there in two minutes. Need to talk to you about last week.

Five minutes later, I walk into the building, am handed a security pass by the receptionist and told to follow the signs to the boardroom. The rest of the team is already there, helping themselves to cups of tea or coffee and Danish pastries covered in icing sugar. Harry is sitting at one end of the large desk in the middle of the room. He looks up as I walk in and gives me a tight smile. I glance at my phone as I pour myself a black coffee. He hasn't replied to my text.

The meeting begins and I nod appropriately in the right places as we discuss the figures for the previous quarter with David Eden, the managing director at Marley Brown's. Whether the losses for the last quarter combined with the budgeted forecasts mean unavoidable redundancies in the branches they want to close down, but I'm not really paying attention. I'm looking discreetly at my phone on my lap, scrolling through the DVLA website until I find what I'm searching for.

Harry waits until we're on our own in the lift after the meeting before he turns to me. 'You look dreadful, Jack.'

'I'm OK,' I say. 'Just a bit tired.'

He looks past me, avoiding direct eye contact. 'Go home, have a sleep this afternoon and come in tomorrow. I'll let the office know.'

'I'm fine, really, I—'

He interrupts me. 'You're not, Jack. You look like shit. I know this last year has been a nightmare for you, I really do, but I'm saying this as your closest friend. Take some time off and get yourself together. I'm doing my best here, but I can't keep covering for you when we're trying to run a business. We looked like idiots in that meeting. You barely said a word. I'm sure everyone could tell you weren't really listening.'

I don't reply.

He opens his mouth as if he's going to say something else, but he's interrupted by his phone buzzing and he looks at the screen. 'That's David again now. I need to go. I'll tell him you weren't feeling well and just hope he's not too pissed off. We really can't afford to lose them as a client.'

As he walks off, I realise I didn't get a chance to ask him if he can remember what happened at dinner last week. Perhaps he'll respond later when he sees my text.

I rub my hand over my face. Ali used to say I had a five o'clock shadow by lunchtime even when I had shaved in the morning. Another unwelcome genetic trait I'd inherited from my father. I know it makes me look worse than I feel and I hadn't been surprised when Harry told me to go home. I'd hoped he would; I need the afternoon off.

I dial Sarah's number as I walk back to the bus stop.

'Ms Henderson's office. May I ask who's calling?'

I hesitate. 'It's Jack Reynolds.' The line goes silent and there's a long pause before the voice returns.

'I'm afraid she's not available at the moment. Can I take a message?' The receptionist's tone is supposed to convey this is only a minor, temporary inconvenience, but I know better; Sarah doesn't want to talk to me.

'When will she be available?' I ask.

This time there isn't any hesitation. 'I'm afraid she has a very full diary today. Would you like me to let her know you called?'

I don't answer.

'Or I can take a message?' she adds helpfully.

'Yes. Can you tell her I rang and ask her to contact me? Say I'm waiting to hear from her. It's urgent.' I know she won't call me back, but I don't need her to. I only phoned so I could check whether she's at work. She might not want to see me, but she can't avoid me forever. Ali always told me I needed to stick up for myself more. I used to ignore problems and hope they'd disappear, I'm not going to do that anymore. Not after what happened. I know only too well how quickly things can go wrong when you're not paying attention.

I get home and change out of my work clothes, digging around in the drawer of the coffee table for some brown paper. I take one of my books off the shelf in the sitting room and wrap it up, copying her name and address from the letter in my bag, sticking on a barcode label that I cut off a recent Amazon delivery. I wind Sellotape around the whole package and check it's fastened securely before picking it up with my car keys and the form from the DVLA website that's sitting in my printer tray. I've run through what I'm going to do in my head and just hope I haven't forgotten anything.

I get in my car and retrace the route I took on Monday, turning into the building entrance and driving slowly past the parking spaces marked clearly in white lines on the tarmac until I spot the black vehicle Sarah got into on Monday evening. I pull over and write the details of her number plate on the form I've printed out and scan the completed document onto my phone, emailing it back to the DVLA with their fee, paying extra for the fast-track service. I hope it's worth it.

I take a deep breath as I pick up the parcel off the passenger seat and walk in through the glass doors, which slide open automatically to let me inside. I smile as I walk up to the counter of the reception desk, glancing at the security barriers beside it.

'Amazon delivery? I've got a parcel for a Sarah Henderson?'

The girl standing behind reception smiles back. *A little courtesy goes a long way.* The phrase pops into my head, unbidden. My father had made my mother repeat it like a mantra, even when her face had been so swollen I'd barely been able to make out her words.

'I can take that for you,' she says.

She doesn't seem to notice my lips stick to my teeth as I speak. 'I'm really supposed to deliver it in person. Can you tell me which office I should take it to?'

The receptionist's smile fades. 'All post is distributed internally,' she replies. 'I'm afraid I can't let you into the building.'

I hesitate, pointing at the label. 'Could you maybe give this person a call, so I can confirm it's been collected? I really need to see a signature.'

She narrows her eyes and then presses a few buttons on the keyboard in front of her to dial an extension. I step away from the desk, pretending to look at my phone as I keep my eyes on the doors on the other side of the floor. Come on. How long does it take to get down a couple of flights of stairs? I glance back at the receptionist, who's pretending she's not watching me.

The barriers next to the reception are similar to the ones in my office; large metal blocks where you have to hold a security pass over a panel to get the prongs to revolve to let you in. They aren't high. Not much more than a metre.

There's a pinging sound as the lift arrives on the ground floor. The doors slide open. Sarah steps out and starts to walk in my direction and then stops as she recognises me. She hesitates for a fraction of a second, then turns back towards the lift, but the doors have already shut. I begin to climb over the barrier, the bottom of my jeans catching on the metal edges. It's harder than I thought. Sarah presses the button on the wall several times as she looks behind her.

'You didn't phone me back,' I shout as I clamber over.

She ignores me, but I know she's heard by the way she glances at the receptionist, checking she's already calling for help.

'Did you even look at what was in the envelope? Did you give it to Ali?' I hop awkwardly as I land on the other side of the barrier, almost falling over, disregarding the shouts coming from reception.

An alarm sounds and a few other people appear, alerted by the noise. The lift doors slide open. I start to run. Sarah steps inside, waiting to be taken out of my reach. I'm so close. She shrinks away from me.

'I just want to talk to you. I need you to tell me where she is,' I say. Her expression doesn't alter. She doesn't understand how much Ali means to me. What I'll do in order to see her. The doors close slowly as I get to them. I push the button repeatedly and bang the wall with my fist. A small crowd has gathered in the reception area and they're all watching me. As the doors open again, Sarah's eyes widen as I step towards her.

Before I can ask her if she's spoken to Ali again, there's a sudden commotion and I'm hauled backwards. Two security guards have hold of my sweatshirt and then I'm on the floor, my arms pinned down so I can't move. Sarah disappears. The alarm stops ringing as they pull me to my feet and drag me towards the entrance of the building.

One of the guards speaks into his radio whilst the other holds onto me. I don't fight him. There isn't any point. I've got what I needed. She does know where Ali is. I could see it in her eyes when I stepped into the lift.

'That's your final warning.' The guard who's been talking on his radio stands in front of me. 'Get up. You can't come in here without authorisation. Next time we'll have to get the police involved. D'you understand?'

I nod, the adrenaline that flooded my body now draining away.

They lead me out of the glass doors and walk either side of me until we get back to my car.

One meeting, Ali. That's all I want. I've stayed away, I've been so patient and still you refuse to see me. You don't understand I'm only trying to do what's best for you. I had hoped I wouldn't have to do this, but you really haven't left me with any other option.

NOW

Alison

I stick my head under the bathroom tap and swallow thirstily. At least it's Saturday and I don't have to face going to work. A few droplets run down the side of the sink, and I make a bet with myself which one will get to the plughole first. Fat beads, like transparent snake heads detached from their bodies that slide between the tiny hemispheres, swallowing them in their wake. A smaller one finds a quicker path, a route designed for speed, and it slithers down with an unexpected momentum, overtaking all the others around it. They make me think of Sarah – I hadn't seen her coming and I can't shake the feeling that unless I can remember where I've met her before, she's going to hurt me all over again.

I take my toothbrush out of its plastic cup and fill it with water, sipping some off the top so it doesn't spill as I carry it. Setting it down on my bedside table, I get back under the covers, pulling them up to my chin and moving my feet around in circles until the sheet warms up enough for me to be able to stretch out. I hate having cold feet. I always used to warm them on Jack's legs, using him as a hot-water bottle, but by the end we'd become so emotionally distant that although his body had been there, it had been like lying beside a stranger, and I'd felt colder next to him than I had been sleeping alone. I don't want to think about that so I get up again and gather my clothes off the floor, where I dumped them the previous night; a faint smell of stale perspiration clinging to the material as I put them in the washing basket.

I catch sight of the piece of paper as I carry my bowl of cereal into the sitting room. It's creased where it's been folded in half at some point, but now it lies open, in the middle of the grey cushion at one end of my sofa. I can see it's his writing, even from a distance. I chew on a mouthful of cornflakes whilst sitting on the arm of the chair, staring at it. I wonder if it's even really there, or if it will vanish when I try to reach for it, like Jack did yesterday. I decide if I can still see it when I've finished my breakfast, I'll read it.

Five minutes later, I take my empty bowl into the kitchen, refusing to give in to the temptation that tries to persuade me to look at it straight away. I wash up, stack the bowl in the cupboard and wipe some crumbs off the counter before going back into the sitting room. It's still there.

I take a deep breath and pick it up. Black fountain-pen ink on thick, cream writing paper. Jack never skimped on quality. If he did something, he did it properly. He'd done that with my engagement ring – designed it himself and chosen the diamond to have set into it. I look down at my bare fingers. It wouldn't fit me now, even if I still had it. They're too swollen, like the rest of me.

His cursive script loops across the page; the familiarity

making my chest constrict with a pang of bitterness.

> *Ali,*
> *When I last saw you, I told you I loved you. Much has*
> *happened since then, but I need you to remember how we used*
> *to be and what I said to you. I wish you'd write to me.*
> *Jack*

For a moment, I am numb. Intense anger and frustration sweep over me and I feel physically sick.

I read it again, picking at a piece of chapped skin on my lip with my teeth. He's referring to what he said to me yesterday on the stairwell and I'm struck by the thought that he must have come here afterwards to leave this for me. I thought I was safe here. I don't understand how he's managed to find me.

I retrieve the second letter from where I've filed it in my notebook in the kitchen, taking it into the sitting room to put it next to the one I've just read. Definitely the same writing, but not the same paper. No dates on either letter, and I realise, no postmark on the envelope. It must have been hand-delivered. Which means he must have been here. In my flat. The thought makes me run to the toilet and retch, bringing up mouthfuls of half-digested cornflakes. I grip the plastic seat until my stomach's empty and pull off some loo roll to wipe my eyes and mouth, sitting down on the floor to catch my breath. If Jack's been here, I need to work out how he got in and if he's left anything else for me to find.

An energy possesses me, my earlier headache and lethargy forgotten. I start by pulling the cushions off the sofa and shove my hand down the gap at the back of the chair, feeling for anything other than seat fabric. I unzip the grey cushion covers and take them off. I empty every cupboard in the kitchen, making sure I've run my hand over the shelves in each one. I drag my clothes out of my wardrobe and drawers, pile them onto the bed and search every pocket. I strip off the bedlinen, unfolding the spare covers and sheets from the drawer under the bed and shake them out to check nothing is hidden in the folds of material. By the time I finish, my flat resembles the scene of a violent burglary, but I've found two more letters. One tucked underneath my T-shirts, and the other stuffed into a pocket of the navy dress I never wear as I no longer fit into it. I used to have so many dresses, but I got rid of them all; I only have this one left.

As I tidy up everything I've removed from my drawers, I find a small red glove amongst my socks. I can see without trying it on it's far too small for me, and I can't find the other one to make a pair. It looks familiar; the panda face that's stitched in black and white across the red wool is strangely comforting, its faint scent familiar. I tuck it back where I found it. It must belong to me, but I've no idea what it's doing amongst my socks. I wonder if it's something else Jack's left for me to find.

I pick the letters up and smooth them out on the floor next to the ones I've already read. Five pieces of paper if I include the one I ripped up and threw away. I unfold the one that I'd found in the pocket of my dress.

Ali,
I don't know if you're reading this. I've got so many questions.
Why didn't you talk to me? Please write.

Jack

I don't focus on the words and concentrate on reading the last letter. This one looks older; it's folded together so tightly that the paper splits apart to leave a hole across the middle when I open it.

Ali,
Why?
Jack

They make no sense. He's leaving them for me to find but runs away when he has a chance to confront me face-to-face, even though that's the last thing I want. He knows what he's done. He knows we have nothing to talk about. He's caused me enough pain already.

'I don't think you've met my wife.' Jack's arm had been around my waist and he'd smelt of the aftershave he reserved for special occasions. I'd looked at the woman he was introducing me to and wished I'd worn something else. This outfit was too tight, and I'd known she'd thought the same from the way her eyes had flickered over my figure before resting on my face.

She'd smiled. 'No, I haven't. I'm Steph.'

Someone had tapped him on the shoulder and he'd turned around, leaving me alone with her. I'd barely been able to hear anything above the noise of the music. I'd wished they'd turned it down at the office parties. But I knew most people wanted to celebrate.

She'd lifted her glass in a toast.

'Cheers. To Butler Reynolds. Or something.' I'd thought she was already drunk but had raised my empty flute towards hers. 'Jack talks a lot about you,' she'd said.

I'd smiled. 'All good, I hope?'

She'd nodded.

I could see him at the bar with Harry. I hoped he wouldn't be long.

'He's a great guy,' she'd said. 'I was sorry to hear about your . . . difficulties.' I'd tried to keep my face expressionless, but she'd noticed me stiffen and had bitten her lip. 'Oh. I hope I haven't said anything out of order. We tell each other everything in the office. It's difficult to keep things private when you're as close as we all are.' She'd smiled, and I'd sensed a look of triumph in her eyes as I'd forced myself to smile back. 'Don't worry,' she said, lowering her voice, 'I won't say anything to anyone else.'

I'd stared at her, brushing a piece of non-existent lint off my too-tight black dress. It seemed to have shrunk since we'd arrived and now I barely had room to breathe.

'They've done amazingly this year. So many new clients,' I'd replied, determined not to let her see she'd unsettled me. 'Jack loves being here.'

He'd walked back towards us, holding a glass of champagne for me and I'd stepped away as he'd gone to put his arm round my waist. His forehead had creased as he'd noticed my movement.

'Harry wants us for a photo,' he'd said. 'Sorry, Steph, d'you mind? We'll be back in a minute.'

He'd ushered me over to where Harry was waiting and as I'd glanced back I'd seen Steph looking at me, no longer smiling.

I kneel on the lounge floor, trying to organise my thoughts into some kind of logical order. Eventually the sharp tingle of pins and needles forces me to get up and I stamp around the room, trying to get the blood circulating again. Should I go to the police? I could tell them he's found out where I live. That he's been here. But all I have to show them are his letters and I don't know if that's enough to make them believe me. Without a date on them, there's nothing to prove they weren't sent years ago and as they don't have a postmark they won't be able to trace where they're from. They won't believe me if I say I've seen Jack in the library and I know he'll just deny it. They'll want proof.

I rip a piece of paper out of my notebook in the kitchen and fold it into a tiny square. Opening the front door, I put the paper inside the hinge of the frame, holding it in place until the last minute before I shut it. I'm careful not to squash my fingers. When I open it, the paper falls out and drops to the ground. I'll know if someone has been in my flat.

I test it several times. It works, but I can see the paper when it drops onto the carpet. Most people wouldn't notice it, but if I do, Jack certainly will. I try making the square smaller, but it doesn't stay in place. It isn't reliable enough. I think of something else.

Standing outside my flat with the door shut, I stick a small piece of sticky tape at the top, so one end is stuck to the door and the other end to the frame. Now when I open the door the piece of tape comes unstuck. I can see if someone's been in and they'll be completely unaware of it. The tape is practically invisible to anyone who isn't looking for it.

I stick it in place every time I leave the flat for the next few days, trying not to think about how many times Jack's been inside without me knowing. Each time I return it's exactly as I left it. No one's been here. To be completely certain, I line up some pens on the kitchen table in a particular order so I'll know if they've been moved. I balance balled–up pairs of socks on top of one another in a fragile pyramid designed to fall over if anyone opens my chest of drawers. I won't let him back into my life.

By Wednesday afternoon I'm growing steadily impatient to leave work. I've got visions of the piece of sticky tape hanging from the door frame as Jack wanders around my flat, opening cupboards and drawers to glean information about who I am now. Without him. I'm so busy watching the clock, I don't see Sarah walk up to the counter. I've been going down to the canteen as late as possible to avoid her. Her make-up is flawless, but I'm wary of what she's hiding underneath. Her impeccable appearance makes me even more embarrassed to remember that the last time we'd met I'd been a sweaty mess.

'You look like you're miles away!' She waves the book she borrowed in my face. 'I just finished this one, so I thought I'd return it whilst I'm here. And I wanted to see how you were after the other day as I haven't seen you in the canteen this week.'

She waits for an explanation. I don't offer one. I was certain I could remember her hurting me before, but now I'm not so sure. I avoid looking at her by pretending to stare at my computer screen, wondering if it's me that can't be trusted. Perhaps I'm just imagining what she did, confusing her with Jack, and it's his hand on my arm that I can actually remember. I click my mouse a few times as I swallow and try to work out what to say to her as she's still waiting for me to reply.

'I'm fine, thanks,' I say. 'It was just a misunderstanding.'

She raises her eyebrows. 'Are you sure?'

'Yes, I'm good. Shall I take that for you?' I hold out my

hand for the book and she passes it to me.

'Perhaps I'll see you tomorrow for lunch?'

'Sure.' I smile but am already thinking of ways to avoid her as she walks out of the door.

I glance at the clock. It's almost four and I want to get home. Picking up my bag, I shout goodbye in the direction of the shelves where Mrs Painter is sticking up cards on which customers have hand-written reviews of their favourite books. She pulls off strings of Blu-Tack and presses a ball on the back of each card.

'You off then, Alison? I'll see you tomorrow. Can you make sure you log off from the computer?' She marches back up the aisle towards me and glances at the blank screen as she fiddles with the mouse. I know she isn't going to be able to resist ensuring I've done it properly. Ever since the incident in the photocopier room she's been more vigilant in checking up on me. I want to tell her that I know what I'm doing but don't get a chance before she says, 'As long as you've checked it, you're free to go,' and walks back down the aisle. Even though I'm sure I've already done it, I check she's not watching and push a button on the keyboard. I'm reassured when the screen stays blank; I hadn't forgotten.

The sticky tape is still attached to my front door and the frame when I get home. My heart sinks. I'm desperate to prove Jack's been here. There isn't any other logical explanation for the letters. Everything inside is as I left it this morning. My pens are in the same order on the kitchen table. I open my bedroom drawer very slowly. All the balls of socks are stacked up neatly. Nothing has been disturbed.

I take out all the letters from inside my notebook and read

them again slowly. *I wish things could have been different.* Me too. *Why didn't you talk to me?* I did talk to you. At one point, I couldn't stop talking. You never listened. *Please write.* There's no way I'm going to contact you. Not after what you did. *I need you to remember how we used to be.* I don't want to remember.

What do you want with me Jack? You ruined me and now I have nothing left to give. We'd been happy once. Or that's what I'd thought. I know I hadn't just imagined the way you used to look at me. The things you used to whisper in the dark. The way your breathing slowed when my hand reached for yours and held it tightly, reassuring you I was still there. I wish I could forget what you did afterwards. I shudder. I won't let myself think about that.

I stare at the pages in my lap. I've been picking at one of the letters without even realising it, tearing bits off the edges, and now there's only a small piece of paper left with most of the words missing and my trousers are covered in pieces of white confetti. I brush them onto the floor in horror, then gather them up in my hand, trying to work out if I can fix what I've done, but the pieces are too small and it's an impossible task. I can't work out which bit goes where. For a moment I think I'm going to cry, but I realise it's futile. I can't undo something I've ruined beyond the possibility of repair.

THEN

Jack

I leave work early to get something to eat and tidy the flat before Em and Harry come over. All the lights are turned off in Harry's office as I walk past. He didn't tell me he was going home, but I don't blame him, I haven't been particularly helpful this week. The pile of paperwork on his desk is almost as high as the one I've left on mine.

I pick up some prawn crackers and a Thai green curry that looks large enough to feed us all from Marks and Spencer on the way home. They are easy guests; we've been friends for so long, I know they'll eat pretty much anything. I hope Em won't bring up whatever she came round to talk about on Monday as my recollection of the evening I spent at their house is still hazy. I have a vague memory of her putting me in a taxi and shutting the front door before the cab drove off, but I still don't remember our conversation. Harry hasn't replied to my text, so I'm convinced I must have said something to upset her. I'll apologise when I see her later. I hesitate in the last aisle before the checkout, and stick a couple of bottles of Valpolicella in my basket. Ali's favourite.

She'd always had a bottle open on the table when I'd met

her after work in the small Italian restaurant that was halfway between our two offices. The first time we'd been there I'd baulked at the red and white gingham tablecloths, paper napkins and fake plants, but the food had won me over. The owner had got so used to seeing us that he'd stopped giving us menus. Ali had laughed when the waiter handed her a rose alongside her dish of *capesante alla veneziana*, and when we'd walked back to the bus stop, the couple of hours together had replenished the tenderness between us that was too often eroded by everyday life. I'd relied on those evenings during that last round of IVF. They were one of the things that had held us together, even though by then the flavour of the food had been tainted by my guilt.

When I arrive, the bus stop in the centre of town is crammed with commuters, all impatient to get home. I've just missed one and there's a ten-minute wait for the next. I hate travelling at this time in the evening. The smell of offices, of stressful work meetings, lingers unpleasantly on everyone's clothes.

The handle of my cheap plastic carrier bag starts to cut into my palm. When the bus finally pulls up, I stand in the aisle, the bottles bumping against my legs every time we stop, a constant reminder I shouldn't have bought them in the first place. I jump off a couple of stops early and walk the rest of the way back, the indent in my hand growing deeper with each step.

Em and Harry said they'd be here at seven; I have an hour. I hold up my key fob to let myself in through the main entrance and almost reach my flat at the end of the corridor when a man emerges, a couple of doors away. I keep walking and put the key in the lock quietly, hoping he won't notice me.

'Jack?'

I shut my eyes briefly and then look round, a polite smile fixed on my face. I can't remember his name, I think it might be Tom.

'Hi,' I reply, not moving. His keys jangle as he puts them in his pocket.

'Haven't seen you for a while?' he says.

I shake my head, looking back at my front door. 'No, I've been busy.'

'How are you?'

'Yes. Not too bad.' I force myself to keep smiling as I adjust my grip on my shopping. The bottles clink together and he stares at me.

'I saw your father-in-law the other week,' he continues. He hesitates, debating whether to say anything else.

I remain silent, hoping now we've exchanged pleasantries he'll leave. I hardly know him and we've only spoken on the odd occasion when we pass in the corridor. He's got a baby. Gracie, I think he said her name was. I hear her crying sometimes and have to turn up the radio in my kitchen to block out the sound. He's probably heard the rumours and is digging to see what information he can find out to pass onto the local grapevine.

My grin fades as he walks towards me. He's not going anywhere.

He lowers his voice. 'He didn't look well. Poor guy. I guess it's not surprising. Edward, isn't it?'

I fight to turn my key in the lock. 'Yes, it is. But he's fine.'

I'm determined not to lose my temper. 'Anyway, I've got a few things to do, so better get on. Good to see you.'

I finally manage to get the key to turn and almost fall into my hallway in my urgency to get away from him. I sense he's still standing behind me, but I slam the door shut before he has a chance to ask anything else. Taking a deep breath, I dump the food on the counter and put the bottles of wine away in the bottom cupboard. Out of sight, out of mind, I tell myself. And not to be opened tonight. I have too much to do this weekend.

I stick the curry in the oven and attempt to tidy the flat whilst setting the table in the lounge. I rarely make the effort to eat in there now. I gather my unopened letters together into one pile and put them on the kitchen counter. I'll sort through them properly later. I change out of my work clothes, have a quick shower and put on some decent after-shave before I check my email. There's one from the DVLA. I scan through it and see it has all the information I asked for. Good. Everything's ready. There's still nothing from Sarah. I'll give her until tomorrow morning.

At six fifty-five, my phone buzzes. A message from Em.

Slight disaster, Jessica's not well. Harry's going to stay with her as he's not feeling too good either. He thinks he might have the same thing, but I'm still coming if that's OK with you?

I hesitate before texting back.

Great, but only if you're sure.

I sound more enthusiastic than I feel. It would have been easier with Harry here tonight, but Em's been so good to me over the last year, I don't feel I can refuse. The anxiety I felt when she was here on Monday swills around in the bottom of my stomach like the fourth glass I shouldn't have had last night. Em and I had promised not to keep secrets from each other and I've always kept to what we agreed, with just one exception.

I open the door to let in some fresh air as the smell of Thai curry wafts through the flat. It reminds me of the Khao San Road. The first time I'd been abroad further than Spain. The place had been heaving with other students on their gap year, all high on adrenaline and the excitement of being far away from home with no responsibilities. Ali and I had flirted in one of the clubs, pressing up against each other in the dark heat of the dance floor. I had wanted to feel every inch of her skin against my own and hadn't been able to get close enough before the energetic beat forced us apart as the strobe lights flashed faster, leaving my fingers empty, wet with tiny beads of sweat from her neck.

The doorbell chimes and I peer at the video entry screen. It's Em. Unlike other visitors, she stands back calmly from the camera, her image clear on the screen, confident she'll be let in. Most people put their face too close to the panel, desperate to show who they are, which actually makes them more difficult to see.

I squint at myself in the hall mirror, one last check on my appearance before pressing the button on the intercom.

'I'm so sorry I'm late,' she says, sounding out of breath when I open the door moments later. 'What a bloody disaster.

Jessica puked everywhere. I'm just glad to get out and leave Harry to deal with it.' She hands me a bottle of Merlot and glances at her phone. 'He hasn't texted yet, so I presume he's coping.'

'Thanks,' I reply as she steps inside. 'We've got Thai.'

She smiles. 'That sounds great.'

'It's bought, I'm afraid. Not home-made. But at least there's less chance of me poisoning you to make your situation at home any worse.'

She laughs. 'I hadn't considered that possibility. Can I stick my jacket somewhere?'

I nod. She opens the door of the small cupboard in the hall. The light comes on automatically and she hangs it on a hook next to one of Ali's old coats. I keep meaning to give it to Edward. There's no point in me keeping it here.

'D'you need a hand with anything?' she asks.

'I think it's pretty much all done.'

She follows me into the sitting room and pours us both a glass of wine. I fill up my tumbler of water and raise it towards her, swallowing a couple of mouthfuls whilst leaving the dark red liquid in my glass untouched. I glance at the clock. Two minutes to eight. I'll allow myself a mouthful at eight fifteen. I'm determined to make this one last the whole evening.

She looks at me. 'Harry said you were off work yesterday afternoon.'

I blow on a forkful of curry. 'Yes. I felt lousy in a client meeting and had to come home.'

Em hesitates. 'Were you hungover?' she asks.

'No!' My denial is too quick.

She stares at her plate, pushing her rice around with her fork. 'Harry said you looked like you were.' She waits for me to speak.

I give into temptation, reach for my glass and take a large gulp of wine, drowning the words I want to say before they leave my mouth. I still have thirteen minutes to go until eight fifteen, but I can't talk about this without alcohol. I need to tell her. My throat burns as the liquid slides down. 'I wrote to Ali,' I say.

'You did what?' She stops eating.

'Edward and I argued when he came over a couple of weeks ago. He told me Ali didn't want to see me and I didn't believe him, so I wrote to her.'

Em stares at me. 'You've always said you didn't want to see her. What did she say?'

'Nothing. I got an official letter back advising me to stay away from her.'

'Oh, Jack. I'm so sorry,' Em says.

I take another mouthful. 'I don't understand why she won't see me after all this time. I'm still her husband.'

Em fiddles with the stem of her glass as she speaks. 'Edward told me a while ago she'd said she didn't want any contact. But that was months ago and I just assumed . . . when she got . . . that she'd change her mind.'

'Well she hasn't.' I down the dregs left in my glass. 'And I know how long it's been, but I've decided I really want to see her. Every time I close my eyes, I'm taken straight back to—'

Em interrupts me as I cover my face with my hands. 'Don't think about it. It wasn't your fault.' She repeats the same words she's said so many times over the past year, but I look up as this time she says it with a little less conviction than usual.

'It was,' I murmur. 'It hangs over me like some bloody great shadow. The whole time.' I glance at her, searching for reassurance.

'I've said this before, Jack. You can't blame yourself.' Her voice is flat.

'I shouldn't have . . .' I stop myself mid-sentence.

'You shouldn't have what?' Her eyes narrow.

'It doesn't matter.' I want to retract the words that slip out too easily.

'I was Ali's friend too, you know,' she says quietly.

I don't answer.

'Are you sure you told me exactly what happened?'

'Of course,' I lie.

'Because when you came over last week to ours, you talked about her.' Em puts her fork down on her plate. She hasn't eaten much. 'An awful lot about her, actually. You were so drunk. So was Harry. He doesn't remember what you said, but I do.'

The anxiety that's been swilling around in my stomach all evening solidifies into a hard ball and rises up in my chest. I cough and take a sip of water.

Em fixes her eyes on mine as she sits back in her chair and looks at me from the other side of the table. 'Don't you remember?' she asks.

I shake my head, trying to think back through the blank fog. My heart races with a sudden burst of adrenaline and there's a high-pitched whining in my head. Every instinct in my body tells me to leave the room. That I don't want to hear what she's about to say, but I can't move. I have nowhere to go.

'You should do,' Em continues. 'I assumed after I'd put you in a taxi and sent you home that what you'd said had just been the drink talking, but now I'm not so sure.'

I concentrate on keeping my face expressionless. My insides are heavy. I can't believe she knows and I don't even remember telling her.

'You told me what you did to stop Ali leaving,' Em says. 'What happened in the car.'

She looks at me and I don't deny it. The sound of brakes and a sickening thump fills my head, pushing any words out of reach. I blink, not wanting her to see the guilt in my eyes.

'That's why you're drinking so much, Jack.' She's right. It helps to blot out those memories. It doesn't work for others that are so much worse. 'I think you're going to have to admit what you did. This isn't something you're going to be able to keep a secret. It's only a matter of time before someone else finds out.'

NOW

Alison

I can't sleep. I flip my pillow over to try to find a cool spot, tensing my muscles, starting with my toes, until I can't squeeze them any tighter, and then relax. I count slowly to five while I breathe in, and then out. It doesn't work. I can still see his face.

When I'd had nightmares as a child, my dad had sat on the edge of my bed with a beaker of warm milk and stroked my hair until I'd fallen asleep again. I get up and pour myself some milk into a cup. The flat is silent apart from the low humming of the microwave as the mug circles on the turntable. I wrap my dressing gown tighter around me as I wait for the timer to count down to zero, then put the drink down carefully on a mat and pull out the letters from my notebook. Two. Where's the third? I'd put them all away in the same place. I double-check my notebook, flicking through the pages and shaking it upside down to see if the piece of paper has got wedged inside by mistake. It's not there.

Did I throw it away by mistake? I'm convinced I haven't, but to be sure I pull out the small swing-top bin from under the sink and fish through the contents inside. There's very little in it: an empty bread bag, a couple of baked bean pots and a screwed-up piece of toilet roll with a clump of tangled hair peeking out from between the folds. No sign of any letter.

It isn't like I actually need it. The words are etched firmly in my memory. I just want the evidence to prove he's real. That he's been here. That I'm not losing my mind. He'd made me feel like that whenever I was getting too close to the truth. Perhaps that's what he wants me to feel now. It's working.

'You must have said something to her,' I'd said, unzipping my dress a couple of inches at the back so I could breathe in the taxi on our way home.

'I didn't. I told you. She must have overheard us on the phone.' He'd been annoyed. He'd hated evenings when he had to socialise with clients. He'd found it draining.

'Jesus, Jack. You need to be more careful. I told you I don't want everyone in your office knowing our business.'

I'd opened the window slightly to let in some fresh air. I'd felt a bit sick. A combination of too much alcohol and the heater that seemed to be blowing hot air straight into my face in the back seat. And the suspicion that he wasn't telling me the whole truth.

'D'you work with her a lot?' I'd asked, putting my hand on his.

'Who? Steph? Not much.' He'd reached into his jacket pocket to find his wallet as the cab had turned into our road.

'She said you were close.'

He'd pulled away from me. 'No more than anyone else in the team. We all have to get on when we work together for as many hours as we do.' He'd caught the look on my face and frowned. 'If

99

you don't believe me, Ali, perhaps next time we have one of these events you'd better not come.'

I hadn't wanted the evening to end on a sour note as he'd given a couple of twenty-pound notes to the driver and told him to keep the change. I'd slipped my hand into his as we walked up to our front door and ignored the fact it had felt like he'd been trying to pull away, telling myself the stress of the past few months had taken its toll on both of us. That I knew my husband better than some woman he worked with.

As I go to switch off my lamp, I see it. Folded up neatly on the edge of my bedside table. I didn't put it there. I distinctly remember putting it in my notebook with the others. I don't move as I try to reassure myself that no one's been in my flat since I got home. I would have heard them.

I creep out of bed and peer into the darkness of the small rooms to check. Of course there's no one here. Just a heavy silence that permeates into every corner, waiting to be broken as I drift back to sleep wondering how the note had ended up on my bedside table.

In my dream I can't move my arms and panic, then realise I'm not being restrained; my fingers are being stroked, gently. For some reason, I can't open my eyes, but I know, instinctively, this is my dad. It's the same touch that had comforted me after Mum died, the same large hands that had wrapped themselves around mine in an effort to shield them – and the rest of me – from the grief. He's talking to me but his words are muffled and I can't ask him to speak louder as my voice doesn't seem to be working. I've got a horrible feeling I'm supposed to be somewhere and need to get up. Dad starts to help me and then I open my eyes to see Jack's face above me, his brown eyes staring straight into mine.

I sit up with a gasp, fumbling for the lamp switch and squinting in the light that's too bright after the darkness. I kick off my duvet as sweat drips from my skin. My pyjamas are soaked through and the sheet underneath me is damp. It's just a bad dream. There's no one here.

I leave the light on whilst I try to get back to sleep for the three hours until I have to get up for work. The nightmare lingers like a pool of water, invisible in the dark. Each time my eyes begin to close, I jerk awake to stop myself sliding back into the cold liquid. I try to think about something else and concentrate on the feeling of Dad holding me. My dad. He hasn't been over for ages. We'd been so close when Mum died, but since everything happened with Jack, I haven't seen him as much. I need to call him. Get him to visit. I try to remember when he last came over, but my thoughts become muddled with tiredness and I'm still trying to work it out as I fall asleep.

It's only the thought of having to explain my absence to Mrs Painter that gets me out of bed the following morning. I stare at myself in the small mirror in my bathroom as I clean my teeth. My hair hangs in lank sections which don't join together when I brush them. I wish I'd got up earlier to wash it. It's too short to tie up into a ponytail, so I have to leave it and hope people won't look too closely. I double-check my notebook. Three letters. All safe. Jack will come back to my flat at some point. He hasn't finished with me yet, but he doesn't realise I'll know if he gets in here and is waiting for me. I just need to be patient.

Sarah gets in the lift beside me when I arrive at work. I take the opportunity to move away from her as I press the button for the first floor, unsuccessfully stifling a yawn.

'Tired?' she asks.

I nod. 'I didn't sleep well.'

'I hate nights like that. Makes getting up early such an effort.' She clasps her pristine tote handbag, her kitten heels pressed neatly together. I'm suddenly conscious my trousers are creased and there's a stain on my top where I've spilt some of my breakfast. I pull my cardigan tighter around me.

'I overslept,' I add as an afterthought. I'm lying, but it helps to explain my appearance. The lift slides to a halt on the first floor. 'This is me,' I say.

'I know.' She smiles. 'Maybe see you at lunch later?'

'Yes. Maybe.' I'm the epitome of politeness, but my tone is cold as I step out. I'm going to make sure I don't go down to the canteen at my normal time so I can avoid seeing her again.

'You're very quiet today, Alison.' Mrs Painter looks over at me when there's a lull in visitors. I don't comment as I notice an indentation on her finger where her wedding ring used to be. The skin is shiny and new, like when you move a piece of furniture and the carpet underneath has been squashed flat. 'I mean, quieter than usual. You haven't said a word this morning. I don't want to pry, but is something the matter?'

I bite back a wry smile. Sure she doesn't. She always wants to know what's going on in my life. She makes a point of telling me things about her neighbours on a daily basis. I never listen, but I don't tell her that. I've worked with her long enough to recognise that her desire to talk is simply a way of masking her own insecurities. I'm not going to confide in her about getting Jack's letters, that I think I've seen him here at work – I'm too worried as it is about losing my job. She's bombarding me with information that I don't need to know and I just want her to be quiet whilst I try to remember something Sarah said. Something she asked me. I think it's important, but I can't recall what it was. Mrs Painter's constant chatter means I can't focus properly.

'Your ring is missing,' I blurt out. I'm not sure what makes me say it other than a desperate need to stop her talking and for her to see what it feels like when someone pries into your life, peeling apart the layers and digging around.

A crease appears in her forehead as she looks down at her finger. 'That's perceptive of you.' She fiddles with her glasses chain and I can see I've pierced her usually impermeable exterior. Her voice trembles. 'I'm not sure whether I should give it back. He wants me to.' She looks at me and there are tears welling in her eyes. 'Do you think I should?'

I open my mouth to answer, but she carries on talking before I can reply.

'But I think he'll just give it to his new . . . and I don't want . . .' She trails off, waiting for me to respond. It's the first time she's ever asked for my advice, but I'm at a loss as to what to say. I didn't mean to upset her. I know in her own way she's just trying to create a pleasant working environment. She doesn't realise that I'm not like the other staff here; I don't want to discuss the local gossip, I'm too busy worrying about Jack. Now I wish I hadn't said anything.

'How long have you had it?' I ask.

'Forty years. But it doesn't seem right that I've got it now he's—'

I interrupt. 'If he gave it to you, it's yours and you should keep it. If you want to.'

She still looks upset and I search for something I can say to make us both feel better.

'My husband gave me a bracelet once,' I tell her. I still remember picking up the fragile silver chain out of the small velvet box and our skin touching as he'd fastened it round my wrist. He'd bought it as a special present, but it was so long ago, I can't remember what it was for. I think it was our anniversary.

She gives me a strange look.

'What happened to it?' she asks.

'I . . . I don't know. I think I must have lost it.' I try to touch my thumb and forefinger together in a circle round my wrist, but they don't quite reach. They press on my bruise and the throb of pain makes me pull them apart. I look at Mrs Painter and smile briefly before turning away and walking down the row of bookshelves towards the back of the room where people are sitting at the tables. I'll give her some space. I hate being fussed over when I'm feeling unhappy.

Some of the customers are reading, others stare blankly at the screens on their laptops. The library is busy and I'm pleased as it means Mrs Painter is less likely to keep checking on me. I look around the tables to see if anyone is eating. People do it despite the large signs on the walls instructing them not to, all written in capital letters, underlined and punctuated with several exclamation marks. They don't know how unpleasant it is to have to wipe hardened globules of food off plastic covers or separate pages that have been stuck together with an unrecognisable substance. It's another reason why I keep hand sanitiser in my bag.

I walk past the tables to the back of the library by the stairwell, where the double-glazed windows overlook the car park. The air conditioning keeps the temperature inside at a constant eighteen degrees, but outside the cars shimmer in a heat haze and I close my eyes, imagining the smell of warm tarmac. One of the last days of an Indian summer before the earthy, crisp smell of autumn appears in the mornings. Jack's favourite season.

I take advantage of the peace and quiet to try to remember what it was that Sarah said, but it's gone, hiding behind too many other thoughts.

'I'm not good at coping in the heat.' Mrs Painter makes me start as her voice breaks the silence. She's standing behind me as I stare into the dazzling brightness. 'Twenty-eight today apparently. Not what you'd expect in September.' She walks off again, peering over people's shoulders.

I turn back towards the window. A large bumble bee is crawling slowly across the inside of the pane of glass, its fragile feet tentatively searching for an escape route. As it moves, the sunshine catches its wings, reflecting a myriad of colours like miniature stained-glass windows. Mrs Painter doesn't like insects. She keeps a can of Raid in her cupboard and picks up the lifeless bodies with tissues afterwards. I look round for something to put it in.

'What are you looking at?' She's back, her inspection round completed. She follows my gaze. 'Oh . . . that's a big one.' I can detect the panic in her voice. 'I'll get the spray.'

'No!' The vehemence in my voice surprises me. 'I'll find a container for it. We can take it outside.'

Mrs Painter stares at me. 'It's only a bee, Alison, and the windows don't open here. You'd have to take it all the way down to the ground-floor reception, and we've got nothing to put it in.'

She walks back towards her desk. I feel a surge of panic. Picking up a book, I try to get it to crawl onto the cover. It ignores my efforts and keeps flying onto the pane, searching for an escape route. I watch as Mrs Painter advances, can in hand.

'Please. I want to save you.' I whisper the words, hoping I can make it understand my intentions.

There's a lump in the back of my throat as Mrs Painter presses the nozzle in its direction and a cloud of noxious fumes engulfs the struggling figure. The bee falls onto the windowsill on its back, legs waving frantically for a few seconds before freezing stiffly like tiny branches.

'There. All done.' She pauses, pushing the tiny body with the tips of her glasses to check for any signs of life before enveloping it in a wad of tissues. 'Would you mind going on the computer for me? There are people waiting.'

I walk back to the counter. A queue is building up as I pass the scanner over the books, lining up the red light with each barcode in quick succession, trying to not think about the poor creature that didn't belong here. I know how it must have felt. Although I'm grateful for this job, I'm trapped just as much as it was, crawling around amongst all these books, waiting for Jack to find me.

I put my hand on top of the tall pile that the man places in front of me. 'I'm afraid you can't take out more than four at once.' My voice quavers and I have to clear my throat.

'Why not?' he asks, putting his hand on the counter.

'It's library policy. It's stated in the rules. That you signed when you joined.' I'm curt as he's being so rude and I'm still upset about the bee.

'I didn't sign anything.' He's wearing a long-sleeved sweat-shirt that's at least two sizes too big for him and he's sweating profusely, despite the air conditioning.

'You must have, or we wouldn't let you borrow any books.' I look anxiously down the row of bookshelves to see if I can locate Mrs Painter.

'I didn't. I didn't sign anything.'

I keep my hand on top of the stack of books so he can't pick them up. 'Which four would you like to keep?'

'I want all of them.' He moves his sticky hand on top of mine and instinctively I pull away. His touch is repulsive.

'Well, you can't. You need to choose four.' I straighten my posture to full height to demonstrate an air of authority. 'Otherwise I'm going to have to ask you to leave.' Other people are joining the queue and he's holding everyone up.

'I want all of them.' He pulls nervously at his damp sweatshirt.

'Can I help at all?' Mrs Painter walks back towards the counter and the knot in my stomach relaxes.

'He wants to take all these out,' I tell her.

'You know you can't do that, Matthew. You're not allowed to take out more than four. We've told you this before.' She speaks to him slowly before turning towards me. 'Matthew's one of our regulars. Don't you recognise him?'

She walks round the counter and mutters in my ear, 'He's always trying it on. But, you know, he's harmless.'

I grip the scanner, pressing it against the cover of one of the books.

Mrs Painter looks at me whilst I make no effort to move and then takes it out of my hand, laying it down on the surface beside me. 'Don't worry about it, Alison. You deal with the others.'

I step out of her way and signal for the next person in the queue to move down as I reach under the counter for my bag, squeezing out a large blob of sanitiser and rubbing it liberally across both hands. It doesn't get rid of the feeling of being touched by damp flesh, but at least it'll kill the multitude of germs that must be sliding across my skin.

Matthew picks up four books off the counter and grins at Mrs Painter, who smiles back.

She's mistaken. He might be one of her regulars, but I've never seen him before in my life.

THEN

Jack

There's a rasping noise next to me in bed. I'm heavy with sleep, fighting to surface from the nightmare that holds me in its grip. The warmth of her skin lingers on my fingers. I press the switch to turn on my lamp, but nothing happens. The room is pitch black. I reach out to put my arm round her, searching for comfort in the familiarity of the curve of her back, the smoothness of the scar on her right hip where she slipped on a rock on holiday. There's a fleeting second of confusion as I touch a cold sheet before I remember she isn't there. The disappointment hits me as hard as a physical blow. It hasn't lessened with time.

I slide my hand under the duvet and cross my arms over my chest, holding myself tightly. Of course she isn't here. She's been gone for almost a year. I glance at her side of the bed and when I shut my eyes, I can see her turn over towards me, pushing her legs between mine so we're linked together, as one, even in sleep.

It's not real. I rub my eyes to get rid of the images. I'd give anything to go back, even to those few seconds before I wake up when I still think she's still lying beside me.

I realise I'm the one making the rasping noise. I can't seem to catch my breath. Why's it so dark? I fight to control my panic and lie still, concentrating on slowing my breathing. I haven't even got my phone to check what time it is.

I get up slowly, the effect of the wine I drank last night becoming evident as I raise myself from a horizontal position and stagger out of bed. I run my hand over the wall to feel for the light switch. I turn it on and off. Nothing. I take small steps over to the window, feeling with each foot for the hazards I can't see on the floor, and pull back the curtain. I still can't see properly, but at least now I can recognise the outline of the garden table on the patio illuminated in the glow of the nearby street lamps. My rapid heartbeat slows a fraction as I realise there's probably been a power cut.

I grope my way to the kitchen. The walls of the flat look smooth in the daytime, but in the blackness, I can feel the slight bumps in the painted plaster. Nothing's perfect when you look closely enough. The lights don't work in there, either. There are no luminous digits showing on the oven clock.

I pat my hand along the shelf in the hall to find my mobile, scroll up to activate the torch button, and open the coats cupboard to look at the fuse box. The main switch has tripped, along with another, so I push them both back up. There's a series of clicks as objects round the flat spring back into life. Not a power cut, just a bulb blown in one of the kitchen lights.

I pull on my dressing gown and make myself a cup of tea. I take a sip, wince and add a teaspoonful of sugar, taking my mug to sit on the sofa in the half-darkness. I want to try to persuade my brain it's still night-time and it should go back to sleep. The caffeine in the tea probably won't help, but I need something sweet to recover from the shock of waking up and not being able to see anything. I know I'm alone, but in the deep silence of the early morning hours I can almost convince myself she's still here.

So much of her remains. She chose the paint, the ornaments, the furniture. She's ingrained in the walls and the floorboards. I can still see her sitting on the sofa opposite me, legs curled up beneath her, hair tied up in a messy ponytail, laughing at she beats me at Rummy, my cards strewn over the table in frustration. Or lying in bed, pillows propped up behind her, so engrossed in the book she's reading that she jumps as I walk in. Or staring blankly across the kitchen table, refusing to meet my eyes, pushing her plate away, the quiche I've bought us for lunch untouched. I can't help returning to how she was at the end. It's as much as part of us as how we were at the beginning.

My breathing has almost returned to normal. I tell myself it was only a nightmare. I have them so regularly, I should be used to them, but it takes a while for the images to fade. I can't understand how my brain can replicate exactly what her skin feels like, even though I haven't stroked it for a year.

I stare at the mantelpiece whilst I finish my last few mouthfuls of tea. I'm not sure what I'm looking at, but after a few seconds I catch up with what my subconscious is telling me. The bronze buddha figure that sits in the middle of the shelf has moved.

I stand up. I'm certain I haven't touched it, but it's now on the far left-hand side of the shelf. I push it back to the centre. We'd bought it on holiday in Sri Lanka when we'd been trying to conceive and had ended up carrying it round with us for the whole trip. Ali had joked it had been her good luck symbol throughout the rounds of IVF, and even when they hadn't worked she'd refused to get rid of it. I'd reminded her Buddhists considered attachment the ultimate bond to break to ease suffering, so keeping it was ridiculous, but she'd insisted.

Perhaps Jess had wanted to play with it and Harry had got it down for her, but I don't remember noticing it had moved since they'd been over. I'll have to ask him next week. I wonder if Em's told him what we talked about. She's given me the weekend to think about what I'm going to do, but she doesn't know I won't be here by then.

The cup of tea doesn't ease the thumping in my head. I put the empty mug back in the kitchen and fish around in the cupboard for a couple of ibuprofen tablets, which I swallow as I head back into my bedroom.

I'm not sure what makes me turn around. Whether there's really a noise or whether I imagine it. Either way, I find myself looking at the door at the opposite end of the hall-way. My skin prickles. It's open. Only a small crack, but the darkness spills out, swallowing the light as it spreads towards me. For a moment I'm frozen, my senses so alert I'm convinced I can hear every noise in the entire block. People snoring. Dishwashers on a night cycle. Radiator pipes.

I take a step forward and realise the shadows in the hallway are playing tricks on me. The door isn't open. It just looks like it is. The brass handle gleams invitingly. Don't go in there, Jack. Go back to sleep. I retreat a couple of steps backwards. Ignore it.

I walk round the edge of my bed. Even though she's not here, I don't like to lie on her side. I take my phone out of my dressing gown pocket and tuck myself under the duvet, turning over a few times to try to get comfortable. I'm not tired. I check my messages. One from my mum.

I spoke to Edward. Was a bad line but he'll be with you at 11 tomorrow. I might come over too. Would love to see you. Hope you aren't too tired after work xx.

I want to have left before they get here. I'm worried Em will have called them and said something already. Her words go round and round in my head. I know what I've done, she was right in that respect, but I'm not drinking because I can't admit it, I'm drinking because I admitted it to myself, a long time ago. I face the consequences every night as soon as I turn off the light, living through it over and over again in my nightmares.

I sit up and plump my pillows before settling down and shutting my eyes. It's no good. I can't sleep. I get out of bed and stand in the hallway, staring at the door at the other end of the corridor. I walk towards it. I haven't been in there since Edward left after our argument. I put my ear against the wood. There's no sound. Of course there isn't. I'm being stupid. All I can hear is my heart pounding. *Go back to bed, there's nothing in there.* I put my hand on the brass knob and twist it. The door swings open and I step inside onto the thick cream carpet. The blinds are lowered and, in the darkness, I can only make out the indistinct shapes of the few pieces of furniture. I pause at the edge of the room, breathing heavily, and switch on the light.

Em had arranged for a local decorator to come in a week after it happened so I hadn't had to face looking at that wall, but as I peer at it now, I realise I can still see the marks very faintly, under the surface, despite the three coats of new paint. I trace over a couple of them with one finger and scratch them with my nail. A few flakes come off in my hand. I pick up a comb that's lying on the chest of drawers and gouge out a small circle. More flakes fall onto the carpet. I still can't see what's underneath. The savagery is sandwiched somewhere between the plaster and the top layer of paint, not properly visible but preserved for eternity. A constant reminder.

An unopened set of Beatrix Potter and a few books about pregnancy are lined up on the white wooden shelf above the small chest of drawers. I run my hand over them and pull out one that looks familiar. She's marked a page in the chapter about hormone treatment with an old photo of us embracing in front of a Christmas tree, my hair covered in tinsel. She's laughing, her amusement reflected in her eyes. On the back, she's written *Remember to think happy thoughts.* I stare at it until my tears distort the words in front of me and fall onto the paper, smudging the ink until the writing is just a damp blur.

I'm tired of trying to cope. And I'm tired of trying to put my life back together when each time I fix one part, another disintegrates. Alcohol no longer helps me sleep. I want one night that isn't so full of unspeakable terrors that I wake up refreshed. All that greets me in the morning at the moment is the start of another hangover and the realisation she isn't here.

I pick up the photo, slide it inside the book and put them both back on the shelf. I wipe my face on the sleeve of my dressing gown as I look at the empty cot at the side of the room. Tiny stars hang motionlessly from the baby mobile. I touch one and it twists round slowly. As I watch it, I have the strongest sensation she's standing behind me. I can feel her hand on my shoulder. For a few seconds I don't dare to move, and then the pressure eases and I know she's gone. I turn around, but there's no one there. It's a sign, show-ing me this is where she belongs and what I'm about to do is the right thing. I switch off the light and walk into the bedroom.

I pick up my mobile off my bedside table and search for Em's contact details to send her a text.

We need to talk.

I don't expect a response. It's three o'clock in the morning. Now she knows, it's only a matter of time. I can't wait until Monday. I push the thought that it could already be too late out of my head. Shutting my eyes, I sleep dreamlessly, for the first time in as long as I can remember.

I get up before my alarm wakes me in the morning and sit on the sofa with the early-morning sun streaming in through the patio doors, warming the back of my neck. I check my messages one last time. Still nothing from Sarah and no reply from my text to Em last night. It's still early, but there's no excuse to put off what I need to do any longer. Pulling on a pair of jeans and a sweatshirt, I stick a slice of bread in the toaster and call Edward as it pops up.

'Jack?' His normally gruff voice is croaky. I must have woken him up.

'Mum said you were coming over at eleven.'

'Right.' He coughs. 'Does that work for you?'

'Yes, that's fine. Thanks.' There's an awkward pause. 'Edward?'

'Yes?' He coughs again.

I frown. 'Is everything OK?' My voice is mumbled as I'm trying to eat my toast at the same time. 'You don't sound well. I mean . . .'

'Yes, everything's fine. I've just got a bit of a cold.'

'OK. I'll see you at eleven then.' I hesitate. 'And Edward?'

'Yes?'

'I . . . I wanted to thank you. For everything. I really appreciate it and I'm sorry if I let you down.'

There's a pause at the other end of the line. 'You haven't, and you don't need to apologise.' I can hear a noise in the background and grip my phone more tightly, straining to hear, but he coughs again and it's gone. 'I'll be with you at eleven,' he says. 'See you then.' I wish I'd told him he'd been more of a father to me than mine ever had.

I take the box down off the shelf in my wardrobe and pull out the card that's lying amongst the other memories. I'd got it last Christmas, and I stare at the black and white photo on the front cover. I need Ali to realise that no matter how far away she goes, I'll always find her again. We're destined to be together, even if she can't see that yet.

I open her jewellery box that's still on our dressing table and take out her silver charm bracelet, putting it into my jacket pocket and glance round the flat as I open the front door. There's nothing here for me anymore. I just need to find her and I know exactly how I'm going to do it.

NOW

Alison

The Sellotape isn't stuck to the door when I get back to my flat. I double-check by running my finger across the frame to find the raised edge, but the paintwork is completely smooth. My stomach lurches in fear. I open my front door slowly and listen for any noises whilst glancing round to look for anything that's out of place. When we'd first got married, I used to love coming home to find the little presents Jack had left for me: a turquoise leather notebook with my new married initials of *AR* monogrammed on the cover, a terracotta pot of jasmine that I'd put outside on our patio to grow. And then one day his surprises weren't so much fun anymore.

'Hello?' I half-whisper, not wanting a reply, peering into the sitting room and glancing at the empty sofa.

Silence.

I clear my throat and call out again.

No reply.

I leave my bag by the door and keep my shoes on as I search inside. My bedroom is deserted, as are the bathroom and the kitchen. My pens are in same the order that I left them this morning and my socks are still balanced precariously in their stacked pyramid when I open my chest of drawers. But something feels different and I can't work out what it is.

I grip the kitchen counter, turning on the tap to get myself some water as I think about what it could be, reassuring myself as I take a few sips that I'm safe here. That he can't hurt me like he did before.

My heart is still beating faster than usual as I heat up a plastic pot of baked beans in the microwave and sit down to watch TV. The familiar sound of the theme tune for *East-Enders* echoes through the adjoining wall from the flat next door. She never misses an episode. Her baby is quiet this evening; I hear it crying occasionally, a noise that fills me with an inexplicable sense of loneliness. Sounds travel easily through these walls, the partitions between us are paper-thin. I wonder if it's worth asking her if she's seen anyone hanging around. Anyone who looks like Jack.

I jump as the microwave pings and eat my dinner in front of *Celebrity MasterChef*, watching as the contestants rush around the studio kitchen. We used to watch it together, sitting on the sofa, me leaning against him like a cushion, his arms tightly fastened around my waist.

As I rinse my empty plate under the tap, it suddenly dawns on me why my flat feels different. It's the smell. A chemical odour hangs in the air, similar to the one at a public swimming pool. Bleach. They must have cleaned the corridor today. They do it every few months with one of those large machines to get the stains out of the communal carpets and wipe down the paintwork. Maybe they dislodged the Sellotape during the cleaning process? Perhaps Jack hasn't actually been here at all. I wait for the cold stone that's been sitting at the bottom of my stomach to disappear with this realisation, but it doesn't, its weight as heavy as ever.

As I get into bed, I check my notebook. Three letters. All still safe. I open my drawer to put it away out of sight, catching a glimpse of the small red glove lying inside. It's definitely familiar. I stare at the panda design. I don't know why I'd have kept it when it no longer fits, or what I've done with the other one that made a pair. I try putting my hand inside the finger holes, but the wool on my skin makes me feel cold. Freezing in fact. I shiver and pull it off, putting it back in the drawer as I rub my arms to get rid of the goose pimples that have risen up.

I need a distraction to help me sleep, so pick up the book that's sitting on my bedside table. It's one I borrowed from the library some time ago and I haven't read it for a while. I turn to the page that has its corner folded down and run my eyes over the words, but they don't seem familiar. I turn back further and try again, but it still seems as though I'm looking at the words for the first time. It's frustrating to try and piece things together when I'm already tired. I flick back a few more pages and notice something hard inside the front cover of the book.

There's a postcard that I haven't seen before. I take it out and look at the picture on the front. A photo of a British seaside. I screw up my eyes as I stare at the expanse of brown sand and long pier, like a row of scaffolding, jutting into the sea, with a large white building at the far end. I recognise the scene and turn the card over to see if I'm correct. It's blank apart from the small words printed on the back: Weston-super-Mare. My dad had taken me there when I was little.

I remember standing in front of a red and yellow bouncy castle, eating my ice cream whilst we waited to go on the big wheel. Sarah's words that I've been trying to remember come back to me. She'd mentioned this place. And now I'm holding a postcard with a picture of it on the front. Had something happened there? Is this where I can remember her from?

I put down my book and hold the postcard under my bed-side light to see the photo better. Families squashed in next to one another, sprinkled with blue and white striped beach brollies stuck in the sand like giant lollipops. A few discarded buckets and spades. Is Sarah in there somewhere amongst the crowd? Am I?

I'm sitting alone when she walks over to my table in the canteen the following day. My heart sinks. I'd stayed in the library as long as I could to try to avoid her. I begin to eat faster so I can leave.

'I didn't realise you'd started to come down later?' she says, raising her eyebrows.

'Yes. My manager asked me to swap breaks.' I think I sound convincing.

'Shame. I wondered why I hadn't seen you. There's not much left to choose from at this time.'

I smile as I try to think of a way of telling her I'm leaving without sounding rude.

'I can't believe how hot it was yesterday,' she continues. 'Unusual for September. It won't last. It never does.' She hesitates. 'Are you feeling better now?'

I'm not going to talk to her about Jack; I don't want to talk to her about anything. I give the briefest nod.

'Do you mind if we change the subject?' I ask as I fold the napkin on my tray into a series of elaborate triangles before screwing it up into a small ball and pressing it down hard on some crumbs so they end up embedded in the paper. I imagine they're the questions she's asking me. The things I don't want her to remind me of.

'OK, but you know where I am if you need someone to talk to.' She blows on a forkful of chicken and pastry. 'This is boiling. I think they incinerate it here before serving it.' She looks at the large fridge near the cashier. 'I'm going to grab something to drink. D'you want anything?' I shake my head as I open my yoghurt.

As she walks off, I realise she's forgotten to take her purse with her. It's sticking out of the top of her bag that she's left lying on the table. I search the queue but can't see her until she emerges from the crowd carrying a bottle of water in her hand. As I pull her purse out of her bag to take it over to her, a piece of paper falls onto my tray, which I pick up and stuff back inside. A letter. I catch a glimpse of the words written on it and freeze.

Black ink. It's Jack's handwriting. I'd recognise it anywhere.

THEN

Jack

I call Sarah once I'm outside. Now Em knows, there's not enough time to delay what I'm going to do any longer. I scroll through my contacts to find her details. I just need to check she's not in her office. I don't expect her to be there as it's the weekend, and if she's not, I know where to find her. I squeeze the charms attached to Ali's silver bracelet hard between my fingers.

A receptionist answers. 'Ms Henderson's office?'

'Can I speak to her please?' I say.

'Can I ask who's calling?'

I hesitate. 'I'd rather not give my name. It's a sensitive matter regarding one of her clients.'

'I'm afraid she's not in today,' she says. 'Can I ask what it's regarding and I can pass on a message?'

I hang up. I've found out what I need to know.

I open my emails to find the reply sent by the DVLA yesterday. The short message sympathises with the loss of revenue I've suffered and lists the details I'd asked for in my original request. I hadn't been totally truthful. I'd told them I'd listed an armchair for sale on eBay, which I had, but the buyer hadn't driven off with the item as I'd stated on the form. They also hadn't been driving Sarah's car, although it was her registration I'd provided. I'd never lied on an official document before, but it had seemed like the easiest way to find out where she lived. The DVLA had provided her address details as I'd said I wanted to pursue her for compensation. It had been worth paying for the fast-track service. It turns out she doesn't live far from me. I'll do this first and then pay her a visit. I need to hurry. I want to be out of the flat before either Edward or Mum arrives.

I grab my jacket, walk down the corridor and push the main door to get out when I hear someone coming up the corridor behind me.

'Can you hold that open, please?' I turn to see Tom's wife wheeling a pushchair. A few seconds earlier and I'd have avoided her completely. I've lost count of the number of times I've wondered whether the last year would have been different if I'd been a bit quicker.

I stand with my foot against the door to stop it swinging shut and she smiles as she walks towards me.

'Thanks. It's tricky to manage when you've got one of these.' She glances down at the buggy as her cheeks colour, perhaps realising what she's said.

I let the door slam behind us and don't reply. I'm not going to play the role of the person who makes others feel comfortable.

'Are you off to the shops?' she continues, clearly anxious to break the silence.

I wonder if she's embarrassed at having to make conversation. Perhaps Tom told her about our exchange the other day and now she wishes she didn't have to talk to me at all. A few of the neighbours had been like that after they heard what happened. Avoiding eye contact in the corridor. Ignoring me when I'd said hello. I can't blame them. I shake my head.

'No, I'm off to see . . . a friend.'

She nods politely, ignoring my obvious lie.

'I'm taking Gracie to the park,' she says. 'We're going to feed the ducks.' She points at a bag full of breadcrumbs in the hood of the buggy as she looks at the couple of steps out onto the pavement. 'D'you mind giving me a hand?'

I'm irritated, knowing I have a lot to do, but not wanting to be rude.

'I saw her,' she says as I lift the front of the buggy.

I frown. 'Sorry?'

'Your wife,' she says.

I let go of the buggy earlier than I should and it drops to the ground roughly. Gracie's mum ignores me staring at her and leans over to check her daughter.

'You saw my wife? When?'

'Yes. Just before . . . before she left. Alison, wasn't it?' she asks.

I nod dumbly. I don't want to have this conversation. I don't want to know what she saw. I look down at the buggy and concentrate on the wheels as they roll along the damp paving stones, picking up bits of grit, which make a crunching sound as we continue down the road.

'I heard someone outside our flat that morning,' she continues. 'I'm often up early with Gracie and I looked out of the window to see who it was. I didn't speak to her. I'm so sorry. If I'd have known . . .'

The buggy gets stuck on a kerbstone and I walk ahead as we negotiate a gap in the railings. I pray she'll stop talking. I don't understand why she's telling me this now. A year too late. A year in which she's obviously harboured a feeling of guilt, a burden which she thinks I'm going to relieve. It might ease her suffering, but it doesn't help me. It makes me feel worse. Perhaps it's her way of trying to tell me there's something I should have seen, that I could have done.

She stops briefly at the end of the road to adjust the strap on the buggy which has come loose and I step away from her, at a loss as to how to end the conversation.

'We're heading this way.' She points towards the park.

I seize the opportunity. 'My friend lives over there,' I say, tilting my head in the opposite direction. I need to get away from her. I don't want to hear anything else she has to say. Each revelation about Ali pierces my skin like a knife. I don't want a stranger telling me things I didn't know about my wife. I walk away as fast as I can, my guilt feeling heavier with every step.

I head down the road, crossing over to walk up the hill towards the bridge. I haven't been here for a year and I'd forgotten how intimidating the concrete tower at the entrance is. It sticks up out of the landscape like a castle in a game of chess. I keep to the left of it to reach the pedestrian path that runs alongside the road. It's narrower than I expected. Walking out to the middle of the bridge, I stop and look out over the metal barrier. The view stretches for miles, the trees in the distance merging into one dark green blur. The river looks as if it's motionless from this height, reflecting the road and buildings along its length like a pane of glass. I can't bring myself to look straight down. It's too far. Way too far.

I put my hand in my pocket and pull out Ali's bracelet. The silver strands sparkle in the sun. I remember how her face had lit up when she'd unwrapped it. That's how I want to remember her. And us. Not what happened after. I shut my eyes. The image in my head evaporates as I remember Em's words. *It's only a matter of time before someone else finds out.* She's right. And once Edward, or my mum knows, everything will be different. They'll never let me see her. I don't have long. I hold the bracelet over the edge of the barrier, feeling the breeze on my fingers. It would be so easy to let go. But I don't. I'm not giving her a way out that easily. I turn back the way I came, stopping on the small patch of grass at the end of the bridge to sit down on a bench.

I check my watch. It's only ten o'clock. I have an hour before anyone arrives at the flat. I check my phone. No messages, but I know my mum will text me before she leaves. I need to see Sarah. Once I've talked to her she'll tell me how I can find Ali. And then we can be together. Ali will understand how sorry I am for what I did when I've had a chance to explain.

I swallow the things I don't want to remember. The things that make my stomach twist into a knot with guilt. How I'd agreed to meet him in that bar after work. How I'd hoped he'd be different. How he'd stared at my wedding ring as I'd handed over the money. How I'd lied to Ali about it when I'd got home, and then the lies had grown ever more complicated, trapping me between layers of deceit until there hadn't been a way out. How nausea burned in my throat like acid whenever I thought about it, trying to dissolve the words that had already been spoken.

I wish I'd brought a drink and some painkillers with me; my head is thumping and I'm so thirsty. Opening my palm, I stare at the bracelet and then put it back in my pocket. I'll buy Ali a nicer one when I see her. We can choose it together. One she can wear all the time. I think she lied to me about the one I gave her. If she'd liked it that much, she'd have taken it with her.

I punch Sarah Henderson's address into my satnav once I'm back in my car. She won't be expecting me.

It's a house with a name rather than a number, so I have to drive up and down her road twice before I find it, slowing down so I don't scrape the exhaust over the speed bumps. A wooden sign is attached to a tall fence which is partly hidden by an overgrown bush. I park and walk up the brick drive- way that's surrounded on either side by flower beds filled with large rhododendron bushes. The purple flowers are out in bloom. Ali's favourite colour. It's a sign.

Her car is parked next to the house. I'm pleased she's home as it means I don't have to wait for her. I'm tired of waiting. I press the antique-looking doorbell and there's a tinkling noise inside. I can hear footsteps and the large wooden door swings open. She's standing in front of me, wiping her hands on a tea towel.

'Hello, Sarah,' I say. 'I think you've been avoiding me.'

Her smile fades the instant she recognises me. She tries to close her front door, but it's too late, I've put my foot in the frame to stop her wedging it shut.

'Why didn't you give Ali that envelope?' I ask.

'Mr Reynolds, you need to leave. You shouldn't be here.'

'I wouldn't be if you'd done what I asked,' I reply.

She doesn't move. Her green eyes stare at me through the narrow gap.

'I can't talk to you,' she says. 'I explained that when I wrote to you. And I can't tell you what I did with your letters. It isn't personal. It's a matter of confidentiality.'

'It's personal to me,' I reply.

'Have you been drinking?' she asks. I don't reply. She must be able to smell it on me. Or maybe my dishevelled appearance gives it away. 'Please move,' she says.

I stay exactly where I am, one hand in my pocket, holding Ali's bracelet for reassurance. I feel the pressure on my foot ease as she stops trying to push the door shut, opening it wide enough for me to see her properly. She's standing on parquet wooden floorboards in a large hallway. It's at least three times the size of the one in my flat. The door to the room beside her is shut and behind her is an oak bench with a large mirror above it. My reflection stares back at me. I barely recognise myself, I look so tired. Sarah must see the same thing; there's pity in her eyes rather than fear as she glances at my pocket, wondering what I'm hiding.

'Do you have any friends to talk to, Jack?' She remembers who I am. 'Perhaps they could help?' She twists the tea towel in her hand.

I shake my head. 'I need to give you something,' I tell her, taking the bracelet out of my pocket and holding it towards her. 'It's Ali's. I want her to have it.'

She takes it from me slowly, watching my reaction. I can smell something burning. She turns her head as she notices it as well. 'We're having people over for dinner,' she says. 'I'm cooking the beef bourguignon in advance.' She hesitates. 'I should probably rescue it before it's too late.' She glances at the room beside her but doesn't take her hand off the door.

Ali had stood cooking the same thing in our kitchen just after we'd moved into our flat. She'd been wearing the apron my mum had given her over her white T-shirt, her long blonde hair tied back in a messy bun. We'd invited Harry and Em over as our first visitors. I'd only finished decorating just before they'd arrived and had ended up scrubbing my hands with a nail brush in the shower in an attempt to get rid of the paint. I'd got most of it off, but a thin grey line had lurked stubbornly round the edge of each fingernail. Em had fanned herself with a napkin as we'd sat down at the table.

'Are you too hot?' Ali had asked.

Em had shaken her head. 'It's just me. Honestly, it's fine, don't worry.' I'd noticed her and Harry exchange looks.

'I can turn the heating down if you want,' Ali had said. 'How's work?'

'I'm off for another three weeks, thank God. School holidays always go too fast.' Em had covered her glass as I'd tried to pour the wine. 'Sometimes I think I must secretly enjoy torture.' Ali had laughed out loud. 'Anyway,' Em had continued, 'I'm making the most of the break. How about you, Jack? Isn't it your birthday next month?' She'd looked at me.

'Yes, it is. And, before you ask, I'm not having a party. Unless Ali has something planned, which I hope she hasn't, as she knows I'm not one for surprises. Do you want a drink?' I'd indicated Em's empty glass.

'Ooh, yes please. Just some water would be great. Thanks.'

'We should do a toast. To the new flat,' Harry had said when I came back with Em's water. 'Let's hope you manage to keep it in better shape than our house at university.'

I'd smiled at him. 'I think if you remember correctly, you'll find I kept that house tidier than anyone else. One of the only reasons you originally agreed to my suggestion to go into business was that you knew I'd be good at the organisation side of things.'

Harry had laughed. 'Perhaps. You certainly did enough research to win that first client. I don't think they knew what had hit them.' He'd paused as he'd glanced at Em. 'We have some news as well. Do you want to tell them?' She'd shaken her head, smiling. 'OK,' he'd said, 'I'll do it . . . to the new addition to the Butler family.'

Ali had covered her mouth. 'Oh my god, you're not? That's why you're not drinking! Congratulations!' She'd leant over the table and hugged Em.

It had taken me a few seconds to comprehend what Harry was talking about and then I'd remembered to smile. I'd stared at Ali, who'd stared back, an unnatural grin fixed on her face. I'd wanted to stand up, pull out her chair and wrap my arms around her to protect her from the words I knew would follow. But I hadn't. I'd sat, motionless in my seat, leaving her to absorb each one that left a wound deeper than a bullet.

'When are you due?' Ali had asked brightly. Too brightly.

'February. I'm only twelve weeks. We waited for the scan before telling anyone. So, I'm on the delights of water for the next six months. God knows how I'm going to get through next term without alcohol to help me, but I'll just have to find a way to manage.' She'd raised her glass of sparkling water to Ali's wine glass. 'And here's to your flat. I hope you're both really happy here. And I hope Jack manages to get through the painting.'

Ali's grin hadn't slipped as she'd pushed her chair out.

'Just going to the loo. Won't be a mo'.' She'd disappeared into our bathroom.

It hadn't been their fault. They hadn't known. But it couldn't have come at a worse time. We hadn't told anyone we'd been trying for a baby. And this morning had brought yet another disappointment.

'Shall we start or wait for Ali?' Harry had eyed the plate in front of him with eager anticipation.

I'd frowned. 'You guys go ahead. Honestly. It'll get cold. I'll check on her.'

I'd knocked on the bathroom door and had heard the lock click, letting myself in. She'd flushed the tissue she'd been holding down the toilet. I'd reached out to hug her, but she'd backed away from me.

'I'm fine, I'm fine,' she'd whispered. 'Don't touch me or you'll set me off again.'

I'd swallowed the lump in my throat.

'You should tell Em,' I'd said. 'She's your closest friend and she'd want to know.' She'd nodded. 'Just not tonight. I don't want to spoil it for her.'

I'd wished there was something else I could say. 'The doctor might give us answers when we see him on Monday,' I'd added.

She'd looked at me, searching for reassurance that I believed what I was telling her, but I'd had none to give.

Sarah steps away from the front door and the sudden movement snaps me out of my reverie. I think she's trying to get away from me and I grab the handle as a man appears from the room beside her.

'You all right, darling?'

Her husband. I didn't realise anyone else was home.

He looks at her, and then at me, sensing the tension.

'Can I help you?'

I don't answer.

He glances at my hand on the door. 'Is there a problem here?' he asks, taking a couple of steps towards me, but before he can reach me I turn and run. Back past the rhododendron bushes, the heady fragrance of the flowers merging with my hangover as a wave of nausea washes over me. I need to get to my car. I'm not sure if he's following me; I don't want to stop and check. I get the keys out of my pocket, jump inside and lock the doors, looking in the wing mirror. He's standing about halfway down his drive, watching me, talking on his mobile.

I can't catch my breath and have an awful feeling I'm going to be sick. A trickle of cold sweat runs down my back. How much had I drunk last night? My hands tremble as I attempt to start the engine and the car jerks forward as it stalls. I can hear his footsteps coming towards me. I turn the key again and put my foot slowly onto the accelerator. I catch a glimpse of him in my rear-view mirror, shrinking in size as I leave him behind, staring after me. Glancing at the clock on the dashboard, I indicate to turn left onto the main road. Ten forty-five. I should be back before Edward or Mum arrives. I'm so busy thinking what I'm going to say to them as I pull out that it takes me a couple of seconds after the deafening explosion to realise I can no longer feel the steering wheel in my hands. I wonder why I can hear someone shouting and try to remember when I last filled up the tank as there's a horrible smell of petrol before everything goes black.

NOW

Alison

There's a high-pitched humming in my ears as the canteen falls silent. I'm still holding Sarah's purse as I reach across to pull her bag towards me. I must be mistaken about the writing.

I look up as someone touches my shoulder. She's standing in front of me, smiling as she speaks, but my ears aren't registering any sound and I don't understand what she's saying. Her mouth moves in slow motion. She looks at me, her forehead creasing, and waves her hand backwards and forwards in front of my face. I grip the table to steady myself as the hum reaches a crescendo and suddenly the volume kicks back in. I jolt in shock.

'Hello? Earth to Ali? I was saying it would help if I took that with me.' She takes her purse out of my hand as she picks up her bag, putting it on her seat out of my reach. 'Are you OK?' I manage to nod. 'I won't be a mo'.' She heads back towards the cashier.

I need to see that piece of paper. I glance over at her seat. I can't reach her bag now without standing up and stretching over the table and she's watching me as she waits to pay.

I have to see if it's Jack's writing. Why would Sarah have something from Jack? I only caught a brief glimpse of the letter. It could have been from anyone. But I'm convinced it's the same as the ones I have at home. My brain isn't quick enough to come up with a solution to get hold of her bag before she's back, lifting it off her seat so she can sit down.

'God, those queues are a nightmare. They really need to get more staff down here. Want some?' She pours the water into a plastic cup.

'No thanks.' My mother had used to paint her nails the same shade as Sarah is wearing now. A baby shell pink. I remember the *'Ballet Slippers'* label on the bottom of the tiny bottle.

I would sit beside her on the bed when she'd been in one of her good moods, my fingers pressed flat on her dressing table as she carefully ran the small brush over mine so we would match. I had been desperate to be just like her when we were together like that. Sometimes I would sneak up to her room when she had been in the kitchen and open the drawer of her dressing table where she kept all of her make-up, breathing in the smell; of her, of lotions and creams that I wasn't supposed to touch but that I thought would make me beautiful. I would press the powder puff from her compact onto my nose and chin just like I had watched her do and turn the base of her No.7 plum lipstick until the smooth stick appeared, spreading it over my lips and pressing them together in front of the mirror to blend the colour. Then I would pull off a couple of cotton wool pads from the neat cylindrical pile that she kept on her dressing table, squeezing out a few drops of her Oil of Ulay lotion to wipe everything off. I'd thought being grown-up was easy. I had no idea what was to come.

Sarah unzips the side pocket of her bag to put her purse away before cautiously blowing on a piece of pie and starting to eat. She's almost finished when she pauses momentarily, her fork halfway to her mouth, glancing across at another table.

I stare at her. 'What is it?'

Her fork restarts its journey and her gaze switches back to me. 'It's nothing. I thought I spotted someone I work with.'

I seize the opportunity. 'Why don't you go and say hello?'

She shakes her head. 'No, it's fine. I see enough of him in the office.' She's almost finished what's on her plate. I can't let her leave.

'D'you want some dessert?' I'm desperate.

'Dessert?' she looks at me.

'Yes . . . some ice cream or something. As it's hot.' I'm gabbling.

'No, honestly, I'm fine.' She puts her hand on her stomach. 'I can't eat anything else after that pie.' She tips up her cup and swallows the last drops of water.

I look at the empty bottle. I'm not going to get another chance to see that letter and I have to force myself not to just grab her bag from beside her and pull out the piece of paper. I watch as she gets up and I follow her, weaving my way between the tables to the far side of the canteen where we have to return our trays. I hang back deliberately whilst she strides ahead.

'I thought I'd lost you,' she says as I slide my tray onto the runners of the metal stand amongst all the others waiting to be collected.

'That man stopped me,' I tell her.

'Which man?' She looks out across the sea of faces.

I point in the direction of the table where she was looking earlier. 'That one over there. He asked me to ask you to go over.'

She frowns but doesn't move, staring at the table where he's chatting animatedly with his colleagues, not looking in her direction.

'He doesn't seem to be looking for me.'

I shrug. 'I said I'd pass on the message.'

She sighs and starts to walk towards him as I tap her on the shoulder.

'Do you want me to hold that for you?' I point to her bag.

She looks at me. 'No thanks, I'm good.'

My heart sinks as she threads her way across the room through the narrow spaces between the various tables. I watch her speak to the man I pointed at. He stares in my direction and I smile, raising my hand in a wave as if to acknowledge him and the conversation that never took place.

She's frowning when she comes back. 'He says he didn't ask you anything.'

'He did,' I insist. I can tell she doesn't really believe me but isn't sure what to do about it. My body language gives the impression that I'm telling the truth. 'Shall we go?'

As we leave the canteen, I smile at the table whose occupants are all staring in our direction and stroll out down the corridor towards the reception area, praying they don't follow us.

I pull the sleeves of my top down over my knuckles, hiding my hands inside the material as I glance at Sarah's bag. She sees me looking and I force myself to smile at her as I press the button for the lift, wondering what would happen if I asked to look in it. Even if she agreed, I couldn't bear the humiliation if I'm wrong. I feel a stab of anxiety when the lift finally arrives and have to stop myself from running into it and curling up in a ball in the corner.

More people push in behind us; it's always busy at lunch-times. The doors won't shut as it's too full, so the two people who got in last are forced to step out. We're shoved up against one another, invading each other's personal space. I don't trust myself to speak, standing next to Sarah in silence as someone presses the button for the first floor and we all move upwards. She's talking to someone on the other side of her, her leather tote bag pressed against my hip. I can see the piece of paper with the black writing on it. I don't hesitate. I reach carefully between the handles and pull it out, stuffing it deep into my cardigan pocket, keeping my eyes fixed on the back of Sarah's head the whole time. She doesn't seem to notice as she's too busy nodding in response to the woman complaining about the lack of space. The lift reaches the first floor, the doors open and I step out, breathing more freely now I'm no longer squashed into the cramped space. I glance at Sarah, but she's still chatting, not looking at me, oblivious to the rustling in my pocket that it seems only I can hear.

I force myself to walk at a normal pace towards the library, counting to ten before I turn around to check she's not fol-lowing me, but the corridor is empty. I convince myself that any second I'm going to hear the familiar ping of the lift that would signal her return. But I don't.

Mrs Painter is waiting by the counter as I walk up to the reception and as she looks at me, I wait for her to ask why my face is so flushed, but she doesn't mention it.

'I've got some photocopying to do,' she says. 'Can you stay here in case anyone needs anything? We're not busy, so you shouldn't have any problems, but you know where I am if you need me.'

I nod and pick up the scanner, anxiety crawling across my stomach, desperate for her to leave so I can see what's written in the letter.

She gathers up her paperwork, one piece at a time, as she peers at me over the top of her glasses. 'Are you sure you're OK? You look a bit hot.'

I nod and lean against the edge of the counter for support, feeling the lump in my pocket flatten as I press against it, reassuring myself it's still there.

I fiddle with the button on my cardigan, waiting for her to leave, staring at the entrance door, expecting Sarah to re-appear at any moment. Mrs Painter finally disappears down the row of shelves towards the copier room. I make myself wait until she's completely out of sight before I reach into my pocket and draw out a crushed ball of paper, unfolding it and smoothing it out on the reception counter.

It's a letter. The black writing is unmistakable and it's ad-dressed to me.

Ali,
It's been almost a year. I think of you often. Do you think about me too? Nothing is the same without you. I miss you and

Tilly.
Jack

Tilly.

Oh my god.

Tilly.

Part Two

THEN

Alison – *Day One*

She's lying asleep under a pink blanket in the hospital bassinet, dressed in the Babygro that's been tucked in my drawer for more years than I care to remember. Her lips are tightly pressed together, a small indent between her eyebrows making it look like she's frowning. She's everything I've ever wanted, but as I stroke her head all I can feel is a knot in my stomach.

Jack pokes his head through the curtain they've drawn around the bed to give me some privacy. I smile at him.

'Hello, you,' he says. 'I was trying to be quiet. I didn't want to disturb you in case you were dozing.'

I shake my head. 'I'm not tired.' I glance at the clock. He's been gone for ages.

'I've bought you something.' He hands me a small box.

I spot the thin sheets of seaweed and slices of raw tuna through the transparent plastic lid.

'Oh my god, Jack! I can't believe you remembered.'

'I promised you I wouldn't forget,' he says, sitting down beside me and kissing my cheek. 'You feel cold. Have they given you enough blankets?' He puts his arm round my shoulders.

I nod as I rip open the sachet of soy sauce and drizzle it over the cubes of rice, watching the liquid seep between the grains, staining them a dark brown colour. I put a piece into my mouth, savouring the saltiness on my tongue. I've craved this during the past nine months after being told I shouldn't eat it. So many of my desires have been subsumed to her needs, and the taste of something previously forbidden makes me realise how much I've resented the burden of responsibility. Having to watch what I drank. What I ate. Every coveted mouthful spoiled by the bitter aftertaste of fear that I would forever be at fault for damaging the body growing inside me.

'How's she doing?' he asks.

I glance at her. 'She's fine. Dropped off eventually.'

Jack strokes the fine layer of dark down that covers her head. I've never seen him look at anyone apart from me in that way and I feel a sharp pang of envy. I haven't fallen immediately in love with her like everyone said I would. I don't really feel anything. I think I'm still shell-shocked from the birth. I hadn't expected it to be so brutal.

Each hour had slipped away, taking with it a small piece of the person who'd arrived on the ward with her neatly packed overnight bag and carefully written birth plan. The unending contractions had been like a rollercoaster that I couldn't get off; a ride where my eyes had been tightly shut and I'd gripped the sheets in an effort to reassure myself I was still alive, still tethered to reality. When there was barely any of me left, the midwife's smile had become a little less bright, her tone a little more urgent as she'd increased the drugs to a point where my hands had shaken so much I hadn't been able to hold the grey cardboard tray full of yellow bile in front of me, my body's attempt to empty itself from every orifice.

My bed had been wheeled into another room, every bump and turn intensifying the agony. There had been no pain at the end. Just blood. So much blood. I'd felt it hot and sticky, a pool that had coagulated beneath me as they'd pulled her out with an implement that resembled giant metal salad servers. Splashes of crimson smeared over legs that looked like mine but no longer belonged to me after the spinal block. The eyes of the people in long blue gowns and masks had been the only visible sign of their humanity. One had held my hand, their touch insulated from mine by a plastic glove as another had sewn me back together. I'd lain motionless, trying to work out if any pieces of the person I'd been thirty-five hours ago still remained.

Jack squeezes my hand. 'Are you sure you don't want me to watch her so you can have a sleep?'

'I'm fine,' I say. He won't know what to do if she cries.

When I'd found out I was pregnant, I'd imagined her as a swirl of blue, like a viscous liquid that would slip through my fingers if I tried to hold onto it. I'd been there before with the rounds of IVF. Too many times. I'd counted the days, anticipating the flood which never came. Instead she'd matured into a ball of red, a pulsing mass that grew at a surprising rate, pushing everything inside me aside to make room for her expanding body. In these last few weeks, she's turned yellow, basking in the warmth of my hands as they've lovingly stroked her, too big to move beneath my skin stretched as tight as a balloon. And now she's beside me. Disturbingly pink and real.

A midwife pulls back the curtains. 'Everything all right in here?'

I nod.

'Hopefully we can get you out of here soon,' she says. 'We're just waiting for the consultant to officially discharge you. I don't think you'll have too long to wait.' She leans over the cot, staring at the small bundle. 'She's gorgeous, isn't she? Dead to the world.'

'She wasn't last night,' I say and the midwife laughs.

'Ah, they take a while to do that. You can always try and have a nap when she does. I did that with both of mine.' She picks up the clipboard hanging on the bottom of my bed, signs something and puts it back. 'And if you have any questions, you can ask my colleague who'll come and see you tomorrow, as they'll need to check on your stitches – you had to have a few more than we all expected. We'll give you some paracetamol or tramadol and the pain should settle down after a few days. I'll be back in a bit when the consultant's been round. Is there anything else you need at the moment?'

I shake my head.

'I'll leave you in peace then.' She walks off and I turn towards Jack.

'Can you get her car seat? I want one of the midwives to check it's not too big for her. She looks so tiny I'm not sure she'll fit into it properly.'

'Course.' He picks up the empty sushi box off the bed and puts it in the bin on his way out of the ward.

I pull the curtain round the bed. I don't want anyone here whilst I get my daughter ready, watching over my shoulder, passing silent judgement on my awkward efforts. Jack is doing and saying all the right things, but I can tell he's on edge, and I don't think it's just because of the baby. He was like it before I gave birth. Mumbling something in the middle of a conversation that made it completely obvious he hadn't been listening to me and I'd had to repeat everything I'd just said.

I pull on my maternity trousers an inch at a time, leaning against the hospital mattress for support. My body is unfamiliar and my centre of gravity has altered now my bump has shrunk. I don't recognise myself.

My dad said having a baby would change everything, that I'd become a different person. I'd laughed but hadn't believed him. Now I wonder if what he said was true, that creating another life took away something of your own, shaving parts off you in thin slices so you didn't notice until it was too late. After we'd all stood in our kitchen raising a toast to the success of our last round of IVF, I'd seen him talking to Jack, his face serious. Perhaps he'd been warning him about what would happen. I hadn't heard what he'd been saying, only Jack's earnest reassurances that he'd make sure he looked after me.

His mum had phoned me earlier to say she couldn't wait to see her new granddaughter. I'd sensed a catch in her voice just before she rang off, telling me to make sure we still found time for each other. That she'd always be happy to babysit. I hadn't said anything to Jack as I know he already blames himself for his father's behaviour that started straight after he was born. He doesn't need to hear his suspicions confirmed that his mother thinks it was as a result of his arrival too. I've never met the man, but from the few things Jack's said about him, I'm glad he's not a part of our lives.

After the consultant's discharged us, I hold Jack's arm to steady myself as we head out to the car, each step taking twice as long as when I came in. I don't want to go. We're safe in here. I worry we're leaving too soon. I'd rather have stayed in a few more days so the staff could be around to keep an eye on her. They'd reassured me that despite the lengthy delivery she's perfectly healthy, but I'm worried they've missed something. You read that in magazine articles all the time and I know sometimes it takes a while for any complications to show up. Our flat is at least half an hour away from medical treatment – longer if the traffic's bad.

The receptionist smiles as the glass doors open automatically to let us out. I swallow, trying to get some saliva into my mouth. I'm not sure they should trust me to take her home. I don't know what I'm doing.

Jack manoeuvres himself and our new baby through the back door of the car.

'Be careful with her,' I say.

'I'm just making sure her car seat is fixed in properly,' he replies.

I ease myself into the passenger side. Sitting down is painful.

He gets in next to me and I twist round to look at her.

'Are you sure the belt's fastened securely?' I ask.

'Yes,' he says. 'I'm sure.' He thinks I'm being paranoid.

'It's not that I don't trust you,' I say. 'It's just once I've thought about it, I worry something's going to happen. It's a superstition thing. You know. Like saluting with magpies.'

He frowns. It's clear he doesn't have any idea what I'm talking about.

'Do you want to check it if it'll make you feel better?' he asks.

I nod and lever myself out of the car to open the rear door. I run my hand along the belt, pulling it several times to see if it's tight, before manoeuvring myself back into my seat.

'Happy?' he asks.

'Yes.' I run my fingers over my eyebrow as he leans across and kisses the top of my head.

'Then let's go home,' he says.

Our flat doesn't feel like the same one I left less than two days earlier. The décor is old and tired and the vibrancy of new life jars against everything that's already here. The rooms are eerily still after the bustle of the hospital and as I run my hand over the photo frames on our hall shelf it's like touching exhibits in a museum that belong to someone else. I'm a stranger in my own home. Up until today it's been Jack and me. Now it's the three of us and I'm unprepared for the intensity. My whole world is contained within these few walls, shrunk to a fraction of the size it was before.

Jack puts the car seat down in the middle of the hall. I'm not sure what to do with her. I should probably pick her up as she's starting to whimper. Sounds that I know will shortly turn into a high-pitched continuous noise, telling me something is wrong; reinforcing my guilt at not knowing what it is. I'm her mother, I should be able to understand her. I check my watch. She's not due a feed for another fifteen minutes. I undo the harness clips on the car seat and pick her up, hoping she can't tell she's making me anxious.

'I got you something,' Jack says, opening the door of the sitting room.

I glance at her. She's quieter, but I know it's only temporary. 'What?' I ask. 'She's getting fidgety. I think I need to feed her.'

He points at the wall. There's a large canvas painted in countless shades of blue that fade gradually to creamy white as they reach the bottom of the picture. Sea and sky above a beach. Two tiny figures in black stand at the edge of the surf.

'I wanted it to be a surprise,' he says. 'It's supposed to be us. When we were travelling. I found an old photo of us in Australia and asked this guy to paint it. D'you like it?'

'It's beautiful.' I feel a physical ache to be back there. To stand in bare feet on the sand with nothing to do, no responsibilities. I can remember how the salt stung the sunburn on my cheeks when I dived in the sea.

Jack leans down to kiss me. His eyes search my face, looking for praise for his efforts, like a child showing off their first piece of writing. It's like he's trying to prove something.

I look away. He doesn't understand that at the moment I can't cope with his neediness as well as hers. She feels awkward in my arms, reminding me of her presence.

'Where's the other picture?' I ask.

'Which one?' he says.

'The one that was up here before. The one we had framed of us at your office party last year.'

He doesn't look at me as he reaches up and adjusts the canvas on the wall, making sure it's not crooked. 'I put it away,' he says. 'It's in the cupboard.'

I like that picture. Harry had taken it. My figure had still been just slim enough to fit into my favourite black dress then, before I was pregnant.

'Have you thought about what we're going to call her?' he asks, changing the subject.

I haven't. She still has the tiny plastic wristband with *Baby Reynolds* written on it attached round her arm and I can't imagine her being called anything else.

'I don't know,' I say.

'How about Matilda? Your mum's middle name? She could be Tilly for short,' he says.

I hesitate, then nod. I don't mind if he chooses. I've got too many other things to think about.

We walk into the newly decorated nursery which smells of fresh paint. A baby mobile with stars dangling from it hangs over the white wooden cot. The yellow bedding inside is brand new, the small blanket folded neatly on top of the ironed sheet. All ready for her to sleep in. It's not big enough to hold me, but at the moment I wish I could lie down and pull the covers over my head to hide myself away underneath the soft fabric. If I raised my arms, I'd be able to make a tent above my face, like I did when I was little, and stare at the patterns on the material drawn by the sun shining through the window.

'I know it's way too big for her and I've still got the book-shelves to put up before it's finished,' he says, 'but it's getting there. And we need to let the paint dry out. I don't want her in here when it smells like this.'

'She'll sleep in the Moses basket beside our bed for now,' I tell him. 'I need to be able to keep an eye on her and it'll be easier to get her out at night.'

'Do you want me to look after her while you try and have a sleep?' he asks.

'I'm OK.' He's treating me like a child when nothing has changed. I'm not ill; I'm perfectly able to cope.

Tilly arches away from me. She doesn't seem to like me very much. I shut the door of the nursery and walk into our bedroom to feed her. I can hear Jack muttering in the hallway. He must be answering the door.

'Is that my dad?' I shout.

He doesn't reply. I have to stop myself from calling out again as I don't want to disturb Tilly. She's keeping me where she wants me already, confined by obligation, unable to get up until she's finished. She starts to cry when I wind her. The noise grates in my head as I carry her in to where Jack's sitting on the sofa.

'Who was that?' I ask.

Jack frowns. 'Who was what?'

'I thought I heard the door?' I say.

He shakes his head. 'No.'

'Can you take her for a bit?' I ask as I lean down and put Tilly into his arms. She's still grizzling as the doorbell buzzes. This time the noise is unmistakable.

'I'll get it,' Jack says, starting to get up and holding out Tilly as if he's handing back something that's my responsibility.

'It's fine,' I say. 'I'll go.'

My dad's face is surrounded by a bright white halo on the video entry screen as he peers at the camera. I let him in and wait by the door as he walks up the corridor. His hands shake as he adjusts his glasses after he gives me a hug. For years he didn't seem to age at all, but since I got pregnant, I notice it more every time I see him. The start of her new life seems to highlight his own mortality. I don't like being reminded of his frailty, of the fact he won't always be here. I want him to have time to get to know his granddaughter.

He stares at Tilly resting on Jack's shoulder. 'She's beautiful, Ali. What a little sweetheart.'

'You can hold her if you like,' Jack says. 'I thought I'd go out and pick us up a treat from that cake place Ali likes up the road. What d'you fancy? One of those strawberry tart things you usually have?'

I nod.

'I won't be long.' He passes Tilly to my dad, who cradles her in his arms, and her cries quieten. My shoulders relax as the noise stops. 'You must have the magic touch, Edward,' Jack says as he picks up his car keys off the hall shelf and shuts the front door behind him.

I frown and lift Tilly out of my dad's arms.

'She's quiet with me too, you know,' I say defensively.

He smiles, stroking Tilly's hand. 'You were the same, you know. Cried all the time for the first few weeks.' If she does that, I don't know how I'll cope.

I stare at the front door. It feels like Jack's abandoning me. I wonder if it's going to be like this every day. I'll sit waiting for the time to pass while I look after her until he comes home. And then he'll leave the next morning and I'll have to do the same thing all over again.

'Nice of Jack to go and get us a treat,' Edward says. I dismiss the thought that he didn't want to be stuck here with us. I know how well he gets on with my dad. When he hadn't got a bonus last year, it was my dad who had phoned to reassure him he hadn't let anyone down. Had told him not to worry and that he'd lend us the money for another round of IVF.

'I'm here to help you, Ali,' Dad says. 'If you want me to.'

'I'm fine,' I insist.

'You can be so stubborn sometimes,' he says. 'You remind me of your mother.'

'I do?' We rarely talk about Mum. I'd thought of her this morning when I'd looked at Tilly in her cot beside me in hospital. Wondered if she'd felt the same after she had me. That it wasn't at all how she'd expected it to be. Like she was missing something. That she was different from all those other women on the ward whose faces radiated instant happiness as they held their babies. Whether she hid the dread that's replaced the baby in my stomach and is growing faster than she ever did. I can't ask her, so I'll never know.

Tilly starts to grizzle again and I grit my teeth. The sound makes me wince. It crawls over my skin and into my brain, where it scrapes along the surface like nails on a blackboard.

She stops crying if I jiggle her as I walk round the flat. My dad offers to do it, but I refuse, so he rummages around in the hall cupboard and gets out our toolbox to fix the tap that's dripping in our kitchen instead. I'd asked Jack to do it before I went into hospital, but he obviously hasn't got around to it.

I take Tilly into the bathroom and lie her down on her mat to change her, undoing the poppers on each leg of her Babygro and pulling it up to get her nappy off. As the material peels away from her stomach, I notice she has red marks on her skin that look like bruises. A chill runs down my back as I remember the leaflets we'd been given on meningitis. I put my hand on her head. She doesn't feel hot. I stand up and search through the bottles and packets on the shelves in the bathroom cabinet for the digital thermometer we'd bought before she was born. It's in the corner, its packaging still intact, which I hack apart with a pair of scissors, telling myself not to panic. I press the small nozzle into her ear. Thirty-six point four. Normal. I should feel reassured, but I don't. I do it again. Still thirty-six point four. I wonder if it's working properly.

'Dad,' I yell.

There's a mumbling from the kitchen.

'Dad! Can you come here a minute?'

He appears at the bathroom door. 'What is it?'

'Tilly's got marks on her stomach.' I try to keep my voice calm.

He kneels down beside me in the small space, holding onto the door frame for support as he lowers himself slowly onto the floor. 'What? Where?'

I point. He bends over her, running his fingers from left to right just below where I've pulled up her Babygro. He looks at me.

'I can't see anything,' he says.

I point at her stomach, but they're gone. Her skin is smooth and unblemished as she kicks her legs.

'But I . . . They were just . . .' I say.

He pats my arm. 'Perhaps her Babygro was rubbing against her. She looks fine now.' He's staring at me rather than Tilly and I don't know why. I'm not the one he should be concerned about.

I hear the front door open. Jack's come back. Of course he's come back. Dad gets up off the floor whilst I finish changing Tilly and fasten her Babygro. Jack puts his head round the door.

'All OK?' he says. Is he asking about me, or her, or both of us? Perhaps we now come as one indistinguishable unit, permanently fused together.

I nod. My dad looks at me, and then at my husband. I assume he's debating whether to mention the marks I thought I saw, but he doesn't say anything. Neither do I.

I follow Jack into the kitchen as he puts a bag on the counter and pulls out three boxes, all wrapped in pink ribbon.

'Help yourself,' he says. 'I wondered if your dad could give me a hand with the tap,' he says. 'It's still leaking.'

'You weren't here, so he's already done it,' I say. My tone is frosty. I know I'm being unreasonable, but I resent him leaving me alone with Tilly.

Jack frowns and I think he's about to speak, but he changes his mind, perhaps unsure whether I'm trying to make a point. He holds out his hands to take our daughter, but I ignore him, clasping her more tightly in my arms. A mixture of guilt and frustration sweeps over me as I walk out of the room. If he can't stay here when I need him most, I don't see why he should hold her at all.

THEN

Jack – *Day One*

My mum calls whilst we're trying to bathe Tilly, I recognise her voice above the wailing as she leaves a message on the answerphone. I'll have to call her back. We're both struggling to hold onto the tiny slippery body that tries to wriggle out of our grasp. Ali wraps her in a baby towel as I manage to lift her, dripping, out of the water, the small hood fitting neatly over her head. Ali's hands shake as she lies her on the changing mat to fasten her nappy.

'Are you OK?' I ask.

She nods. 'I hate it that she's so upset. I think I'm doing something wrong.'

'Course you're not,' I say, putting my arm round her, but she shrugs me off. 'She's fine; she's just not keen on baths. Perhaps she's more of a shower girl.' I glance at her as I say it, in an attempt to make her smile, but she doesn't smile back and I notice her shoulders stiffen. I hand her the Babygro that's been warming on the radiator.

'I can get it,' she says. 'I'm not totally incompetent.'

I don't reply. I don't want this to turn into a bickering session. I'd wanted Edward to leave earlier in the afternoon, so we could have some time to ourselves, but he hadn't, so now we're left trying to make the best of the most difficult part of the day. The part where I can see how shattered she is and all I want to do is settle Tilly so we can have something to eat.

I take a deep breath. I shouldn't resent Edward. I know he just wants to spend time with his granddaughter and without him we wouldn't even have Tilly. He'd been the one who'd insisted on lending us the money for the last round of IVF. My stomach turns over when I think about how I've deceived him. I'll pay him back as soon as I can afford it.

As I go to play the answerphone message, I notice Ali's taken the framed picture of us out of the cupboard and has balanced it back on the hall shelf. I wish she hadn't done that. I thought she'd forget about it. I look past the man who smiles back at me in his dinner jacket with his arm round his wife to the woman standing behind them. Harry's photo had caught her at a slight angle and she's staring directly at me. I'd thought I could trust her. She'd found me at my most vulnerable when I'd needed someone to talk to. I open the cupboard door and slide the frame back onto one of the shelves inside as I focus on listening to the message my mum has left.

I'll call her back tomorrow, I can't face it tonight. I'm worried she'll be able to tell something's wrong just from my voice. She knows me too well. I haven't told her who I saw last week. It had taken a few seconds to recognise my father's face when it had appeared on the screen of our intercom. I hadn't expected to see him again. I'd warned him he wouldn't be welcome. I'd gone to hang up, but he'd made it clear he wouldn't leave unless he spoke to me. I'd agreed to meet him at the local coffee shop; I certainly wasn't going to let him into the flat.

I'd ordered a large latte at the counter, looking around for him. He'd been sitting at a table at the back, his hair more dishevelled than I remembered. Mum had always made sure he'd cut it regularly, but he must have forgotten now she wasn't there. He'd been wearing the navy blazer and rotary club tie he thought lent an air of formality to his appearance. I'd carried my coffee over and had sat down opposite him.

'A hello would be nice,' he'd said, smiling. He had several different smiles, my father. I'd seen them all. This was the one designed for strangers who didn't know him any better. The one that said it's lovely to meet you, that I can't wait to hear what you have to say. The tiny part of me that had allowed myself to hope he'd asked to meet in order to apologise, or at least reach out and build a relationship, shrivelled up as soon as I saw it.

'I'm not here to exchange pleasantries,' I'd said, not allowing the disappointment to show on my face. 'We agreed you wouldn't come round again.' He'd taken a sip out of the paper coffee cup in front of him and I'd noticed he was drinking water. 'Gone off coffee, have you?' I'd asked.

'No point in paying for something when you don't really want it,' he'd said. 'They've got a legal obligation to provide water. I'd have had something at yours, but you didn't seem very keen to invite me in.'

'I thought we had an agreement,' I'd said.

'That was then,' he'd replied. 'Things have changed since last year.'

I'd adjusted my chair, pushing it back a little further from the table. His eyes had flickered as he noticed the movement.

'What d'you want?' I'd asked. It appeared he wasn't in a rush.

He'd taken another sip of water. 'I miss our chats, Jack.' He was doing this to provoke me. If I'd got up and walked out, I'd have found him on my doorstep again. Probably not today – he enjoyed stringing out the agony – but he'd have appeared when I least expected it. I'd have come home to find him having a conversation with Ali. I assumed he didn't know about the baby and I wanted to keep it that way, it was one less thing he could use against me.

'What do you want?' I'd asked again, keeping my voice calm, refusing to rise to the bait.

'Perhaps if you asked "what d'you want, *Dad*," I might feel more inclined to reply,' he'd said.

I'd swallowed, looking directly into his eyes. They were the same colour as mine, but that's where any similarity ceased. His had no warmth, like looking at glass. I'd seen straight through them to what lay beneath. He'd been playing with me. I'd curled my toes up in the ends of my shoes and forced myself to remember I wasn't a child anymore. I didn't need to seek his approval.

'Either you tell me what you want, or I'm leaving,' I'd said.

He'd stared at me. I'd shrugged and pushed my chair away from the table as I'd stood up.

'I don't think you want to do that, Jack.' He'd squeezed his hands round his cup and the cardboard had crumpled at the edges. I'd turned and taken a couple of steps away from him. 'I'll just come and see you again.' There'd been a tremor in his voice. He hadn't been sure if I was bluffing, and he'd just given away the fact that he was as desperate as I was. Whatever he wanted, he obviously couldn't get it anywhere else. I was his last resort. Even though I'd known he was exploiting me, that fact still hurt more than I wanted to admit. I'd hesitated. 'If you sit down, I'll tell you,' he'd offered.

I'd turned around slowly and lowered myself back into my seat, watching him. He couldn't be underestimated. I'd made that mistake too many times before.

He'd adjusted his cufflinks as I'd waited, not speaking.

'I need you to lend me some money,' he'd said.

I'd kept my face blank. The same request as last time. He'd begged and I'd refused until he'd told me he'd found out where my mother had moved to and was considering paying her a visit. I couldn't let him put her through that again. And I hadn't wanted him anywhere near Ali, hadn't wanted her to meet him, to see the person whose genes I'd inherited and was so ashamed of. I'd given him the five thousand pounds he'd asked for and told him I wouldn't see him again. It had been worth every penny, even though we both knew he'd never pay it back. He hadn't known it came out of our savings for IVF and that I hadn't told Ali what I'd done.

'How much?' I'd asked.

He'd hesitated. 'Another five thousand.'

I'd resisted the urge to laugh. How stupid did he think I was? I wasn't going to hand that amount over again. He'd brought me here for a reason; he must have guessed my reluctance to let him into the flat meant I hadn't told Ali

I'd raided our savings, and he thought he could use that to blackmail me.

'What's it for this time?' I'd asked.

'An investment.'

'I thought that's what it was for last time? Didn't it produce the returns you were expecting?' I'd asked.

He'd reached into the inside pocket of his blazer and had taken out his diary, pulling out a small biro that had been tucked down into the spine, licking his finger as he'd turned the pages. I shouldn't have asked the question. I shouldn't have even been there. I hadn't been able to believe I was related to this man. I'd wondered whether I could behave like he had towards his own child. Whether the same character traits were buried somewhere inside me, just waiting for an opportunity to manifest themselves.

'The fund did brilliantly for months, returned over twenty-six percent, but a few weeks ago it crashed. Might still come back, apparently, but there's a question mark over the conduct of a couple of the directors.'

'And what's it worth now?' I'd asked.

'Around two.' He'd seen me raise my eyebrows before adding, 'Hundred.' If I hadn't known him better, I'd have felt sorry for him. Desperate to keep up with other members in his club, he'd got involved in things he didn't understand. But I had known him better, and it was hard not to feel he'd got what he deserved after all he'd put us through.

'I'm not going to give you any more money.' I'd sat back in my chair, waiting for him to threaten to tell Ali.

He'd looked at me. 'I think you will, Jack.'

'Or what? You'll say something to her?'

He'd continued to stare at me, not speaking.

'Go ahead. I can explain why I did it. She'll believe me over someone she's never even met. I've told her what you're like.' I'd shut my mouth before any more vitriol could escape.

A woman had pointed to the extra chair at our table and asked if she could take it. I'd nodded. The brief moment of interaction with a stranger had made me realise he'd been deliberately antagonising me. My anger had been clouding my judgement, which was exactly what he wanted. I needed to keep a clear head.

'I will tell her,' he'd said.

'Fine, you go ahead.' I'd begun to stand up.

He'd smiled at me, and his lips had narrowed in triumph. Something heavy had slid into my stomach. He'd been hiding something since the start of this conversation. An ugly surprise he'd been saving just for me. I'd gripped the chair. He'd waited, knowing I would too.

'What?' I hadn't been able to help myself.

His lips had twitched, rearranging his original smile into something I'd been more familiar with. The one I'd been used to seeing when he'd walked out of our house, leaving my mother in the sitting room. Lying on the floor. The one that said he knew something I didn't.

'Do you think Ali will forgive you now if you tell her what you did? After you've lied to her for this long? Come on, Jack, think about it from her point of view. If you've lied about this, what else might you not have told her? I hear your company's not doing so well at the moment, have you told her about that?' He'd relished every word as he'd stabbed them into me. How did he know? No one knew that. He'd smiled again, waiting for me to ask, seeing if I could resist the temptation to find out where he'd got the information. I hated him, but I'd asked all the same. I didn't have anything to lose.

'How do you know?' I hadn't bothered trying to deny it. There hadn't been any point. I'd just needed to work out if Ali would hear it from anyone else.

'Someone at my club mentioned something. It's only a rumour, but you know how news likes to travel. Businesses are folding all the time in the current climate. I wouldn't want your clients to get nervous and I don't think Ali should hear about it from me. Do you?'

I'd hesitated, and then shook my head. He hadn't made me beg. Not like he used to do with my mother; he'd kept her on her hands and knees until she was too exhausted to plead anymore. He hadn't needed to do that with me. He'd known he'd already won.

'It's only a temporary cash-flow issue. We'll be fine in a couple of months.' My words sounded hollow.

'I'm sure you will. But it's not something you want people to find out about right now, is it? Especially your wife. Don't worry, Jack, no one else knows. For the moment. And they won't hear anything from me, providing we can sort this out.'

For about the millionth time, I'd wished I'd told Ali what I'd done. I'd panicked, not wanting to face her and tell her we couldn't afford another round of IVF because I'd given the money to my father. I'd known she'd be furious. And part of me had been secretly relieved at the thought we didn't have to go through another round of treatment. As much as I'd wanted us to have a baby, I'd been sick of the dates and cycles and injections and disappointments. I'd thought we could be enough for each other. So I'd come up with a lie that had been easier than telling her the truth. That I hadn't got a bonus and so we couldn't afford it. I thought Ali had accepted it until that phone call from Edward when he'd offered to lend us the money. And I'd taken it and lied to him, too.

My father had studied me. 'You could tell Ali, of course. I'm sure she'd get over it. But I think the timing now she's having a baby is probably something you want to avoid.' I'd stared at him. 'I've seen her,' he'd said, by way of explanation, 'Going into your flat. Hasn't got long to go now, I imagine.' He'd dabbed at a small drop of water he'd spilt on the table with a napkin. 'I'll give you a couple of weeks,' he'd said. 'To sort something out.' He'd circled a date in blue pen in a page of his diary. 'You must still have all my bank details from last time.' He'd got up out of his chair, leaving his half-empty cup on the table. 'I'll expect to hear from you, or I'll be back in touch. Bye, son. I get the impression you won't mind if I don't give you a hug.'

I'd watched him walk out of the door and had swallowed the lump in my throat with my last mouthful of coffee. Despite everything he'd done, I still felt the pain of rejection as fiercely as I had twenty years earlier.

The sound of Tilly crying interrupts my thoughts and I walk into the bedroom, where Ali is sitting on the bed, holding her against her shoulder as she pats her back. Tilly's face is bright red, her fists screwed up into tiny balls, her mouth wide as she screams so loudly her lips tremble.

Ali looks at me. 'I don't know what I'm doing wrong. She doesn't want to feed.' Tears well in her eyes.

I hold out my arms. 'Do you want me to take her for a bit?' I ask.

She nods and I pick her up. Ali's shoulders sag as she massages her forehead.

'She'll be fine in a minute,' I say. 'I'll walk round with her for a bit. See if I can settle her.'

Ali stares at me, but I don't think she's really listening to what I'm saying.

I carry Tilly on my chest round the flat, rubbing her back, waiting for her cries to quieten before I go back into the bedroom. Ali's lying on the bed, curled up on her side and at first I think she's asleep, but then she rolls over, wiping her face on the pillow.

'I don't think I can do this,' she says.

'You can,' I say. 'I'm here to help and it'll get easier. Do you want to see if she'll feed now she's a bit quieter?'

She sits up slowly, wincing as she adjusts her position. I hand her Tilly, who nuzzles into her, latching on this time. I sit next to her silently, trying to think of something to say. I want to remind her she's everything we wanted. That we'd tried for her for so long. That we all just need some sleep. But I don't. I can't find the right words amongst the possibilities that flicker on my tongue before I reject them as unsuitable. The weight in my stomach that I've carried round with me over the past few months feels heavier than ever. Ali looks exhausted. For months I've lied to her about what I've done, and I'm sure she knows I'm hiding something. I daren't consider telling her the truth, but I've no idea where I'm going to find five thousand pounds that we don't have. She closes her eyes as she leans back on her pillows whilst Tilly feeds. I wish I could go back and change what happened. If she finds out now, she'll leave me – and take everything I've ever wanted with her as she walks out of the door.

THEN

Alison – *Day Two*

I lie awake with my eyes shut, Tilly making strange snuffling noises in her Moses basket beside me. It felt like I hadn't slept at all last night – I'd leaned over the side of the bed so many times to check on her. Her eyes had always been shut, even though her tiny body had twitched every now and again. I'd thought she'd lie still at night, like the pictures of babies I'd seen asleep in magazines. I hadn't realised she'd be so noisy. Each time I'd begun to drift off, she'd brought me back to reality with a scuffle or gurgle, my senses somehow tuned into her every move. Without me, she'll die. I know Jack doesn't feel it in the same way. It's all down to me. A duty designed to smother me with its intensity.

Jack hadn't come to bed until late and has been restless for most of the night. My brain won't switch off. It seems a lifetime ago that we found out I was pregnant. I'd held the white stick like a fragile ornament in our bathroom, too scared to look, watching Jack's face when he'd seen the blue line. I hadn't realised until then how hard he'd found the past few years, the three rounds of IVF. How devastated he'd been when he'd thought we couldn't afford a final attempt.

How my anger had transformed into pity when I'd found him crying in the bathroom as he'd told me he hadn't got a bonus and we couldn't justify the expense. He'd wanted it as much as I had, and I'd found a way to get it for both of us. Looking at him lying beside me now, I don't feel anything.

I wait until it's light before I get out of bed, wash my hair and put on some make-up, keeping the bathroom door open so I can keep an eye on Tilly through the glass shower screen. The midwife is due at ten o'clock. Jack keeps telling me she won't care what I look like, that it's not a test. He's naïve. Of course it's a test. And if I fail, she could take Tilly away from me.

I jump up when the buzzer sounds for the front door, leaving Jack sitting in the kitchen, pulling down my top over the remains of my bump. The material's creased. I should have ironed it.

'It's Mrs Reynolds, isn't it?' the midwife says as she steps over the threshold, offering to shake my hand as she takes off her jacket. 'I'm Lisa. Lovely to meet you.'

'Call me Ali.'

'Have you got somewhere we can go and have a chat?' she asks.

'Yes, we can go in the sitting room,' I say. 'Can I get you a cup of tea or anything?'

Lisa shakes her head. 'I'm good, thanks.' She pushes the door of the lounge shut behind her, smiling conspiratorial-ly. 'That's so we're not disturbed.' She can't be older than twenty. She gets out her stethoscope, blood pressure cuff and a large notebook. Tilly makes a gurgling noise in her Moses basket and I pat her blanket gently, hoping she'll settle. 'Did you manage to get any sleep last night?' Lisa asks.

'Some,' I lie.

'Perhaps try and have a rest when she naps today? It's good to catch up if you can.'

I don't like being told what to do by someone so much younger than me; I want to ask her how long she's been qualified. She writes something in her notebook, but I can't see what it says. I think it could be that I'm not getting enough sleep. Surely that's something all new mothers find difficult, not something I could fail her test on. I want to ask her, but I'm worried she'll jot that down too. *Ali asks too many questions. She seems to lack basic knowledge of childcare.* I could tell her I've been to all the NCT classes, I've completed all the exercises. I was confident I knew what I was doing when we'd changed the doll's nappy. But it's all so different when I try and do it in real life, Tilly's delicate limbs flailing around, actively fighting where I try to put them. I wonder if Lisa will write a report on me when she leaves here. Perhaps she'll discuss me with her boss. I press my lips together to stop any more information slipping out.

'Can I?' She holds out her arms as I pick Tilly up. 'She's such a sweetie.'

I hesitate, not wanting to hand her over to this stranger who already doesn't seem to like me. I'm worried she won't give her back. I pass her across reluctantly, hoping she doesn't notice my hands are shaking. She strips off Tilly's Babygro and checks her over. My breathing quickens as I search for any sign of the marks I saw yesterday, but her skin is flawless. Dad was right, they must have been from what she was wearing. I wince as Lisa holds the cold metal chest piece onto

Tilly's skin to listen to her breathing. I wait, half-expecting her to tell me there's something wrong, but she passes her back to me whilst she packs her stethoscope away.

'Do you have any children?' I ask. I bet she doesn't.

Tilly starts to whimper and I put her on my shoulder, rubbing her back. I plead with her silently in my head not to cry. Not to embarrass me in front of Lisa.

'Not yet. I've got enough on my plate dealing with other people's.' She smiles. How she can possibly understand what this is like when she doesn't have any of her own? 'Your husband,' she says. 'Jack, isn't it?' I nod. 'It's great he's got a bit of time off work. Good to have another pair of hands around to help you.' I think she's already questioning my capabilities. I wonder if it says Tilly was an IVF baby on my notes. That I'd already been marked out as having failed at the first step of parenthood before I'd even started.

'Have you looked after many new babies?' I ask.

'Quite a few.' She's sidestepping the question. A few. That could mean three or thirty, and if it's only three I want someone with more experience, who'll notice if something's wrong. I'm worried she missed something when she listened to Tilly's breathing, but I can't ask her to do it again. I wonder if I can ask to swap to another midwife.

I rub my forehead. She's talking to me, but my head hurts and it's difficult to hear what she's saying.

'Do you want to pop your trousers off, so we can take a look at those stitches? Your notes say you had a difficult labour, so I just need to make sure everything's healing properly.'

I put Tilly, quiet for now, back in her basket, take my trousers off and lie down on the sofa. My top is stuck to me, the material damp with perspiration. I'm dreading Lisa touching me. Lying with my knickers off in front of a stranger in hospital is one thing, but in my own home I'm acutely aware of my nakedness and my protruding stomach that makes me look like I'm still pregnant. I want to tell her to fuck off, to leave me alone, to stop this assault on my vulnerability, an anger instantly welling up inside of me. But I don't. I lie mute as she puts on a pair of plastic gloves and peers between my legs, prodding parts of me that are tender, making me wince before telling me to put my clothes back on. I'm tempted to add more layers next time. To cover up my body and give it a chance to hide. She sits back, a slight frown on her forehead as she peels the gloves off.

'Have you felt unwell, Ali? Since you left hospital? A temperature?'

I shake my head as I hear voices in the hall and sit up, reaching for my pants. I hadn't heard the buzzer. Doesn't Jack realise I don't want visitors at the moment? 'I'm not expecting anyone,' I say, stretching my top down to cover my trousers as I pull them up. I'm panicking they'll open the door before I've had a chance to get dressed properly.

'Sorry?' Lisa looks at me.

'I . . . I didn't know someone was coming.'

She looks confused. 'Where?'

'Here,' I say, putting my finger to my lips. 'Listen. Someone's talking. In the hall.'

Lisa frowns. 'I can't hear anything.' She turns her head to the side. 'No . . . nothing.'

'Jack?' I shout.

'What?' He puts his head round the door.

'Is anyone out there with you?' I ask him.

He looks confused. 'No. Why?'

'I thought I heard something. Ignore me. Sorry.'

Lisa repeats her question as Jack goes back into the kitchen. 'And you're sure you don't feel unwell at all?'

'No,' I say. 'I'm fine.'

Lisa finishes scribbling in her notes and puts them in her bag. I wonder if she'll give me a copy when she leaves. 'I'd better make a move, Ali, unless there's anything else you'd like to ask me?'

A dozen questions pop into my mouth, but I swallow them and shake my head.

'I'm going to come back tomorrow, just to check on those stitches. I think they're OK but everything still looks a bit raw, so I'd rather keep an eye on them. It's nice to meet you. You've got a beautiful daughter.'

I stare at Tilly, her face scrunched up and blotchy. 'I know,' I reply. 'I'm so lucky.'

'You're driving too fast,' I say as Jack swings the car round a bend, and I reach for the handle above the passenger seat.

I had to get out of the flat. Tilly's grizzling had become unbearable. Eating into my brain until there hadn't been an inch left to escape into. At least she sleeps in the car. I twist round to look over my shoulder to check her seat is fastened firmly in the back. She seems fine, but it's difficult to tell when she's facing away from me. We need to get a mirror put up so I can see her properly.

'Do you think we should stop to make sure she's OK?' I ask.

'There's no point. We're almost there now,' he says.

I've read about the statistics for cot death. Four babies a week. I wonder if you can get a monitor for the car, like the one we have at home next to her Moses basket. Last night I'd watched the small green dots light up in time with her breathing and had made a plan of what I'd do if they'd stopped, working out how long it would take for an ambulance to arrive or whether it would be quicker to get her to hospital in our car. I'd drawn up an emergency list on the notes app on my phone of the essentials I'd need to take with us if it happened. Best to be prepared. Just in case.

We sit in silence as Jack reverses into an empty space in the supermarket and pulls on the handbrake.

'Are you getting out then?' he asks.

'No,' I reply. 'I don't want to. Tilly will be safer in here with me. People will breathe all over her if we take her inside. There's too many germs in there.'

'But you said you wanted to bring her?' He hesitates before pulling his keys out of the ignition.

'I did, but I hadn't thought about the possibility of her getting ill.'

He doesn't reply and slams the driver's door as he gets out. Tilly stirs briefly but settles back to sleep. I watch as he walks across the car park towards the entrance before I switch the radio on, not loud enough to disturb her. I close my eyes as I listen to the murmurs I can hear alongside the music in my head. I can tell Jack's irritated. It doesn't take much to make him fly off the handle at the moment. I think the lack of sleep last night is getting to him.

I'm jolted out of my doze as the car door opens. I'd only

shut my eyes for a few seconds. I sit up with a start and look behind me. Tilly's fine, she's still dozing. I need to be more vigilant. What if someone had opened the door, taken her out? I dig my nails into my palms as Jack looks at me.

'You don't have to wake up,' he says. 'You rest and I'll drive home.'

'No, it's fine,' I say as I get out and walk round to the driver's side. 'I want to.' I don't trust him not to go as fast as he did on the way here. He doesn't mean to take risks, but he doesn't realise how vulnerable she is. It's my job to protect her. To keep her safe.

His mouth is in a tight line as he gets in beside me and clicks the seat belt into place. I pull out of the car park hoping she stays asleep on the journey home. I like it when she's asleep. I start talking in the hope it'll wake me up a bit.

'Stop!' Jack bellows and hits his hand on the dashboard. 'Jesus, Ali. It was red. Didn't you see it?'

I look across at him, confused. 'See what?'

'The traffic light! You went straight through it. You could've killed us. How could you not see it?'

'I didn't . . .'

'Pull over.' He's yelling.

'Don't shout at me.'

'Pull over, Ali. I'll drive. I knew you shouldn't be behind the wheel.'

I indicate and stop the car next to the kerb.

'You're overreacting,' I mutter, my face hot. I can't bring myself to look at him. I don't even remember seeing the traffic light. Or what colour it was. There's a moment of silence until I glance across at him. He's still looking at me, concern now showing in his eyes rather than terror. I could have killed Tilly. Or Jack. Or all of us. A few cars accelerate as they drive past us and I shrink down in my seat, hoping they didn't see what happened.

'You're lucky it's not busier.' He fumbles to undo his seat belt. Tilly's still fast asleep.

I get out, my legs trembling and he steps into the driver's side; his cheeks flushed.

We drive home in silence.

He turns to me as we walk through the door of the flat.

'You need to sleep,' he says. 'No arguments. I'll wake you if Tilly needs you.'

I don't try to contradict him. There's no point in having a row. I walk off into the bedroom, draw the curtains and lie down. Half an hour later, I hear him coming down the hall. He peers through the dim light to look at me. I lie motionless under the duvet and shut my eyes. Satisfied, he tiptoes out again, pulling the door shut behind him. Wide awake, I pick up my notebook from where I've set it down on my bedside table and continue writing. Words flow onto the page as the noises in my head gather together into something coherent. Now I understand. They want to start a conversation.

THEN

Jack – *Day Three*

I press the button on the intercom as it buzzes to let Lisa in and wait for her to walk up the corridor, holding the mug of untouched cold tea I took Ali earlier. Guilt slops around in my stomach like the liquid in the cup. I should have told her everything a year ago.

'Morning, Jack. It's lovely out there today. How was your night?' Lisa asks.

'Fine.' I lie. My father's smile had appeared every time I shut my eyes. At five o'clock, I hadn't been able to stand it any longer and had got up. The conversation I'd had with him got out of bed with me as well, attaching itself round my waist like a belt that had been fastened too tightly. It squeezes my stomach every now and again, just to make sure I haven't forgotten about it.

'Are they in the bedroom? Is it OK for me to go through?' Lisa asks.

I nod and she disappears up the hallway. I take the mug into the kitchen, pour away the cold drink and put the kettle on. I hope Ali's less tired today. I think she'd managed to get more sleep last night. At least Tilly hadn't cried so much.

I log onto my computer and open an email from the bank. It confirms what I thought: the balance in our savings account isn't nearly enough to pay my father what he wants, and they won't lend me the difference as my credit score is too low. I'm searching through loan companies online when Lisa walks back into the kitchen.

'Your wife and daughter are both doing really well,' she says.

I nod. I don't trust myself to speak in case she detects my cynicism. Ali clearly hasn't told her she'd jumped a red light yesterday.

'She told me she managed to get about five hours' sleep last night, which is great. Perhaps you could encourage her to go for a walk to get some fresh air? And make sure she eats some lunch? You're lucky with the flat being on the ground floor, you can sit out on your patio when the weather's like this.'

'Sure,' I say. I've got stuff in the fridge to make that prawn salad she really likes.

'And there isn't anything you want to ask?' she says, staring at me.

I glance at the door, wondering if our conversation can be heard in the bedroom. I have got questions, but I don't want Ali to hear me. Are all new mothers reluctant to let anyone else hold their baby? Do they all want to spend so much time in their bedroom? I don't want Lisa to think I'm questioning Ali's decisions. Or her behaviour. Harry had said it took a while for them to adjust when Josh had first come home. And I'm not in a position to judge. I shake my head and Lisa lets herself out.

As I'm walking to the bedroom I hear whispering, which

stops as soon as I open the door. Ali smiles at me, wrinkling her nose.

'She needs a change,' she says.

'I'll do it.'

I don't give her an opportunity to refuse. I pick Tilly up and carry her through to the bathroom and lie her on her changing mat. My fingers fumble with the poppers on her Babygro as I undo them awkwardly. She starts to cry. Ali's standing behind me, watching everything I'm doing. I take a deep breath and clean Tilly with the wet wipes, discarding the dirty ones into a plastic bag. I unfold a clean nappy, carefully avoiding the stump of her umbilical cord and once it's in place, fasten her Babygro back up, my fingers slippery.

I wonder if my father ever did this with me. I can't imagine him changing a nappy. That had been the kind of job he'd left to my mother. I wonder if we'd bonded better from the start, whether he'd have seen me as more than just a rival for my mother's attention.

Ali holds out her arms for Tilly.

'I'll take her for a bit,' I say.

'It's fine, honestly,' she says, scooping Tilly out of my grasp.

'I'm . . . I'm only trying . . . to help.' Her dismissal and my thoughts about my father make me stumble over the words. I wonder if she's deliberately trying to hurt me. If she is, I probably deserve it.

I walk away into the kitchen to get a glass of water. Swallowing a mouthful doesn't get rid of the rejection that tastes bitter in my mouth.

★

We push the pram along the pavement in the muggy summer heat. It needs a storm to clear the air, but it's still more pleasant than being cooped up in the flat. Tilly stares at the stripy zebra Ali's fixed to the hood which twirls and swings as we walk. I'm not sure she can actually see it, but Ali insists newborns can distinguish black and white. I put my arm round her shoulders. She doesn't push me away. Her hair falls over my bare skin and I shiver. Before we'd had Tilly, I'd have pulled her towards me, kissed her perhaps, but now there's a tightness between us that holds me back and I keep walking straight ahead.

'I think she's putting on weight,' Ali says. 'She seems heavier than she was in hospital. And I think we should have her christened.'

I pause. This isn't something we've discussed.

'Ali, I think we should—'

She interrupts. 'And we need to get her name registered. I'm not sure where we have to go to, but I think there's something about it in those pamphlets that I was given. Em said she'd pop over tomorrow. Do you know if Harry's coming as well? We'll have to get some food if they are.'

'I don't think they're going to expect anything to—'

'We can grab something on the way back from the park,' she says. She seems like a different person today, perhaps we're starting to get into a routine. She's talking more. A lot more. I can barely get a word in.

We stroll across the small car park and along the path that leads to the entrance gate of the local park. I hold it open whilst Ali pushes the pram over a couple of bumps and sits down on a bench shaded by some tall lime trees. A short distance away, children scramble over a wooden pirate ship and throw themselves down a slide in a playground surrounded by a low fence. The grass in front of us is covered in a patchwork quilt of picnic rugs.

'Do you want a drink?' I ask her. 'I'll get us something from the café.'

She nods as she brushes some tree pollen off her skirt and the hood of Tilly's pram.

'I'll have an Earl Grey tea.' She adjusts the stripy toy.

'OK. I won't be a minute.' I walk off down the narrow path across the grass, kicking a football back to its owner as it lands in front of me.

The café is busy; a long queue of customers stands waiting to be served in front of the small counter. By the time I've ordered, I'm desperate to be back outside in the fresh air. I pay the teenage cashier, who is bathed in a sheen of sweat, and carry the paper cups carefully as they've run out of lids.

Ali's sitting with one hand on Tilly's pram. She's talking to a woman I don't recognise. I screw up my eyes against the glare of the sun as I struggle to keep the hot tea from spilling over the side of the cup onto my foot. By the time I reach her, she's lifted Tilly out of the pram. I go to hand her the cup before I realise that she's crying.

'What is it?' I put my arm on her shoulder. 'What's the matter?'

'That woman.' She pulls at the front of my T-shirt, her eyes wide.

'What? What happened?' I say. I look at the back of the figure who is rapidly walking away.

'She told me I was an awful mother. That I don't deserve to have Tilly.' Her voice is shaky.

I glance at the woman again and then back at my wife, in disbelief that anyone could be so rude.

'Stay here,' I say.

I put the cups on the ground by the bench and run along the footpath, trying to avoid tripping over buggies and legs of toddlers. I tap the woman on the shoulder and she turns around.

'Excuse me,' I say, out of breath. 'I believe you just spoke to my wife.'

She looks confused but smiles when she sees me pointing at Ali. 'Oh, yes. The lady with the baby. So cute.'

I'm confused. There's an uncomfortable pause whilst she waits for an explanation.

I clear my throat. 'Can I ask what you said to her?' The words sound ridiculous as soon as they're out of my mouth.

She frowns. 'Just that her baby was really sweet. She's still so tiny. Why?'

'I . . . I just needed to check . . .something. Thank you.'

She walks off, leaving me standing in the middle of the path, flushed with embarrassment. I look at the other families on the grass who are eating their sandwiches and packets of crisps and feel more alone than I did before we had a child.

'Are you sure you heard her properly?' I ask Ali as I help her put Tilly back in the pram.

'Are you saying I'm lying?' She pulls away from me.

'No . . .' I choose my words carefully. 'I just wonder if there was a misunderstanding.'

'I didn't misunderstand anything. Some woman just had

a go at me and now you're sticking up for her. How d'you think that makes me feel, Jack?' A couple sitting nearby stare as she raises her voice. 'Let's go. I don't want to stay here.' She picks up the cup of tea that I've just bought and pours it on the grass.

I glance back at the couple, who smile at me in sympathy. I remember those looks. I'd seen them a lot when I was younger whenever we'd been on a family outing. My father hadn't cared who'd been listening when he'd raged, as long as it wasn't anyone we knew. Amongst his friends he'd behaved like a perfect husband. My mother hadn't had any friends of her own. They were all his. Recruited to bolster his ego until her identity had been absorbed into his and the person she once was had been slowly eradicated.

We walk home in silence, the pram wheels juddering along the pavement as she speeds up. I don't understand what's just happened. A nagging voice at the back of my head tells me I don't believe Ali's version of events, but I don't want her to think I don't trust her. What I've lied about is so much worse. I need to make her realise she can rely on me to be the father Tilly deserves. That we can get through this without anyone else's help.

She's walking in the middle of the pavement and there's not enough room for me to fit next to her without getting precariously close to the edge of the kerb. The pram wheel catches on a bump in the pavement and she shoves it roughly to get it to move forwards. I open my mouth to tell her to be careful, but stop myself. I can see Tilly's face under the hood and step forward to grab the handle of the pram to bring it to a halt.

'Please, Ali. Don't be cross.'

She turns towards me, her knuckles white. 'Don't tell me what to feel. I know you don't believe me.' She has tears in her eyes.

'It's not that I don't believe you. I just . . . I don't know what to say.' At the moment it seems every word has sharp edges which we use to cut into each other. I put my hand over hers on the pram and she stares at me, as if she's searching for something.

'There's something you don't . . .' she says, in barely a whisper.

'What?' I ask.

She can't seem to find what she's looking for and the moment passes. She looks away. 'It doesn't matter,' she replies. 'Can we go home?'

I move my hand to let go of the pram and she walks off.

My mum comes over in the afternoon and I swallow the lump in my throat as I put Tilly into her arms for the first time.

'How are you finding it so far?' she asks Ali.

'There's so many things that I'm not sure about,' she replies. 'I was thinking about them all last night. I'm not sure if she's supposed to have so many layers on. I'm not sure when I'm supposed to feed her. I don't know if I should be winding her more. I don't understand when—'

My mum glances at me and I can see the familiar crease in her forehead appear. 'Don't worry so much, love,' she says. 'She looks fine to me.'

'But you're not an expert, are you?' Ali retorts.

'Ali!' I say.

She looks at my mum, embarrassed. 'Sorry, I didn't mean . . .'

'It's fine . . . really. I can remember what it's like.' My mum smiles at her. She hates any kind of confrontation.

There's an awkward silence. I'm worried about Ali, but if I say anything to anyone, she'd consider it a betrayal. *I think my wife is imagining things.* She'd be furious. I wasn't there, I keep reminding myself. I didn't actually hear what that woman said. I know I should tell Lisa. *I don't think my wife is sleeping.* She might be able to recommend something to help. Maybe I could say something to my mum. Maybe all new mothers are like this. Maybe my mum was. I try to ignore the small voice inside me that tells me it's why my dad ended up behaving like he did. That her behaviour meant he got fed up of teetering on the edge of a precipice, trying not to say the wrong thing that would tip them both over the edge. What if I turn out like him? The person I least want to be? I won't say anything about Ali yet. It's still early days. We just need to get ourselves into a proper routine.

When I come to bed, Ali's sitting up, writing something in what looks like a baby book.

'Can I see?' I ask.

She raises her head and snaps the pages shut. 'Not at the moment, no. You can look when it's finished. I'm going to sleep.' She puts it on her bedside table and closes her eyes.

I stare at her lying on the pillow beside me.

'What?' she asks as she opens her eyes briefly to see me

staring at her eyebrows and runs a finger over the sparse line of hairs.

'Nothing,' I say a little too quickly as she frowns. 'It just . . . it looks like you've been pulling them out.' I lean over to touch her, but she flinches and moves her head away. I realise she's been avoiding me since she had Tilly and her response freezes something in my chest, making it difficult for me to breathe. She won't even look at me, shutting her eyes so if I didn't know better I'd assume she was asleep. I don't think she trusts me anymore, and I can't tell her she's right not to.

I watch as she reaches across with one hand and twists her engagement ring round on her finger, as if she can read my thoughts as they spill out of my head. She pulls off the ring and puts it on her bedside table.

'It feels too tight,' she says in the uncomfortable silence. 'My fingers are swollen.'

I switch off the light, waiting for her to say something else, but she doesn't. There's just my own voice in the darkness, telling me that I've missed something important and as a result I think Ali's found out what I did last year.

THEN

Alison – *Day Four*

Don't let her in. I don't have a choice. She's knocking on the door. *She'll take Tilly away.* She won't. She needs to check on her. *You said you'd listen to me.* I am, but I can't ignore Lisa. *You promised.* I understand what I've got to do, but I need to let her in. *Prove it.* I can't prove it right now. She'll wonder why I'm not answering. *You agreed to do what I said.*

I shut my eyes and press my fingers into the lids as hard as I can, watching the colours change from black to a dizzying array of stars that burn with a whiteness that's so bright I have to open them again to get away from it. I know it's hiding in there somewhere, I just can't see it. I need it to leave me alone so I can sleep. I rub my face, blinking to clear the flashing lights.

I glance in the Moses basket next to my bed, plucking up the courage to call out and let Lisa know she can come in. I wish I didn't have to. *Don't do it.* Tilly's asleep, one hand tucked under her cheek, her mouth slightly open, relaxing in an unselfconscious slumber. I reach out to stroke her face when I notice the blood. A slow trickle that seeps out of her nose, down towards her mouth, where it drips onto her pristine white sheet. It spreads out in a circle like ink on blotting paper. I freeze, too terrified to move, as a mottled pale grey colour spreads across her skin. My baby.

There's a more insistent knock on the door. *I told you not to let her in. I told you.*

I step forward to touch Tilly's back with the tips of my fingers, terrified she's going to feel stiff, like one of those mice our neighbour's cat leaves outside our patio door. A tiny, cold body that's unnaturally rigid when I wrap it in a plastic bag. I force my hand forward those last few centimetres. Her skin is still warm. Soft. She's breathing. I scoop her into my arms, pressing her into me tightly as I look at her face. No blood. Nothing on her or me. A spotless white sheet lies in the Moses basket. I gasp, letting the air rush back into my lungs. My heart thuds so hard, I think it might leave my chest. *This is what will happen to her. This is what Jack will do. I can help you.*

'Leave her alone,' I whisper over her head to the empty room.

The handle turns on the door as Lisa lets herself in. 'Ali?' she says. 'I wasn't sure if you could hear me?'

I'm holding Tilly against my chest. There is no blood. No blood. I stroke her head, inhaling her baby vanilla scent as I sit down on the edge of the bed to hide the fact my legs are trembling.

'Sorry. I was just changing her and didn't hear you.' There's a catch in my voice.

Lisa sits down next to me. 'You sure you're OK? You're a bit pale.'

'I'm fine.'

'Jack said you went to the park yesterday,' she says.

'Yes.' I'm not really listening to her, focusing instead on the movement of Tilly's back under my hand as she breathes softly in and out.

'Ah, I bet that was nice. It's good to get a bit of fresh air.'

I don't reply. It's getting harder to work out who's talking to me.

'Let's have a look at Tilly, then.' Lisa reaches out to take her and I hesitate, petrified I'll see smears of blood on her Babygro, but there's only white. Nothing red.

I run my hands through my hair to give myself something to do, twisting it up into a ponytail.

'How are you feeling?' Lisa asks.

'I'm good.' *You need something to protect you.*

'Not too tired?'

'No. I slept quite well last night.' *You didn't. We talked. All the time.*

'Did you? Jack said you were a bit restless.' *Of course he did. He's telling tales.*

'I was for a while, but I managed to get a few hours.'

'Good. And everything else is OK?'

'Yes.' *There's something that would help you in the kitchen drawer.*

'Are you sure? You seem rather . . .' Lisa hesitates and shifts her position on the bed, leaning towards me as if she's confiding something. 'You can tell me if you're struggling with anything,' she says. *Told you Jack's been telling her about you.*

'I'm fine, honestly.' *No, you're not.*

Lisa nods. 'Well, do say if there's something you're worried

about. It's quite normal to have concerns as a new mum.
Everyone does.'

Smile. Agree with her. I smile. She passes Tilly back to me
and I snuggle her into my chest, hoping she can't see my
hands are still shaking.

'It might be nice if you let Jack do a few things with Tilly
on his own,' she adds. 'Let him take her for a walk or something. It'll give you a break. Most new mums would kill
for the chance to be on their own for a while.' She pauses,
smoothing non-existent creases out of the duvet cover. 'It
doesn't mean you love Tilly any less if you let other people
help you,' she says.

I don't reply. She's got no idea what she's talking about,
what I need to do to protect my daughter. No one else can
do that. She doesn't understand Jack shouldn't be allowed on
his own with her. He's going to hurt her. I know it. *Jack's
waiting until you're asleep and then he'll take her. Somewhere you'll
never find her again. You need something to protect you.*

Lisa sees I'm not going to answer, so changes the subject.
'Let's check those stitches again.'

I go through the familiar routine of stripping off and looking at the ceiling as she stares between my legs.

'They're not looking too bad,' she says. 'You can put your
trousers back on. Those deeper ones still look a bit red, so I'll
check them again tomorrow.' She smiles. 'Are you going to
have some lunch?'

I look at the clock. I hadn't realised how late it was.

'Not yet. I'll come and get some in a minute.'

I lie Tilly back in her Moses basket as Lisa walks out and
pick up my notebook. If I write it all down, it'll be out of my

head and I'll have some space. It never stops. My mind is so crammed with everything it's telling me, I'm losing crucial information as it spills over the edges. I can't hold it all in.

I can hear them talking in the kitchen. Holding Tilly with one arm, I open the bedroom door a crack and peer out. Their voices are muffled and I can't make out what they're saying. I wonder if he's telling her I didn't sleep last night. Making me out to be a liar. The kitchen door begins to open and I shut mine slowly, careful it doesn't make a noise.

I know he's hiding something. He never whispers unless there's something he doesn't want me to hear. A couple of days before I went into labour his mum had come over. She'd given us a teddy and a blanket, which I'd taken and put in our bedroom to stop Jack getting paint all over them. When I'd emerged, I'd listened to their hushed voices in the kitchen, which had stopped the minute I'd walked through the door. I'd asked him about it later when we'd been lying in bed.

'Why was your mum saying she couldn't believe you'd been so stupid?'

He'd paused and swallowed before he'd answered, telling me something about a project at work, but I hadn't believed him then, either.

He's left his laptop in the bedroom and I open the cover, watching the screen light up before typing in his password. I click on the tab which shows all his emails and scan down them whilst listening to their voices in the hall. I read the one that he got yesterday from the bank. An application and rejection for a loan. The thought we could be in financial difficulties makes me go cold. Tilly's future is suddenly uncertain, and I wonder what else he's hiding from me.

I shut the laptop and pull out the folder where I know he keeps all our bank statements. I can hear him opening the front door to let Lisa out. I don't have much time. It doesn't take long to spot it, an amount so large it stands out amongst the other payments. Five thousand pounds to a Mr John Reynolds last year. His father. Who he'd said he had no contact with. He'd given away our money without even telling me. As I hear the front door shut and Lisa's footsteps retreat up the hallway outside, I look at the dates again and realise with a jolt this means we'd had the money for our last round of IVF – Jack just obviously hadn't wanted to go through with it. And then my dad had lent it to us and he hadn't had a choice.

Jack has never wanted Tilly, and now he's planning how to get rid of her.

'Em's supposed to be coming over this afternoon,' he says, standing at the foot of our bed. 'D'you want me to cancel?'

'No, why would we do that?' I stare at him.

'I wondered if you felt up to it.'

'I'm fine. She can give me some tips on how to handle the first few weeks.'

'Great.' He smiles, but I don't smile back.

'Don't patronise me, Jack. You're treating me like a five-year-old. It's nice Em's coming over, I'm looking forward to it. It doesn't mean I'm happy you're saying things to Lisa about me.'

'I haven't . . .'

'I heard you talking to her in the kitchen. Before you go

telling tales, can you at least speak to me first?' I turn away from him and pick up my notebook, making it clear the conversation is over.

He stares at me. 'Christ, Ali, can you drop the attitude? I'm just trying to help. I want to spend time with you and Tilly, but you seem to resent me being here at all. You haven't asked if I'm OK, if I need anything.' He falters. 'I've got stuff going on as well, you know.' I don't reply. He rubs his hand over his face as he mumbles something about his father. He's a good actor, but I can see through the pretence.

I walk into the bathroom and shut the door. I need to ask him what he did with our money, but I don't want him realising I know yet. I need to find out what else he's lied to me about.

I can hear him pacing around the flat. *He's biding his time. Not long left.*

'You awake?' Em taps on the bedroom door. 'Hi, lovely. How are you? Jack said you were here. Is it OK to come in?'

I nod and she walks over to where I'm sitting on top of the duvet, pillows piled up behind me, and gives me a large hug.

'I don't want to intrude.'

'You're not. It's good to see you.' I force myself to smile.

'Isn't she gorgeous?' Em peers over the side of the Moses basket. 'What a cutie. I've left Josh and Jessica with my mum. I thought they might be too much to cope with. Can I have a cuddle?'

I nod. *Don't tell her about me. You haven't fetched it out of the drawer. You need to hurry.*

She picks Tilly up. 'How are you finding things?'

'OK.' I shut my eyes briefly.

'Is she waking up lots? Jessica was dreadful for that. Six weeks of hell. You probably remember better than I do. You were so supportive.'

I stare at her blankly. 'I . . . I didn't really do anything,' I say. What had I done? I can't remember. My head's too full. I can't think back to before I had Tilly. She's made everything so intense, so real. Anything that came before runs through my mind like water, diluted versions of memories that escape before I can hold onto them. It's there, somewhere, hidden under all the noise, but I can't find it.

I think really hard, making a supreme effort to block out the voices which are babbling so fast they're an incomprehensible blur. Yes, there it is. I'd gone to stay with her for a couple of nights when Josh had been ill. I have hazy memories of taking her tissues and cups of tea. It all seems so unimportant, as if it was never part of my life. I smile, but I hope she doesn't stay long. I need to get something from the kitchen.

Jack pushes open the door. 'Sorry to interrupt,' he says. 'Just wondered if Harry was in the office today, Em? I was going to give him a call. I need to ask him a favour.'

She nods.

He hasn't shaved for a couple of days and his stubble combined with the circles under his eyes make his face darker than usual. He looks at me as if he can read my thoughts. I blink them away, concealing them out of sight.

Em strokes the foot of Tilly's sleepsuit that's poking out from under her blanket and I notice them glance at each other. *They've been planning.*

'Are you sure you're not tired, Ali?' Em asks. 'We can take

Tilly out for a walk so you can get your head down for a bit. It did me the world of good.'

They're going to take her away.

'I'm fine.' That glance again. 'But I could try and have a nap. Just a quick one.' This time there's no mistaking the look that passes between them.

'Great.' Jack can't hide the elation in his voice. *Of course he can't. He wants to get his hands on her.* 'I'll take her down the road if you like, let you get some proper rest. Em can come to make sure I don't leave her anywhere.' He laughs, but I don't smile at his feeble attempt at a joke.

Em waits until he's gone. 'He's just worried about you, Ali.'

I want to tell her what Jack's going to do. Not to trust him. That he's hiding things from me. *She won't understand.* I can't tell her when Jack's in the flat. He might hear me. I'll show her instead. She'll understand when she reads it.

'I've got something for you,' I tell her. 'It's an early birthday present.' I hand her my notebook, which I've put inside a small paper bag that was in my bedside cupboard. 'You can't open it until your actual birthday though, promise?'

Em laughs. 'Ah, thanks, Ali. You're too kind. I'm surprised you remembered.'

'Em . . . I . . .' I trail off, not really sure what I want to say as the voice babbles in my ear. *You need to get it. Then I'll show you what to do.*

'What?' she asks.

'Did you feel like there was a lot to do when you first had Josh? A lot of things going on, I mean. Hard to keep everything in your head?' *She won't believe you. She'll tell Jack.*

You shouldn't have given her the book.

She lets out a snort. 'I concentrated on getting through a day at a time, to be honest.'

I nod. I'm already doing that. She doesn't understand. My head is overflowing with what I'm supposed to remember and I can't work out what's important and what's not. It's so hard when someone's talking to you all the time.

Em puts her hand on mine. 'You're doing a great job.' She stands up. 'You get some rest whilst we take Tilly out.' She smiles at me. 'Don't worry, I'll keep an eye on them both.'

They might not come back. This could be the last time you see her. 'Thanks.'

She walks out of the bedroom and I hear them chatting as they get the pram ready. Jack's asking her about the loan they got for their car last year. We don't need a new car; Tilly fits into the one we've got. Why does Jack need to borrow money? We're not overdrawn. The balance in our current account isn't any worse than usual. I wonder how much trouble we're in, what it is that he hasn't told me.

The front door shuts behind them and the flat is silent apart from the voice in my head. I wait until I hear the thud in the corridor of the main door closing before I get up and wander down the hall to Tilly's new bedroom that she hasn't spent a night in. The smell of fresh paint still hangs in the air even though Jack's opened the window. He's only just finished the last coat after putting up the bookshelves. He'd said we shouldn't take Tilly in there until everything's completely dry. We've got all her clothes and nappies in a pile in our bedroom. I wind up the star mobile that's fastened to the side of the cot, the high-pitched nursery rhyme droning as it circles round slowly. A row of picture books sit waiting to be read on top of the matching chest of drawers. The various cuddly toys we've bought, as well as the ones we've been given as gifts from people at work, sit in the cot, waiting for her to play with. *This is the place. This is where you need to do it.*

I've given Em my notebook. I thought it was finished. I don't have space to write anything else. *There will always be more. Until you come with me and I can show you.* I want Em to know the truth. To open her eyes to the light. But now I'm not sure I've done the right thing. I think she's working with Jack. He pretends to care, but he doesn't. *We both know the truth.* I'm not going to be able to pretend for much longer. He doesn't understand what I'm trying to fit inside my head. What I have to do. *Go and get it.*

I pull open the drawer in the kitchen, hesitating as I glance at the knives in the cutlery tray on one side before picking up a black marker pen and walking back into Tilly's room. Standing on a chair, I start on the wall beside her cot and begin to write what it tells me across the cream paint. Words, symbols and numbers. Everything that's in my head. The feeling of relief as the black marks appear on the surface is immeasurable. It pours out of me, one line after another, temporarily halting the flood that threatens to drown me. *Soon.* I didn't realise how everything fits together in the universe. It's so obvious once you understand. We're all part of one another and I can see how things are supposed to be.

Finally I run out of clean wall as the black marker starts to turn grey. I stand back and look at what I've done. That's the pattern. Now they'll understand why I had to do it. *You have to come with me.* I don't think it'll wait much longer.

I close the door firmly behind me and curl up under my duvet to wait for Tilly to come back. I need to get us out of the flat and away from Jack. We're running out of time.

THEN

Jack – *Day Five*

'Ali? Are you OK?' I knock on the bathroom door for the third time. 'You've been in there forever. Come on, let's go. I thought you wanted to get to the shops before Lisa comes over this afternoon.'

There's no answer. She hasn't said a word to me since she woke up. I had stayed on my side of the bed, focusing on the cold strip of sheet between our bodies, moving my foot backwards and forwards over the edge of it, too scared to reach across to the other side in case she'd pushed me away. I had pretended to doze whilst she'd stared at the wall as she'd fed Tilly. I'd wanted to say something but hadn't found the right words, dismissing the possibilities one by one until I had none left, our breathing being the only sound punctuating the uncomfortable silence.

'Ali?' I rattle the handle. My irritation spills over into anger after another disturbed night. I'd got into bed long after I thought she was asleep, sliding in beside her before I realised she was still awake, staring at Tilly's monitor. I'd put my arm around her, but she'd stayed stiff, and I hadn't dared ask what the matter was, eventually succumbing to the softness of sleep before she had.

I'd stayed up late last night, spending hours surfing the internet, searching through companies who offered personal loans but hadn't found one who would lend the amount I needed at a rate we could afford to repay. The firm Harry had recommended wasn't any use. I don't know where to go next and I'm conscious I haven't got many days left.

I knock again. 'Can you talk to me please?'

Silence. Panic rises on tiny wings and flutters around inside my stomach. Has my father said something to her already? She'd been a bit quiet when I came back from the walk with Em yesterday, but surely she'd have told me if he'd contacted her?

'I'm going to unscrew this lock if you don't answer me.'

Nothing. What's she playing at? She's been in there at least twenty minutes.

I put my ear to the door but can't hear anything except running water. I thump the wooden panel with the edge of my fist. 'Ali! Let me in, for God's sake.'

I'm about to go and search for a screwdriver when the lock clicks back. I turn the handle. She's bent over the sink at an unnatural angle, holding her hand under the tap. Scarlet beads of water are splashed over the sides of the basin, leaving jagged trails that run towards the plughole. A red flannel lies on the floor beside her. I stare at it, momentarily confused. We don't own any red flannels.

Ali doesn't look at me. 'I couldn't help it,' she murmurs.

'Jesus.' Blood oozes from a deep gash across her palm and down her wrist. I pull her hand away from the tap, grab the nearest towel and press it against her skin. 'What the hell happened?' I shout.

She clutches my arm in a vice-like grip and shakes her head frantically.

'It told me . . . I did it,' she whispers.

'What? What did you do?' I ask. There's a broken disposable razor on the bathroom shelf. I look round the room, fitting the pieces together, refusing to acknowledge the inevitable conclusion.

'It was an accident,' she mutters blankly, not meeting my eyes.

I sit her down on the toilet seat. 'Hold this tightly.' I push her uninjured hand down on top of the towel.

'I was trying to get the cover off the razor and it snapped,' she says. 'It was an accident.'

I fish through the various bottles and packets that line the shelves in the bathroom cabinet to find the roll of Elastoplast.

'You believe me, don't you?' She's shaking.

I nod dumbly and lift the towel up. I pull some Elastoplast off the roll, ripping it with my teeth and stick it along the length of her sliced skin.

'Ali . . .' I start to say.

She clenches her fists into balls. 'Don't. Just don't.'

'We need to see a doctor,' I tell her.

'No. I can't leave the flat.' She's insistent.

'Why not?'

'I just can't.'

I take her hand in mine and kneel down in front of her. 'We need to get you seen by someone. You might need stitches.' I put one hand on the tiles, letting the coolness seep into my skin to steady myself. The panic I felt earlier expands in my stomach; hundreds of trapped birds flapping helplessly to get out.

'I can't. You don't understand,' she says.

The Elastoplast appears to have stopped the flow. I find a length of gauze bandage in the cupboard and wrap it round her wrist to keep the plaster covered. I have a horrible, sick feeling. Something is very wrong with my wife.

She looks over my shoulder and I glance behind me, half-expecting to see someone standing there. I hear my mum's words in my head: *How could you have been so stupid.* I'd done this. It's my fault. I need to fix it.

'Explain it to me.' My words are short, heavy. I want her to reassure me my father hasn't been here. I refuse to think what could have happened if she'd pressed the blade any harder.

She glances towards the bedroom where we'd left normality. Tilly is silent in her Moses basket.

'She's fine,' I say. 'She's asleep.'

Ali stares at her bandage, not speaking.

'We need to go to the hospital,' I add.

'I'm not going anywhere.'

'At least come and sit in the bedroom whilst I . . . sort this out.'

For a moment I don't think Ali's going to move but then she gets up and I help her walk to the bed and sit her on the duvet before going back to pick up the bloodstained cloths. I hold them by one corner and carry them out to the kitchen, wrapping the flannel in a plastic bag and throwing it in the bin. I fling the towel in the washing machine and walk back to the bathroom, pulling off some toilet roll to wipe the red streaks off the sink and opening the window to let in some air before I shut the bathroom door behind me and go back into the bedroom.

'I'm sorry, Jack. It was an accident. It just slipped.' Her self-assuredness has returned. She's buried the brief moment of vulnerability I witnessed and now she's lying to me. I don't respond. 'It looks worse than it is,' she adds. Perhaps my father hasn't been here. Maybe she doesn't know.

Our landline starts ringing in the hall. Ali stands up to answer it.

'Leave it,' I say. 'We need to talk about this. Let it go to the answerphone.'

'It might be important,' she says, her unbandaged arm already reaching for the bedroom door.

I glance at Tilly, still asleep. I want to tell Ali that we're more important, but she's already left the room. I can hear the ringing stop as she picks it up. I pull back the door to see her sitting in the hallway, the phone next to her ear.

'Yes. That would be nice, Dad. Any time's good.'

I raise my eyebrows, silently mouthing 'Not today' at her.

She frowns and shakes her head. 'Yes, she's good. Slept a bit more last night. Yes, he's here, d'you want a word?'

I shake my head. I don't know what to say to him.

She covers the phone with her hand and holds it out. 'He wants to speak to you,' she says.

'You're going to have to tell him,' I whisper. She stares at me. 'The truth,' I say.

'Yes,' she hisses as she presses her hand over the mouth-piece, 'because you're so good at that. I'll tell him that the razor broke and cut me.'

'You and I both know that's not what happened.'

She stares at me, expressionless, no longer bothering to whisper. 'That *is* what happened.'

I hesitate. 'I'm not going to lie for you, Ali.'

'Will you just speak to him.' She holds out the phone and I lift it slowly to my ear.

'Hi, Edward,' I say.

'I hope I didn't disturb you.' I wonder if he could hear our muffled conversation.

I swallow. 'No . . . you didn't.'

'Oh good. I just wanted to see how Tilly was this morning.'

'Tilly's fine,' I say.

Ali walks back into the bedroom, sits on the bed and looks at her in the Moses basket.

'Ali said she'd slept a bit better,' he says.

'Uh-huh.' I try to be non-committal. I just want to get off the phone.

'And Ali's all right?'

I hesitate. She looks up at me from the bed. I shut my eyes briefly. 'Ali's fine.' A wave of guilt washes over me. I've lied to him twice now. I know what she's just done wasn't an accident, just as much as I know I hadn't told the truth when he'd offered to lend us that money. We're hiding everything and I wonder if either of us are capable of being honest anymore. Every word I say is twisted, bent out of shape by the deceit that came before. I grip the handset. 'Edward, Ali had a . . . bit of an accident.'

There's a silence on the end of the line and Ali gets off the bed and walks towards me, holding out her hand for the phone. I wave her away.

'Edward? Are you still there?'

I can hear him clearing his throat.

'I'm here, Jack. What happened? Is she OK?'

'She's fine. Physically. She just cut herself. On her hand . . . well, hand and wrist. I just thought you should know.'

There's another silence. Perhaps I should have broken it more gently. He's usually so calm, dependable.

Ali's standing in front of me, her jaw clenched as she pulls the phone out of my grasp. 'Dad?' I pretend I can't hear the note of hysteria at the edge of her voice. 'A razor just slipped and broke. I'm fine, honestly.' She waves her arm around as if she's suffered a small scratch rather than a four-inch gash. 'I'm OK.'

I shake my head at her and walk into the kitchen, trying not to think about the red stains in the sink as I run the tap to get a glass of water.

I take it into the sitting room, where Ali is now perched on the sofa holding the phone, trying to give reassuring responses to the questions Edward must be asking. She leans forward suddenly, putting down her unbandaged hand on the coffee table to steady herself as the colour drains out of her face. I stand up and push past the coffee table to reach her, picking up the phone from where she's dropped it in her lap. I can hear Edward's voice repeating her name.

She leans back against the cushions, and I put my hand on her forehead. She feels clammy. She reaches for the phone, but I don't let go of it.

'Edward?' I say.

'Jack? Where's Ali? Is she OK?'

She looks at me, her face as white and crumpled as a piece of paper.

'She's fine,' I lie. 'She just felt a bit faint, but to be on the safe side we're going to get her checked over by a doctor. I'd better go.'

There's another silence.

'Edward?'

Nothing. I need him to say goodbye. I don't want to hang up on him.

'I saw it. Sticking out under the door,' he says quietly.

I have no idea what he's talking about but I have to get him off the phone.

'I'm going to have to call you back later,' I say and this time I do hang up.

I pass Ali my glass of water. Her hands tremble as she sips it.

'I'm fine,' she says.

'No, you're not,' I retort. 'You almost passed out. We're going to the doctor.'

'I—'

'I'm not arguing about this, Ali, we're going.' I hope my insistence hides how terrified I am at this situation which seems to be unravelling around me faster than I can grab one of the loose threads to pull it back together. I pick up the car seat in the hall and lift Tilly into it before ushering Ali reluctantly out of the front door.

We head outside and walk slowly down the pavement. I'm holding the handle of the car seat with Tilly inside and see him before we reach the car. He's standing on the other side of the road, behind the row of parked vehicles, staring at us.

He looks at me and smiles. That smile. My stomach turns to ice.

Ali hasn't noticed, she's too busy opening the passenger door. I help her into her seat and shut it behind me. He raises his hand slowly, still smiling, putting three fingers in the air. I shiver. I think he means I have three days left, but I'm not sure. Now he's seen Tilly, I'm more worried he's trying to tell me he knows there's three of us, and so many more possibilities.

As I walk round to the driver's side, I don't look at him. I can't bear to see him gloat.

'I can't . . .' Ali says as I start the engine and pull away.

I glance across at her. Her face is ashen.

'I really can't go,' she says.

'Why not, Ali, why can't you go?' I thump the steering wheel. 'You need to be checked over by a doctor.'

She looks at Tilly in the back seat, not answering.

'I'm not discussing this,' I say. 'We're going.'

I turn out onto the main road. The traffic isn't busy and the surgery's only a couple of miles away.

'You don't understand.'

'What don't I understand?' I ask.

She doesn't reply. Her knee twitches. She goes rigid and presses both hands to the sides of her head.

'No. I can't. Don't make me go, Jack. I know you're going to take her away.' She begins to rock, the seatbelt locking mechanism the only thing restricting her movement.

'Stop it, Ali.'

She rocks harder. I glance in the mirror. There's a line of cars behind us. She begins humming, a horrible monotonous sound.

'Stop doing that,' I say. She raises her voice. 'Stop humming. You're going to upset Tilly.' I can't stand it and reach out to grab her wrist. 'Stop fucking humming! I'm not taking Tilly anywhere. All this . . . everything you keep saying . . . it's all in your head,' I scream at her, the stress of the last few days overflowing in an explosion of anger.

She pulls away from me with a screech, undoing her seatbelt, flailing her limbs as her humming turns into an inhuman wail so loud it makes me wince. I have no idea how to deal with this situation. She jerks away and reaches for the door handle, trying to pull it open.

'Don't do that!' I shout, but she's not listening.

I pull into a side road without indicating and brake to slow down. She grabs at the steering wheel and I fight to keep control. We're going to crash. I jam my foot on the brake, praying no one's following behind us, and try to push her away, but she's still fumbling for the wheel and her hair's in front of my face. I can't see anything. I'm so scared for Tilly and the pavement's getting closer and I don't know what to do, but I need her to stop and I slap her across the face. A blow where I feel her cheekbone hard under my fingers and her head twists sideways with the force. The sound reverberates around the car in the silence that follows as we screech to a halt, the tyres bumping as they hit the kerb.

I tell myself I didn't have a choice. I'd been protecting Tilly. We'd narrowly avoided crashing into someone's garden wall. God knows what would have happened if she'd managed to open the door. But in the seconds after my anger evaporates, I wonder if that's really the whole truth. I clasp my hands in front of me, pretending they don't remind me of my father's, not quite believing what I've done.

Trembling, Ali touches her face and the shame that descends like a thick cloud makes me think I'm going to be sick. I can't bring myself to look at her.

I fumble to get out, ripping the knee of my jeans on the metal catch of the car door as I slam it shut behind me. I take large gulps of air. A few people drive past me along the residential road, but none slow down to give me a second glance. I walk over to the low red-brick wall in front of the house I'd almost crashed into and sit down. There's no movement from inside the car.

I wonder if Ali will flinch like I'd seen my mum do when my father touched her. Whether she'll hold back those last few words in an argument in case they provoke me too far. I've turned into the man I despise most and wish more than anything I could erase the last few minutes.

I walk back to the car and open the passenger door. Ali's unbandaged hand is pressed against her cheek. She stares ahead, refusing to look at me.

'I'm so sorry,' I say. 'I'm so, so sorry. I shouldn't have done that.' She doesn't move. 'You scared me . . .' I mumble. 'I didn't know how to make you stop.'

She moves her hand away from her face, revealing an angry red mark.

'I'm not going to the doctor's,' she says, looking at the windscreen in front of her. 'I'll tell them you hit me. Take me home, please.'

'Ali, you're not—'

'I want to go back to the flat.' She pulls the passenger door shut, and I'm forced to snatch my hand out of the way to avoid trapping my fingers. Remorse prickles over my skin. I can't risk going to the surgery; the evidence of my guilt is on the side of her face.

I get back in the car. Tilly's still asleep. Thank God she hasn't witnessed any of this.

'You need to see someone, Ali.'

She shakes her head.

I try a different approach. 'Will you talk to Lisa instead?' It's a compromise on my part, but at least Lisa's medically trained. I don't think I can deal with this situation anymore on my own. I'm terrified of what could happen if I lose control again.

Ali nods as she whispers something that sounds like she's agreeing with the suggestion, and then looks straight ahead, her eyes fixed on the windscreen. She doesn't speak for the entire journey.

I pull into our road, searching the pavement for any sign of my father, but there's no one there. Ali gets out and unclips Tilly from her car seat. I follow her, pausing before I put the key fob up against the panel by the front door.

'I'm so sorry, Ali. I really am. I just lost it. You were going—'

'Let me inside, please,' she says.

I open the door and we walk up the corridor in silence into the flat.

She holds out her mobile. 'I've put Tilly in her Moses basket for a nap. Can you call Lisa?'

'Why?' I ask.

'I don't want her coming over today,' she replies.

I hesitate. 'You just agreed you'd see her.'

'No, I didn't.'

'In the car. You agreed to talk to her if we didn't go to the doctor's. She needs to check on you to make sure you're OK.' We'd had the conversation less than thirty minutes ago. She must remember.

'Well, I'm not, am I. Clearly. D'you want her seeing this down the side of my face?' She points to her cheek. The mark is less livid but still noticeable. I look down at the floor. 'Call her,' she says.

I take a deep breath. 'Ali, we need help. I think you should let her come over.'

'No.'

I put the empty car seat down on the floor in the hall. 'You need to tell her what's going on.' I hesitate. 'And I mean what's actually going on.' I look at the bandage round her wrist.

'Is this some kind of tit-for-tat thing?' she asks. 'I won't tell her if you don't?' Her voice is cold.

'I didn't mean it like that,' I say.

'Call her.' She presses her phone into my hand.

'We need some help,' I plead.

'I don't need help. I don't need anyone.'

'Please, Ali.' She covers her face with her hands and sinks to the floor. I put my arms round her, expecting to be rejected, but she doesn't push me away. 'You've got to talk to someone,' I say.

'OK. I'll talk to her. But not right now. Get her to come over tomorrow. I can't deal with her today.'

I can feel her tears as they slide off her face onto my neck. Maybe this is a turning point.

I give in. We sit beside each other on the floor as I dial Lisa's number and tell more lies. This time about my wife. I lie that she's tired and wants to have a sleep this afternoon. I lie that she's been eating well and her stitches haven't been hurting any more than usual and that she slept better last night. I lie that everything is fine and we don't need to see her until tomorrow.

I hand the phone back to Ali. I've given in to save myself. I pray she'll stick to her word. I look at her sitting next to me, staring into the distance, the mark from my hand still visible on her face, and feel sick with guilt. For so many reasons. She doesn't speak, but as I stare more closely, I see her lips are moving, as if she's having a silent conversation.

THEN

Alison – *Day Five*

We're both awake, lying next to each other, pretending to be asleep. I could lean over and touch him, but there's such a distance between us now, I can't see the point. I glance across at the familiar outline of his face in the dark. His eyes are shut and he's breathing steadily, but I know he won't let himself drift into unconsciousness. The muscle in his jaw flickers despite his efforts to appear relaxed and I know he's waiting until I doze off as he doesn't want to leave me alone. I'm not giving him the opportunity to be with Tilly without me. *Stay awake.* It fires the words like bullets, every couple of minutes, as waves of sleep lap at the edges of my mind.

I move my tongue round the inside of my cheek, stretching the skin, feeling the twinges of soreness where he hit me. It hurts, but the pain in my chest hurts more. He's shown me what he's capable of. In that one small movement, he's destroyed all the trust I ever had in him. All the things I thought he was, I cannot be sure of anymore. The man lying beside me is a stranger. He's betrayed me in the worst possible way. A father is supposed to love and protect their family. He's just been pretending he wants this, pretending that he loves me and he loves Tilly, but he doesn't. He's lied to us about so many things and after what he did yesterday, I know I can't leave him alone with my daughter.

My stitches are irritating me. My body feels like I've borrowed someone else's. I spent nine months with my stomach expanding, my skin getting tighter and tighter as Tilly grew bigger. I knew every inch, every curve. I used to run my hands over her, feeling her early flutters, and, later, full-on kicks and punches just below the smooth surface. My tummy button, which was once a neat hole, had been pushed out into a bump, like a small flesh-coloured mushroom, every last millimetre of skin straining to contain her growing body. One minute she'd been part of me and now she's lying in her Moses basket, a separate person. I'd created something perfect but didn't realise it would leave me broken.

My stomach sags in rolls, its tautness gone forever. All the handfuls of cream I'd rubbed in were a waste of time; it's scarred irreparably with lines that criss-cross the surface like a cracked egg. Some have turned a shiny white colour; smooth and hairless, they run like rivers across the sea of flesh. Lisa said I'm healing, but I don't believe her. I can't be repaired and am only held together with string.

I scratch between my thighs where one of the stitches digs into me, catching one of the black knots with my fingertips. It's stiff and hard. Someone in our NCT group said they're made from catgut. Part of an animal is entwined into my skin. I have a new body and it's not even human. I pick at the loop that feels like thick cotton between my fingers. It doesn't hurt. I pull harder. Something unravels. I tug again. Something inside me falls apart. The thread zigzags across my skin, unstitching my insides from my stomach to my chest, leaving a gaping wound. I search through the layers of flesh, through the fat and blood vessels, delving down to the muscle, to see if I can find the remains of my once familiar body.

'Ali.'

I open my eyes. I flinch as he touches my arm.

'You're mumbling. Are you OK?'

I nod and turn over so I'm facing away from him. *Stay awake.* I run my hand over my stomach. No holes I'm intact but have never felt so empty. I wait until his breathing falls into a regular pattern and his mouth goes slack. I have to be vigilant. I'm bombarded with random thoughts that make my brain run around in circles, jumping from one idea to the next. I am invincible.

Jack's trying to keep us here. I'd been warned about him from the start. That I should get out, that I should run. I hadn't believed what the voice in my head had kept telling me, but I've been proved wrong over and over again. How many minutes Tilly had cried for when I put her down to sleep. How many drips had come out of the shower after I'd turned it off. How often Jack blew his nose in the bathroom in the morning. I am told the answers, and I count. Sometimes my head hurts, but I have to keep going. I'm not allowed to stop. There are so many numbers and patterns, I can't keep track of them all.

I'd only been right once. I'd counted five steps to get from the bedroom to the bathroom when I was told it would take four. I had to go back and do it again, taking larger strides each time until it worked. When I wrote on Tilly's bedroom wall yesterday, I finally saw how everything fitted together. Jack still hasn't been in there. It's only a matter of time. I hope he understands when he sees it, but by then I'll be gone.

We play games. If Jack puts his toothbrush in the holder so it points towards the window, it shows he wants to hurt his daughter. He does, despite me concentrating all my thoughts to get him to point it towards the door, so we play again. If he puts on the navy socks and not the grey, I lose. I plead for one last chance, but I'm told the game is over. Two out of three. I've lost, fair and square. The bandage on my wrist shows what happens when I don't do as I'm told.

Jack knows it's his fault. The look in his eyes when he opened the bathroom door yesterday told me what I needed to know. Guilt. He wants to get rid of Tilly. I wonder if he's told his mother. Perhaps it's what I overheard them talking about and they're both hiding it from me. I won't let them hurt her. Blood is thicker than water. And his is contaminated. You should protect your child at all costs. Just like I'm protecting Tilly.

I've been told where I need to go. I'm worried she'll be cold. It's windy despite the warm weather. Jack doesn't understand. How can he? He isn't part of the plan. He hasn't seen the things I've been shown. I don't think he realises what he's capable of if he's left alone with her. I know it's the right time; I can't wait any longer.

I ease back the duvet and pick up Tilly out of her Moses basket. She lets out a small cry.

'What are you doing?' Jack sits up sharply in bed, already alert, his eyes focused on the blanket in my arms.

'I . . . I need to go.'

'What are you talking about? It's . . .' he turns his lamp on and squints at the beside clock, 'half-past three in the morning.' He throws off the covers as I press myself against the wall. 'It's the middle of the night. You're not even dressed.'

'We're not safe,' I say. 'I need to leave. Tilly's in danger.'

'You're not making any sense. Of course she's safe. Come back to bed.'

I retreat away from him. This is part of his plan; I was told he'd try to do this. Take her away from me. I clutch her tighter whilst he stands up and starts to walk towards me.

'Talk to me, Ali. What are you doing?'

'I don't want to talk to you.' I stand rigidly and watch as he edges towards the doorway, blocking it with his body. He's trying to stop me leaving.

'You're not thinking clearly,' he says.

'I am. I know what you're trying to do. I've been told. And I've written everything down and given it to Em. She'll tell people if something happens to me or Tilly. She believes me. She's got it all as evidence.'

'Ali, I don't understand what you're talking about.' He stares at me, but I can see through the layers of pretence he's covered himself with like a coat of a thousand colours, trying to distract me from the blackness that lies at the heart of him.

'I know you've lied to me, Jack,' I say.

He hesitates. 'No, I haven't.'

'You have. You've inherited your father's genes. You told me he was a liar. You're turning into him, Jack. Lying to me. Destroying our future. Hitting me. You said you'd never do what he did. What if you do it to Tilly? I'm not going to let you. It's me and her. It's always going to be me and her.'

'Ali, put Tilly down. I'm not my father. I couldn't be more different to the person he is, and if you knew him, you'd understand what an insult that is.' Jack spreads out his hands across the door frame, making himself as wide as possible.

I clutch the blanket more tightly.

'You have his eyes. I saw it in his photo,' I say.

He glances at his wardrobe. 'Have you been going through my things?' he asks.

I don't answer his question. 'Stay away from me. You're not coming near her. I won't let you. You don't understand. She's special. You never wanted her and you never understood how much I did.'

He stares at me, not speaking, a look of incredulity on his face.

I gaze at Tilly in my arms. 'Do you think I haven't overheard you and your mum whispering when you don't think I can hear? That I hadn't noticed that woman at your office party last year who kept giving me strange looks and then told me how close you were? Are you paying her as well as your father?'

He shakes his head and stammers as he starts to speak. 'Ali, you've misunderstood. I told Steph about us needing to have treatment for IVF. That's all. I'd been feeling so stressed about it and she was there when I needed to talk. I didn't tell you because I knew you wanted it kept a secret. I don't know why she said what she did at that party. She was drunk. There's nothing going on between us. I promise you. And I wasn't whispering to—'

I interrupt him. 'You're lying. I know you're lying. You're keeping things from me, but you don't realise I'm hiding

220

something, too. I knew you didn't want a baby, but I tried to have one anyway. Why d'you think I realised something was wrong so quickly? Because it wasn't quick. We'd been trying for ages without you realising. I made the decision for us as I knew you'd never make it on your own. Not being able to get pregnant was my punishment. I carried it around without you ever knowing. And it grew inside me, just like the baby I wanted should have been doing, but this was something dark that sat rotting in my stomach, stopping anything else from thriving the longer I hid it.'

He looks at me, stunned. 'You wouldn't have done that, Ali. This isn't you talking. Put Tilly down.'

Her face is so tiny. She's still asleep, I can see the iridescent surface of a small bubble rise and fall in the gap between her lips as she breathes. She doesn't know how much I love her. I'd die to protect her. She has no idea how much I've been through to have her. And I know he wants to take her away from me. She needs me to be strong. He isn't going to let me leave. *You need to find a better time.* The thought is burned so brightly into my head, I see the imprint every time I shut my eyes. *Wait. Have patience.* I lay Tilly back down in her Moses basket and sit on the mattress.

'How can you think I'd ever hurt her?' Jack asks, the deep crease in his forehead softening now I've sat back down. 'I love her. And I love you. I really do, Ali. What are you doing trying to run away in the middle of the night?'

He looks into my eyes as he tucks my hair behind my ear and puts his arms around me. I go to pull away, but he slides his hands round my wrists, where his fingers dig into my skin. It's uncomfortable. I try to push him off, but he holds on more tightly. 'I mean it, Ali,' he says. 'You can't leave. I won't let you.'

'Please, get off me.' I slide out of his grip off the bed onto the floor. He doesn't seem to hear me as he kicks out, scuffing the Dove Grey walls he'd once painted.

'I want to help you, Ali, but you need to listen to me. D'you understand? Saying I'm turning into my father . . .' He sinks down on the floor in front of my feet. 'I know what that man is capable of, Ali. I could never do the things he's done. Why d'you think I gave him our money? I'd have done anything to keep him away from us. I'm ashamed we're even related. He almost destroyed my mother and he'll destroy me if he gets the chance. I'm nothing like him. Nothing.'

I put my hand up to touch my cheek where there's still a very faint bruise and tears well in his eyes.

He picks up Tilly's blanket that I'd dropped when I put her in her basket. 'You know how much I love you, don't you?' he says.

The voice in my head is so loud, I press my head into my knees and shut my eyes to try to escape into the darkness. *Find a better time. Not yet.*

He puts his hand on my shoulder and I look up.

'I'm sorry,' I say, 'I'm just scared. It took so long to have her and she's so special . . . I'll talk to Lisa tomorrow if you think it'll help.'

Jack pushes himself up off the floor and steps forward to hand me Tilly's blanket before he picks her up out of her basket, his hands gently stroking her back to calm her. 'You promise?'

'I promise,' I lie as I stand up slowly and sit back on the bed.

'She's hungry,' he says tonelessly. 'She needs feeding. I'll sit with you.' I know he's only doing it so he can watch me, but I reach out my arms as he passes her to me and she latches on whilst I rest against the pillows. He sits beside me, staring blankly at the wall ahead.

A million tiny pinpricks of light dance round in my head. *Patience. He's tired. He'll fall asleep soon.* I glance at him as he rubs his hand over his face and strains to suppress a yawn. I don't think I'll have long to wait.

THEN

Jack – *Day Six*

I lie next to her and watch as the duvet rises and falls in a constant rhythm. She's asleep. Finally. I edge to the side of the bed, a centimetre at a time, attempting to muffle the sound of my skin as it slides across the sheet. She doesn't stir. Tilly's motionless in the basket beside her, satiated from her last feed. I creep across the floor and out of the bedroom, groping in the dark for my phone on the hall shelf. I shut the door to the kitchen with exaggerated slowness, wincing at every creak, and scroll down my list of contacts.

'Hello?' A groggy voice answers.

'Em. It's Jack,' I mutter quietly.

'Jack? What d'you . . . it's . . . oh god . . . it's five a.m. . . . . what are you doing calling at . . .'

I interrupt her, whispering frantically. 'It's Ali.'

The bleariness in her voice vanishes. 'What's wrong with Ali? Why are you whispering?'

'She doesn't know I'm calling. She's . . . not coping.'

'Where are you?'

'At home. I think she's having some kind of . . . I don't know . . . She's saying all these things and I woke up to find her trying to leave the flat. She thinks I want to hurt Tilly. She's asleep at the moment, but I don't know what to do, Em. I don't think I should leave her on her own.'

'Hang on a minute.' There's rustling as Em moves the phone around, adjusting her position. 'She seemed OK the other day when I called round.'

'Can you come over?' I ask. 'She trusts you.'

'Sure. Give me a few minutes to get dressed?'

'She's literally just fallen asleep. She must be knackered even though she keeps insisting she's not. Can you get here for half-six?'

'Yes, no problem,' she says. 'Harry can stay with Josh and Jessica.'

'Thanks. She won't listen to me. It's as if I'm talking to a stranger.'

'I'll speak to her. It's all crazy to start with when you have your first.'

I don't contradict her, but she doesn't understand how bad things are. 'Thanks. And, Em, don't press the buzzer on the intercom.'

'All right,' she says. 'Go and sit with her. Try not to worry.'

I walk into the sitting room and draw back the curtains. The sun is starting to come up. Dark grey clouds sit on top of an orange glow, squeezing it into an ever more concentrated colour towards the horizon. At the lowest point is a line of dark crimson, as if someone has pricked their finger and smudged it angrily across the skyline. I shiver as a gust of wind blows across the patio, flapping the material of the umbrella that shades the garden table.

I feel sick at the thought she knows I've lied to her. How did she find out I paid my father? She must have looked through my bank statements. And now she thinks there's some kind of conspiracy going on. I need to explain it to her. Like I should have done last year. Tell her about my father. Tell her that she'd only heard my mother and I whispering because I'd asked Mum to lend me some money and she'd refused, telling me I was stupid to get myself into debt with a baby on the way. I hadn't told her I needed the money for my dad. Or that I'd given him money before. I hadn't wanted her to think she was in some way responsible, or worse, that she'd pluck up the courage to confront him about it and he'd get the opportunity to pull her back into a relationship. I wasn't sure she'd have the strength to get out again.

I wonder how many times Ali has searched through my things. I know the photo she's talking about. The only one of him that I've kept. I'd taken it. He and my mother had been holding hands, looking directly at the camera. Unless you knew to look closely, you'd never have seen the knuckles on his fist were white as he squeezed hers a little too tightly. That the shadow on her face wasn't really a shadow at all. I look down at my hands as thoughts of what happened in the car run through my head. Perhaps Ali's right. Perhaps I am turning into him.

I press the button to start a new message on my phone. He's listed in my contacts under his name, John, rather than Dad. I begin to type.

I'm not giving you another penny. Feel free to tell whoever you want what you think you know. Jack.

I spend a few minutes re-reading the words, adding some more and then deleting them. There's no point in trying to say I never want to see him again; he already knows and doesn't care. He'll reappear no matter what I write. That's the thing about families, you're bound to them forever by blood. I'm scared about how much of him is in me. What I'm capable of.

I press send. He's used to getting what he wants, so my refusal to comply with his demands might come as a surprise. I don't know if he'll try to contact Ali, but at the moment I don't even care. She knows I've given him money already and I have to acknowledge there's a part of me that wants the truth to come out so that we can get back to some semblance of normality. To confess my guilt and start again. How could she possibly think I'd hurt Tilly? The child we'd tried so hard for. I don't understand. The woman in the room next door isn't my wife. In less than a week she's turned into someone I don't recognise. Who scares me. I don't know how to reach her – she doesn't even look at me when I speak to her anymore, focusing instead on something that seems to hover behind my head. Something's taken her and turned her into a stranger who's living in our flat. I've made excuses for her behaviour but there's no denying it anymore. I wish I could speed up time until Lisa's due to arrive. Ali needs to see someone and I'm guilty of helping her avoid getting the help she needs. Lowering my head, I pray. It's the only thing I can think of to do as the veneer of adulthood I've stuck over my emotions is ripped away.

I'd held Mum's hand as she had sat on the floor, her lip swollen. I hadn't wanted to speak until I was sure he'd gone. Sometimes he'd hide outside until we'd thought it was safe before he'd reappear, that smile on his face as he'd knelt down beside her again. When I was sure I couldn't hear anything apart from her wheezing, I'd crawled to the back door and turned the handle. It had swung open. No one had stepped out.

'Carn ya geth thum iyth?' she'd asked.

I'd passed her a piece of kitchen roll to press onto where her lip had split. It had come away bloody when she'd dabbed at it. I'd opened the freezer and had taken a packet of peas out of the drawer.

'An a thee thowel.'

I'd pulled one off the oven handle. She'd wrapped the peas in the material and held it on the side of her face. I'd sat beside her.

'I'm so sorry,' I'd mumbled.

She'd shaken her head. 'Noth your faulth.' She'd stroked my cheek with her free hand.

'Should I get someone?' I'd asked.

She'd shaken her head again.

It had been my fault. I had watched through the banisters and had known what he was going to do. I'd always known what he was going to do. So had she. I could have gone in. I could have opened the kitchen door. Sometimes he'd stopped when I'd opened the door. But I hadn't. I'd sat at the bottom of the stairs, my vantage point concealed, and looked on whilst the shouting got louder until I'd finally heard the familiar dull thuds.

She'd have understood if I'd told her. She'd have said I was scared, that it wasn't my problem, that I didn't need to feel responsible. It wasn't my job to protect her. I'd have nodded and we'd have carried on as normal, me taking myself to school and her absence noted by the other mothers at the school gate.

But I hadn't been scared. I'd been used to the shouting. I hadn't

*helped because I'd been hoping he'd hit her. That he'd hit her so
hard that she'd have to go to hospital and people would see what
he'd done and then he'd have to leave us alone. So I hadn't done
anything. I'd been a fraud, holding her hand, when I'd known it
was safe. Five minutes earlier, I'd been wishing he'd hit her harder.
I'd wondered when I'd pay for that.*

At six-fifteen I creep back into our bedroom, inching the
door open a fraction at a time so the noise of it catching on
the carpet doesn't wake Ali. She doesn't move as her blonde
hair fans out over the pillow. She looks at peace. Angelic
almost. I fumble for my trousers that lie on the floor. My
T-shirt stinks of stale sweat but I'm not going to risk the
noise of getting another one out of the drawer. I peer into
the Moses basket. Tilly's sound asleep. She lies on her back,
completely relaxed, both arms raised up with her hands either
side of her head.

I creep out of the room, open the front door of our flat
and walk down the corridor to wait by the main entrance for
Em to arrive. There's normally a quiet calmness in the early
hours that's soothing, but this morning the echoing stillness
that surrounds me in the hallway is heavy with unexpected
dread. I hope Em can make Ali see reason. But as I head
towards the door to let her inside, I have a horrible feeling I
may already be too late.

THEN

Alison – *Day Six*

I lie awake with my eyes shut, listening to my breathing, steadily in, steadily out. *Relax every muscle. Make him believe it.* Now and again I raise my lids just enough to peer from beneath my eyelashes, watching him as he creeps around our bedroom. I'd heard him on the phone. He'd called them to come and get me. They'll be here soon. *Told you.* I'd known he would. And once I'm gone, he'll take Tilly away to somewhere I won't be able to find her. Where she'll be in danger. There's no way I'm going to let that happen.

I wish I had time to tell my dad. He'll understand when he sees what I've written. Why I had to do it to protect my daughter. He'd have done the same thing.

I've been shown the bridge in my dreams. It's waiting for us. I've been told we need to strip ourselves of everything that keeps us tethered to this mundane existence and move forwards towards the light. Until now, a small part of me has been scared. I'd wanted to stay here, in this room, but tonight I've been reassured I'm doing the right thing. There's nothing left for me and Tilly here. I need to take her where she'll be safe. My mind isn't big enough to hold in everything I've been told. It spills over, running out of my mouth and down my face in rivers of brightness, invisible to anyone except those like us. I want to tell everyone why we're really here, but no one will believe me. I can only show them. And then she'll be out of harm's way forever.

I wait for Jack to leave and grab a used plastic carrier bag out of the waste-paper bin in the corner of the bedroom. I shove in Tilly's blanket and search the room for any other essentials. *There isn't enough time.* He'll only be gone for a few minutes and then he'll come back and take her away. *Hurry up.* There's too much to remember. I consider taking different objects off my dressing table, but I'm unable to make a decision. What do I really need? What are the absolute essentials? Her hat. My jacket. I realise I'm only taking the bag to make it look like I'm carrying something. Less of a reason for anyone who sees me to stop and ask questions. I don't actually need anything. Other than Tilly. *He'll be back any second.*

I pick up the photo that sits on my bedside table of us in a restaurant in Amalfi. We'd framed the shot the waiter had taken after the one we'd originally posed for, when a large bee had flown into my hair. I'd ruined the first one by frantically flapping my hands, but he'd caught us a few moments later, where for a split second we were looking at each other, our simultaneous laughter mirroring each other's relief. It had used to make me smile every time I'd looked at it. When things had been different. *Now. You need to go now. He'll be back any minute.* I think about putting it in the bag but change my mind and leave it where it is. It belongs to our past, not my future.

A week ago seems a lifetime. Everything before I had her seems indistinct; fuzzy oddments of memories that feel like they belong to someone else. I put my dressing gown on and pick Tilly up gently from her basket before walking a few steps and realising it's too awkward to carry both her and the bag at the same time. I drop the bag on the sofa, pulling out her blanket and wrap it round her instead. I leave everything else. I leave my keys on the sitting-room table next to my mobile. There are three missed calls from my dad. *Hurry. You need to hurry.* I can hear footsteps in the corridor outside the flat. He's coming back. I unlock the sitting-room doors to get out onto the patio, the fresh air helping to clear my head. Holding Tilly tight in my arms, I unfasten the gate in our fence with one hand, push it open and step out onto the street, walking towards the bridge and our salvation.

The breeze is stronger than I'd anticipated. I'd put my slippers on before I left the flat, but the pavement is cold beneath my feet, making the soles of my feet numb. Tilly's asleep. I head down our road and cut through the narrow gap that takes me between the stone buildings onto the street parallel to mine. *Walk faster.*

I walk past the Georgian flats with their symmetrical rectangular windows, all staring at me. Some already have lights on inside, and I can see people having breakfast. The knowledge I have makes me realise how pointless our bland lives are. I cross over the road, heading up the hill. I can see the bridge in front of me, the stone towers at each end looming like castle turrets, guarding its entrance. The iron chains holding the bridge up fall away from the tower, suspended like pulleys on a giant's drawbridge, dwarfing the traffic that runs across it. I look down at Tilly, whose forehead is partly hidden by the blanket wrapped around her. Her eyes are tightly shut and her lips are pressed together, making her look like she's smiling. I can feel her warmth through the front of my dressing gown. My baby girl. This is the only way to keep her safe.

A car slows down beside me and the driver stares through the window but doesn't stop. I wait for it to pass before I step off the pavement and walk over the small green that leads to the footpath that runs alongside the road across the bridge. It's the beginning of rush hour and already a line of traffic snakes slowly along beside me. The wind is much stronger here.

I walk to the middle of the bridge and climb over the barrier, holding Tilly to my chest, and look out.

This is why you are here. You will both be safe with me.

It's much harder to grip the railing than I had expected. The cold metal bites into my hand until I can't tell if it's attached to my body, the last brittle anchor holding me in place. A crowd gathers a short distance away from me on the bridge; some watching through their car windows, others standing with their vehicle doors wide open.

Remember how he's lied. Remember how he wants to hurt Tilly. Remember how he wouldn't let you go.

A woman points in my direction, her shouts muffled by the noise of the wind. The strands of hair that whip across my face sting my eyes, and I reach up to tuck them behind my ear. A sudden gust nudges me off balance and my stomach lurches, momentarily suspended, before I scrabble to retrieve the iron bar beneath my fingers.

Remember how he doesn't believe in you. Remember he won't let you follow the rules. Remember how he's called people to come and take Tilly away.

Ripples appear as tiny white flecks on the muddy surface of the river far below me. The two giant towers guarding each end of the bridge look on in anticipation and I draw strength from their solidity. I glance back at the gathering ensemble whose numbers swell as their sense of urgency escalates. I wonder what Jack would say if he was here. What he would do.

Remember how he hit you. Remember the sound of his hand on your face. Remember he'll end up like his father. He can't escape who he really is.

I'd watched him this morning as he'd pulled on his trousers and T-shirt, and had realised I was staring at a complete stranger. The urge to get up and unpeel his skin to see if I could reveal something familiar underneath, some evidence that would prove we were once connected, had been almost irresistible. He'd walked out of the bedroom without speaking whilst I'd feigned sleep, my breath trapped under the edge of the duvet, warm against my chin.

He's been observing my every move, waiting for an opportunity to vent the anger that flows just beneath the surface of our daily lives. I know he's hiding something from me. He denies it, but his eyes say he's lying every time we look at each other. As soon as he left the room, I knew I would do it. Now I'm standing on the narrow girder, there is no fear.

I believe in you. I've shown you the truth. I'm waiting for you.

Someone in the crowd breaks away from the group and walks slowly towards me, his hands held up in a gesture of surrender. The noise of wailing sirens grows louder. The stranger keeps coming, his confidence and pace increasing as he makes eye contact and smiles nervously. I turn my face back towards the river and look down. He sees the movement of my head and cries out. I hear his footsteps speed up as he tries to reach the barrier that separates us. He won't make it.

Have no fear.

I let go of the railing, feeling the pressure of the wind against my face that offers up a final moment of contemplation. Then the breeze tapers off, as if acknowledging the decision has already been made, and I step forward into the silence.

THEN

Jack – *Day Six*

Em is already standing behind the door when I open it, pulling her grey throw around her against the early-morning chill. She steps forward and envelops me in a large hug. I shiver. I'm not sure whether it's because I'm cold or tired or both.

'Thanks for doing this,' I murmur.

'Don't mention it,' she replies.

I shut the door, pressing the handle down to stop it rising up too quickly so the lock doesn't make a noise as it clicks back into place. We head up the empty corridor to the flat.

'Is Ali still asleep?' Em whispers.

I nod. I've left the front door ajar. I walk towards the bedroom, inching the door open. In the darkness, I can make out the contours of the large mound in the duvet, so I tiptoe out again. There's a loud bang and I wince, waiting for a cry from Tilly which doesn't materialise.

Em stands in the doorway to the hall holding an empty plastic carrier bag in one hand and Ali's jacket in the other. 'The patio door was open,' she says. She doesn't bother to whisper.

'What?'

'Your door. To the patio. It was open.'

I frown as I walk into the sitting room.

'The wind slammed it shut,' she adds. 'That's what the noise was.'

I open it again and step out onto the crazy paving. The small space is empty, the road behind the flat visible through the gate in our fence, which swings gently on its hinges. A sense of unease flutters in my chest. I run back inside, past Em, towards the bedroom, throwing back the door as I reach for the light switch. Brightness illuminates the white duvet lying rumpled in a heap on the bed. Tilly's Moses basket is empty. My stomach lurches.

I open the bathroom door. Please let her be in here. Please don't let it be like yesterday. I flinch, but the room is spotless. And silent. I can't catch my breath as I step back into the hall and the pain in my stomach forces me to bend over. I lower myself to the ground, my fingers pressing into the carpet.

'She's gone,' I say. 'And she's taken Tilly with her.'

Em doesn't speak. I wonder if she understands what I'm saying. Dropping Ali's jacket and the bag, she walks towards me and puts her hand on my arm. I think she's trying to comfort me, but it feels like she's clutching me for support.

'She can't have gone far,' she says. 'Have you checked Tilly's room?'

'She won't be in there,' I reply. 'We haven't used it yet. It's not finished.'

But I get up and go down the hall to look, Em following. I switch on the light and we stand in stunned silence as we absorb what's on the wall in front of us. Black writing covers the entire surface of the cream paint. Words and numbers in abstract patterns. Odd sentences I can read, but their meaning is terrifying in its incomprehensibility.

I shut my eyes, pretending I haven't seen it, but the picture is imprinted on the inside of my eyelids, and the letters move around, rearranging themselves to spell out my guilt. I know Ali's done this, but my brain struggles to find another explanation, however far-fetched. Could someone have broken in? Was she forced to write this?

I look at Em, who's glancing around the room, and realise she's doing the same thing; searching for signs of an intruder.

'Oh, Ali,' I mumble. Something has burrowed inside her, hiding itself in the darkness where others can't see it, wrapping itself round her thoughts like a parasite, poisoning them until I wonder if there's any of the Ali I know still left. It's been sly, revealing its true nature in tiny glimpses that were over so fast, it made me question whether I actually saw them.

Em presses her back against the chest of drawers, distancing herself from the horror in front of her. 'Do you have any idea where she'd have gone?' she asks.

I shake my head. 'No . . . I don't know.' I can't think.

Em hesitates. 'Has she taken the car?'

I feel for my keys in my pocket and run into the hall. I can't see hers in the bowl on the shelf where we normally keep them, but there's a set lying on the table in the sitting room.

'She's left them in here with her mobile,' I say.

Em walks towards me, shutting the door of Tilly's room behind her, concentrating on organising practicalities in an effort to stay calm. Neither of us mention what's on the wall.

238

'If she's walking, she can't have got far,' Em says. Is she reassuring me or herself? 'My car's here, I'll drive and we'll go and look for her. You call Harry and warn him in case she heads to ours, then phone the police.'

Acid bile churns in whirlpools in my stomach.

I dial Harry's number and he picks up immediately. 'Jack?'

'Yes, it's me. Listen, Ali's gone. She's taken Tilly.'

There's a short silence whilst my words sink in. 'What?' he asks, sounding confused. 'Where to?'

'I don't know,' I reply. 'She must have left the flat whilst I was letting Em in. We're in the car now looking for her. Can you call me if she comes to yours?'

'Course,' he says quickly, and then hesitates, but I know what he's going to say next. 'I think you should call the police, Jack.'

'Yes,' I tell him. 'I'm doing it now.'

As I end the call, we reach the top of the road.

'Left, or right?' Em asks.

I scan both ways but can't see Ali in either direction. I don't know which way to choose and turn my head from side to side with paralysing indecision, trying to spot something to help me make up my mind.

Em makes the choice for me as she turns left and heads up the road, driving slower than the thirty miles an hour speed limit so we don't miss Ali. We're far enough away from the town centre to avoid most of the rush-hour traffic, but cars overtake us at regular intervals, the low morning sun casting long shadows that shroud us in gloom each time they go past. The momentary drop in temperature makes me shiver.

I dial the same three digits on my phone and wait to be connected.

'Operator speaking. Which service do you require?'

'Police.'

'Hold the line please.' There's a short pause.

'Thank you, caller,' a different voice states, 'you're through to the police. What's the nature of your emergency?'

'It's my wife. She's gone missing with my daughter.'

'Can you tell me your name and location?'

'Jack Reynolds,' I say. 'I'm in a friend's car in Clifton and we're out looking for them now.'

'What's your wife's name, Jack?'

'Alison. Alison Reynolds.'

'Right. And did she tell you she was going out?'

'No. I just left our flat for a minute and when I came back they were both gone.'

'How old is your daughter?'

'She's six days old.'

'Have you tried contacting your wife?'

'I can't. She left her mobile in our flat. I'm worried she's . . . I'm worried about her mental state.'

'Did you have an argument before she left?'

'No.' I wonder if the person on the other end of the phone notices the tiny pause before I answer.

'Does your wife have any relatives or friends who live nearby that she might have gone to see?'

'Her dad doesn't live too far away.' I wave frantically at Em and press the mute button on my mobile. 'Station. Head for the station.' She indicates and turns right as I take the mute button off again. 'But there's something in our flat I need you to see. She's written on one of our walls.'

There's a short pause. 'Like graffiti?'

'No. Not like graffiti. It's just lots of words. I can't really describe it, someone needs to see it.' I can hear a couple of voices murmuring on the other end of the phone before someone speaks to me again.

'I'm going to send someone out to you. What's your address, Jack?'

'15 York Crescent, Bristol.'

'They'll be there as soon as they can.'

'Thank you.' I put my mobile on my lap. 'She might be going to see her dad,' I say to Em.

She nods. 'Maybe.' She doesn't sound convinced. 'You don't want to check anywhere else first?'

I stare at her. 'Like where?'

'I don't know. I'm just worried she might—'

'She'd never hurt Tilly,' I interrupt flatly.

'I'm not saying she would.' She doesn't mention the wall, but I know she's thinking about it. I am too. I try to focus on keeping my mind like a blank page. I will not take any notice of what she wrote. She's not that person. Em grips the steering wheel and stares straight ahead.

'Let's check the station.' I'm confident. 'I think she's going to her dad's. He's only a couple of stops away.'

She hesitates, then turns right.

I try calling Edward but his landline goes to answerphone and his mobile is switched off; he never remembers to charge it. I don't leave a message. I don't know what to say. I don't want to tell him Ali's taken his granddaughter and they're

241

missing. Not yet. She'll turn up in a minute and I'll have worried him for no reason.

We drive up the suburban roads, searching the grey pavements that are quiet in the early-morning light. A mother carrying a baby should be easy to spot, but there's no sign of them.

I jump out of the car when Em pulls into the station, leaving her to turn the car around. I scour the platform and ticket hall. A few commuters stare at the departure boards, but I can't see Ali.

Em lowers her window as I walk back across the tarmac.

I shake my head. 'She might have gone to the main one in town,' I say hopefully.

'She couldn't have walked that distance,' Em replies. 'She'd have had to get a bus. I think it's unlikely.' She looks at her watch. 'It's been fifteen minutes. We need to get back to yours so we're there when the police arrive. Try Harry again. He might not have been able to get through when you were on the phone.'

I can tell by the tone of his voice before he says the words that he hasn't heard from her. I squeeze the phone tightly.

'We need to head back,' Em says. I search for something in her face but there's nothing to reassure me.

'OK,' I say reluctantly.

She looks away and as she wipes something off her cheek, I notice her hands are shaking.

The traffic is starting to build up and I can hear sirens faintly in the distance. The police must be on their way over. At least they're treating it urgently. I don't want Em to leave me on my own. I have no idea what I'm going to say to them. She pulls up in my road and looks at me as she puts the handbrake on.

Em hesitates before she asks, 'Had you been arguing?'

I swallow, looking out of the window to avoid her question, and see my father standing outside the entrance to our block of flats. He's staring at me. I blink in case I'm imagining it, but it's definitely him. Wearing his blazer. He smiles as he sees me notice him. I didn't think he'd come this quickly after my text, but he doesn't realise he's already too late. His grin falters slightly as he puts his hands into his pockets. He was expecting to see me panic. He doesn't understand he can't make things any worse than they already are.

I turn back to Em who's trying to see what I'm looking at. 'What d'you mean?' I ask.

'You know what I mean,' she says. 'You paused before you answered the question when you were on the phone to the police.'

I don't reply. My face is hot. I don't want to tell her how we'd screamed at each other when I'd found Ali trying to leave last night. That she'd accused me of trying to hurt Tilly. It hadn't been an argument. It had felt like the obliteration of our relationship. And every time I think about what happened yesterday in the car, I feel sick.

Em turns off the engine and reaches into the footwell by my feet for her bag. I glance out of the window but my father hasn't moved. She hands me a small notebook. 'Ali gave me this when I saw her a few days ago. Told me it was a birthday present and not to open it until the weekend. You can read it if you want, but I think we should give it to the police.' She looks in her mirror as a marked car pulls up behind us and a couple of policemen get out.

'What's in it?' I ask.

'I don't know exactly. I only had a quick look when we stopped at the station. I forgot she'd given it to me, to be honest. I'd left it in the car. It's like the stuff she's written on the wall of Tilly's room. Something about a voice. That she's been chosen. Rules telling her what she can and can't do.' She hesitates. 'That you're trying to take Tilly away from her.'

I swallow hard as I flick through the pages, tiny narrow lines covered with ink. It doesn't even look like Ali's handwriting.

The officers walk towards me and I slide the book into my pocket as I wind down the window.

'Mr Reynolds?'

I nod.

'I'm Sergeant Turner and this is my colleague PC Simmons. Shall we talk inside?'

I nod and open the car door. We walk side by side, Em following behind, up the pavement to the entrance. My father sees us coming and I stare at him as we get closer. He's no longer smiling. We almost reach him before he breaks eye contact and doesn't acknowledge me as he steps away from the iron railings and heads out onto the street. He doesn't realise who the police are here for. Threatening my wife won't get him what he wants. Ali's already gone.

My hands tremble as I push open the main door and we head down the corridor, the waterproof material of their uniform rubbing against itself, the rhythmic swishing sound exaggerated in the silence.

'Can I get you anything . . .?' I stammer when we get into the flat.

'No thanks.' The sergeant is polite but brisk. His colleague shakes her head. I can see them glance round the flat, looking to see if anything seems out of place.

I usher them into the sitting room, where we sit awkwardly on the sofas. I try to ignore Ali's jacket and the pink teddy that lies on top of the empty plastic bag on the floor.

'So, Mr Reynolds, you say your wife left here this morning around six-thirty?' he asks, pulling out a notebook.

'Yes.' I clear my throat.

'Can you tell me what happened?'

'I'd left the flat to go and open the main front door to let Em in. Ali must have got out of bed and taken Tilly . . . our daughter . . . and gone out that way.' I point at the patio doors. 'They were open when we came back.'

'And you're Em?' the sergeant queries.

'Yes. Emma Butler. I live in Percival Road. About five minutes' drive away. With my husband, who is currently looking after our two children. Ali's one of my closest friends.'

The PC is writing as Em speaks.

I cut across her. 'I'd called Em earlier to ask her to come over because I was worried about Ali. She hasn't been . . . well.'

The police officers exchange a glance.

'And what time was that?' the sergeant asks.

'Around five o'clock.'

'In the morning?' He raises his eyebrows.

'Yes . . .' I mutter. 'Ali wasn't herself last night—'

He interrupts. 'How d'you mean, not herself, Mr Reynolds?'

'I mean not herself. Not how she used to be. Since she had Tilly, she's been . . . different. Saying things that aren't true.'

'Like?' The PC doesn't smile as she speaks.

I take a deep breath. 'Like, she thinks I want to hurt Tilly.'

The sergeant studies me as he speaks. 'And you'd never do that.'

'Of course not,' I reply.

'And you've never hurt Tilly or your wife in anyway?' he continues.

'No. Never.' An image of a red mark imprinted on Ali's cheek rises in my head and I feel my face colour. The sergeant doesn't comment but I can tell he's seen it.

Em nudges me.

'Ali gave this to Em last week.' I hold out the notebook. 'I didn't know about it. She said it was for Em's birthday, which isn't until the weekend.'

The PC flicks through the pages, a frown settling on her face.

'How old is your daughter, Mr Reynolds?' the sergeant asks.

'Six days old. And please call me Jack.'

'And did the midwife have any concerns when she visited?' he continues.

I hesitate. 'Not really. I told her a couple of days ago Ali wasn't sleeping well.'

'And since then?'

'She hasn't been back. She said to call if we needed her, and we agreed she'd visit today.' I clasp my hands together and take a deep breath. 'There's something you should see.'

They follow me into Tilly's nursery, where I point at the wall.

'Ali must have done this yesterday or the day before. I'd told her not to take Tilly in there whilst the paint was still drying. I only finished putting the bookshelf up in here two days ago and it obviously wasn't here then. I haven't been in there since and only saw it this morning.'

The PC stares at her colleague, who walks out into the hall and begins talking into his radio.

'He's calling our control room,' she says. 'Let's go back in the sitting room and you can get me your midwife's contact details.'

I walk past the sergeant into the kitchen and search for Lisa's details amongst the various piles of paper. I can hear Em's voice as she interrupts the PC in the other room. My vision blurs when I finally find them, paper-clipped to Ali's hospital notes. I separate the pieces of paper and go into the sitting room to hand the details to the policewoman.

'I'll give her a call now, if you don't mind, to get her take on things,' she says. 'Try not to panic. Have you got a photo of your wife we can circulate?'

I nod, fetching the one of us in a restaurant in Amalfi a few years ago from her bedside table. I love that picture of her. We'd both been laughing with relief after she'd shaken off a bee that had flown into her hair.

'Here.' I hand it to her. 'It's a bit old, but she hasn't changed much.'

'Thanks.' She undoes the frame and clips the picture to her notebook. 'Have you got one of Tilly?'

'Yes.' I show her one on my phone that I'd taken when she was in the hospital crib and she nods.

'Can you get a copy of that one for me?'

I send it to our printer, my hands shaking as I load in the photo paper.

'I thought she might have gone to her dad's. He only lives locally. Just the other side of town. It's a couple of stops on the train,' I blurt out.

The PC nods. 'I'll need his contact details and address so we can check. You said you weren't sure what she was wearing when she left. Can you have a look?'

'Yes.'

I go into our bedroom. It's so empty without them. The sight of Tilly's bare Moses basket makes me shudder. I pick up one of her Babygros, which is lying on the floor. It smells of her as I hold it against my face. Where are you? I need you to come home. I sink down on my knees at the side of the crib, a tear falling onto the white sheet that's covering the small mattress.

The PC makes me jump as she puts her hand on my shoulder. 'I'm sure we'll find them,' she says.

I wipe my face.

'It doesn't look like Ali's taken any clothes with her,' I say. 'There's nothing obvious I can see, anyway.'

'Don't worry, Jack,' she speaks gently. 'I just wanted you to check in case you noticed something in particular. Are her pyjamas still here?'

I look on the floor and behind the pillows on the bed.

'I can't see them, so I think she must still be wearing them.' I push back the bedroom door to reveal an empty hook. 'Her dressing gown's gone. It's a white towelling one.'

The PC nods.

I look at her. 'You think they're in danger, don't you?' I grip the side of the dressing table.

'I'm not going to assume anything at this stage. Let's just concentrate on doing what we can to find them. Come back into the sitting room and write down her father's details, and anyone else you think she might have contacted. Any other friends, or family.'

I sit on the sofa next to the sergeant, who's now off his radio. The PC hands me a piece of paper and a pen. I write down a few names, including my mum's and Ali's work address.

I show Em and she nods before adding, 'I can't think of anyone else. Her work colleagues might know more. But she hasn't been there for the past month or so. She's been on maternity leave.'

The sergeant's radio crackles. He picks it up.

''Scuse me, I need to take this.' He walks out of the sitting room.

'What are you going to do now?' Em addresses the PC directly.

'Well, we'll circulate the photos and a description and have a drive round locally ourselves. I'm going to try your midwife again as she didn't pick up when I called her before. We'll also contact your wife's father and visit her work to see if anyone knows anything there.'

I hesitate, my frustration hardening into anger. 'She's in her pyjamas. Walking the streets at . . .' I check my watch, 'not even eight o'clock in the morning. With a newborn baby. She won't be heading into her office. She's not think-ing logically.'

Em puts her hand on my arm. 'They're doing their best, Jack.'

I stand up. 'I know. But it's not enough. I'm going to go and look for them.' I can't bear to sit here any longer doing nothing.

The sergeant puts his head round the door. 'Can I have a word?' He motions to his colleague and she walks out of the room.

I don't feel I can leave whilst they're still talking in the hall so I pace up and down by the sofa.

'They're doing everything they can,' Em tries to reassure me. 'I'll come with you to look if you want me to.'

The two officers come back in. The sergeant looks at me.

'Mr Reynolds, I think you should sit down.'

'Have you found them?'

He motions towards the sofa. 'Please sit down.'

I sit next to Em. The sergeant and PC sit opposite us. He clasps his hands together on the table and glances at his colleague.

'Oh my God, what . . .?' I can't bring myself to say the words. The two police officers seem very far away, and my mind isn't in the room with them at all. Ali fills my head. The way she sticks the tip of her tongue out when she's con-centrating on something. The way she always puts three ice cubes in her gin and tonic. The way she can't ever manage to fasten a necklace and lifts up her hair for me to do it. The way she picks coriander out of anything she eats. The way she refuses to kill spiders, trapping them instead in a glass with a piece of cardboard before carrying them carefully out of the flat.

I'd know if something had happened to her. I would have felt something. I know I would. She was here less than two hours ago. I don't want to listen to what the sergeant's going to say next. I'm not capable of hearing the words.

The room tips further over and the last thing I see is the PC's arms reaching out to catch me as I fall forwards off the sofa.

Part Three

NOW

Alison

I'm standing behind the library counter, Jack's crumpled letter in one hand, oblivious to the person holding out their book for me to scan. Tilly. My baby. Where is she? Why isn't she with me? I don't understand why Sarah has a letter from Jack in her bag. I glance at it again. He says he misses us. Tendrils of fear unwind themselves from the knot in my stomach and reach into my chest, squeezing my lungs so I can't breathe.

I have to find Sarah. Now. She might know where Tilly is. When did I last see her? I can't remember. I put the letter down on the counter and cover my face with my hands, searching for her in the blackness. There's nothing there. Nothing that tells me where she is, just a rising panic that turns my vision from black to red as the sound of blood pumps in my ears.

I'll go upstairs to the fourth floor and wait outside the door until they let me in. I'll break in if I have to. I walk away from the computer, leaving a customer calling after me. I ignore him and head towards the stairwell at the back of the library, walking down the narrow row of bookshelves whilst images of a tiny person with dark hair, dressed in a white Babygro, flash before me. Faster and faster they appear. It's like flicking through the pages of a book. Shutting my eyes doesn't make any difference. They're like a tap I can't turn off and they fill up my head until I'm drowning. I reach the tables and grasp one of the chairs for support as the room swims in front of me. Tilly. Oh God. I have to find her.

When I look up, Jack is standing in front of me. I think I must be imagining him as I can see straight through him to the bookshelves behind, but I want him to be real and his image becomes sharper and more solid each time I shut my eyes. He's still wearing the T-shirt that's covered in paint splashes. He pulls the chair out from under the table so I can sit down, puts his hands gently on my shoulders and looks into my eyes as he smiles at me.

'I've been waiting for you to remember,' he says.

'Where are we going, Mummy?' I'd asked, tracing round the pink and green flowers on the wallpaper in our hallway with my finger, my red anorak zipped up, my panda gloves in my pockets.

'Just down to the shops.' She'd smiled at me.

'Can we walk?'

'No, sweetheart. We're going to drive.'

'But it's not far.' I'd jumped up and down on the spot, waiting for her to get ready.

'I know. We'll walk another day.' She'd grabbed her bag, pulling up the zips on her boots.

'Aren't you going to wear your coat, Mummy?'

'No, I'll be fine.'

'It's a bit cold. You make me wear my coat.'

'That's because you're only eight, Ali-bear, and I'm a lot older.

Mummies can look after themselves.' She'd knelt down in front of me, smoothing down a stray wisp of hair firmly behind my ear. 'You know I love you, baby-boo.'

'Yes. I love you too, Mummy.'

'How much?' she'd asked.

'To the moon and back,' I'd told her. We'd played this game a lot and I always gave the same answer.

'Exactly.' She'd wrapped her arms around me and planted a kiss on my forehead. When she'd pulled away, her eyes were wet.

'Are you sad, Mummy?'

'No, darling. I'm fine. I just had something in my eye.'

'Can we go then? You said we could get sweets. Can we get sweets?'

'I think you've still got a few packets left over from the ones Father Christmas brought you in your stocking, but, yes, we can get sweets.'

'I don't have many left, Mummy. Only about sixty-two hundred.'

She'd shut her eyes for a few seconds and her face looked like she'd swallowed something that tasted horrid, and then it had straightened out again. I'd tried to hold her hand, but she'd pulled away.

'Come on then, Mummy, let's go.'

She'd taken a long time to shut the front door. I'd reached the garage first, the gravel on our driveway crunching under my feet as I'd run across it. She'd pulled on the handle so the large metal door swung up and over to reveal our car.

'Can I sit in the front with you?' I'd asked.

'If you want, sweetheart. You get in. Careful with the door.'

I'd opened it slowly so as not to chip the blue paint on the garage wall and had climbed across to the passenger side, snuggling myself down into the brown plastic seat. I'd put my panda gloves on top of the dashboard, in front of the windscreen so they could see out, and had watched as my mother had pulled the handle to seal the entrance before she'd got into the car.

'Why've you shut the door, Mummy? It's all dark now. We can't drive to the shops with the door shut.'

'I thought we'd play a little game before we go to the shops. I'm going to start the car and we're going to sing some songs.'

'What kind of songs?'

She had turned the engine on.

'We can start with some nursery rhymes. What's your favourite?'

'Panda likes "Rock-a-bye Baby".'

'I like that one too. Let's start with that. You sing.'

'Rock-a-bye baby on the tree top. When the wind blows, the cradle will rock. When the bough breaks, the cradle will fall, and down will come baby . . . Mummy, can we put the window up? It's cold and it smells funny.'

'Soon, sweetheart. Come and give me a cuddle.'

'Panda wants a cuddle too.' I'd picked up my gloves and crawled onto my mother's lap. *'I wish Daddy was here. He could sing "The Grand Old Duke of York". It's his favourite.'* I'd hummed the nursery rhyme for a bit. *'I'm a bit sleepy now, Mummy.'*

'Me too, sweetheart.'

'Are we going to the shops?'

'In a minute, baby-boo. I love you, Ali-bear.'

'I love you too, Mummy.'

I open my eyes to find tears trickling down my face. Now I've seen her, I realise how much I miss her. I wish I hadn't remembered at all. Jack's letter is lying on the table in front of me, but now there's no sign of him. I can feel the imprint of his hands on my shoulders. He was just here and although I know what he did to me, I wish he hadn't left.

My world is disintegrating. Where is my child? Why can't I remember? I touch the letters on the paper, running my fingers over their shapes, hoping they'll tell me how to find her. If I could just understand them, I'd be able to work it out, but the longer I stare at them, the less sense they make, until I can't even read the words at all.

I put my head down on the table. The other chairs around me are empty, but I don't care who sees me. Memories trickle through my brain like sand, gathering above the table in heavy piles. I run my fingers through them, but they fall away before I can piece them together enough to make sense. Someone is ringing the bell on the counter for assistance. There's a part of my brain that normally jumps at that sound; Mrs Painter has conditioned me to remember it's my responsibility, but I'm not moving. They can help themselves. She's going to be really angry, but I don't care. All I need to do is find Tilly. A void has opened up inside me and I don't know what I've filled it with until now. I wipe the tears away with my sleeve as they slide down the side of my nose. When my vision clears, Jack is facing me, sitting in the chair beside me, lying with his head on the table too. He tucks my hair behind my ear and reaches for my hand.

'It wasn't your fault you know,' he says.

Mummy was asleep. The car smelled really bad now. I'd tried waking her up but she'd made a funny noise and hadn't opened her eyes. Panda hadn't liked it at all. I'd thought how cross Daddy would be that we hadn't been to the shops. He'd been cross a lot this week. He'd wanted fish fingers for tea and Mummy hadn't got them. I don't think I wanted any tea. I felt a bit sick. The smell had made my head woozy, but I hadn't wanted to go to sleep without

Daddy knowing where we were. He'd be worried if he came home and couldn't find us. Then he'd get all cross and shouty.

I'd opened the door of the car and squeezed out through the small gap. I'd been extra specially careful so I hadn't chipped the paint on the garage wall, even though it had been so dark. I'd tried pushing the garage door, but it hadn't moved. I'd tried again and when I'd pushed really, really hard, I'd made a tiny gap at the very bottom. I'd slid one of my gloves underneath so it had stuck out under the door and took a breath of the nice air. Panda would tell Daddy where we were. My pandas went with me everywhere. Even in the summer I'd put them in my pocket when I'd gone out. Daddy had given them to me last Christmas. He'd said every explorer needed a good pair of gloves as they helped to keep you safe in the harshest of conditions. I hadn't been sure what the harshest of conditions were, but they'd kept my hands warm when I'd got stuck up a tree. I'd been really cold then.

I'd felt my way back to the handle on the car door and had climbed onto Mummy's lap. She was still asleep. I'd wait for her to wake up and then we'd go to the shops. I thought we should turn the engine off whilst we were sleeping. It was noisy and it might wake Mummy up. She needed a lot of rest at the moment. Daddy had told me yesterday she hadn't been well and that I should try and be especially good for her. I hoped I was being good.

I'd reached over and turned the keys round to pull them out like I'd seen her do. It had gone quiet. That was better. It had still smelled funny though. I'd given Mummy a goodnight kiss and then I'd gone back to lie down next to panda, my head by the bottom of the garage door where I'd felt the nice air on the tips of my fingers. It had made them cold, but I hadn't minded. It had felt like someone was stroking them. I'd sung my 'Rock-a-bye Baby' lullaby to myself and had waited for Daddy to come home.

I wonder how long it had taken my mother to plan what she'd done. Had she simply woken up that morning and decided she didn't want to live anymore? We hadn't talked about it properly at home after it happened. People had mentioned a tragic accident in hushed whispers, and when I'd asked Dad, he'd mumbled something about her being in a car. He'd looked so stricken at the direct question, I hadn't dared to ask again. I had a vague memory of being in hospital, but Dad had said it was because I'd suffered an asthma attack. I don't understand why he'd never told me what she'd done. I don't know if I'm crying for her or for Tilly.

I keep my eyes closed and don't move my head off the table. I know if I open them Jack won't be there, but if I keep them shut, I can feel him holding my hand.

'Why did she do it?' I ask.

'She was ill, Ali,' he whispers, his face so close to mine I can feel his breath on my skin. 'Really ill.'

'But why me? Why did she take me with her?'

'Why do you think?' he asks.

'I can't begin to explain something like that.'

'I can,' he says. 'She loved you. More than anything. She didn't trust anyone else to love you as much as she did. It was her way of making sure she was always going to be there to look after you.'

I keep my eyes shut.

'Where's Tilly, Jack? Something happened, didn't it?'

He doesn't answer and I can't feel his hand anymore. I open my eyes. He's gone.

'Alison!' I raise my head as Mrs Painter shouts my name.

'There are people waiting here!' She can see me, but I don't care. I don't care if they have to wait. I don't care about anything except finding Tilly. I stare at her as she approaches, marching down the row of bookshelves, her skirt swishing with every step. 'Alison!' She stands beside me. 'Alison?' she repeats, expecting an answer. I don't move. She reaches out hesitantly and puts a hand on my shoulder. 'Are you all right?'

'I need to find Tilly,' I murmur.

'I thought you were looking after the reception desk,' she replies. 'Didn't you hear the bell ringing? It's chaos up there. There's customers everywhere and no one can scan anything out.' She realises I still haven't moved and she bends down in front of me. 'Are you not feeling well?' she asks. I don't reply. 'Alison, can you look at me, please?' She pulls out the chair Jack was on and sits down opposite me. I want to ask her if she's seen him. She studies my face. 'You look pale. Are you ill?'

'I don't know,' I tell her. Perhaps I am ill. I'm not sure how I feel anymore.

'I think we need to get someone to take a look at you. Can you walk if you hold my arm? We're going to go back to my office.'

I put one hand on the table and one hand on her arm and get to my feet. Something is stirring in my head. Things I've buried deep down are beginning to float up to the surface. The floor is liquid under my feet. I'm walking through water, one step at a time, slow and heavy. She guides me to her office.

'Can everyone please take a step back.' She shouts the command in a shrill voice. People are buzzing angrily around the counter. 'I have someone here who isn't well and I need to deal with her first. Can you all please wait in an orderly queue for a couple of minutes or come back later if it isn't convenient.' The small crowd spreads out into a line. I recognise Matthew, the others keeping their distance from him. 'Sit down here, Alison.' She pulls out her chair as she picks up the phone on her desk. 'It's Julia Painter. Library, first floor. If you can send someone down, please. Yes, it's urgent. Thank you.' She pats my arm. 'Someone will be down in a minute. You've got some of your colour back. Would you like a glass of water?' I shake my head. She looks at the queue of people in front of the counter. 'Will you be OK if I go and scan those people's books whilst we're waiting? I'll be right there if you need me.' I nod blankly as I'm not listening to her.

There's something . . . something I can almost remember.

I sit and watch as she bleeps the scanner over the barcode. Book after book. Open cover, scan barcode, repeat. Open cover. I'd written a book once. The thought flashes into my mind. A notebook. I remember the pages of black ink. Lots of instructions. I can't remember what they were for, but I remember they were really important. There's something heavy in the bottom of my stomach when I think about it. It's how I'd felt when I hadn't followed the instructions.

Sarah appears through the doors at the end of the corridor. I need to ask her about the letter. At least I don't have to go to the effort of finding her. Mrs Painter sees her, smiles and puts down the scanner. She walks back to where I'm sitting. My heart starts to thump in my chest.

'Mrs Painter . . .' I stammer. 'D'you know her?'

'Who?' she asks.

I point towards the rapidly advancing figure. 'Her. The woman in the red jacket.'

'What, Dr Henderson?'

'She's a doctor?'

Mrs Painter looks at me. 'Yes, she's a doctor. Dr Sarah Henderson. She's hardly a patient, is she?' She smiles. 'She's come down to check you over.' I watch as she walks closer, the weight in my stomach drops down further, so heavy that I'm anchored to my seat.

'Hi, Alison.' She squats beside me. 'Mrs Painter says you're not feeling well.'

I stare at her. 'You're a doctor?'

'Yes,' she replies.

'You never told me,' I say accusingly.

'Can you give me your wrist? I need to check your pulse.' She takes hold of my arm.

I flinch, expecting her nails to dig into me again as I stare at her. 'You know about Tilly, don't you?' I say and she stops, mid-count, her fingers sliding off my wrist.

'Do you remember?' she asks.

'Of course I remember. She's my daughter. I found the letter in your bag from Jack. Where is she?'

'Alison,' she says, putting her hand back on my arm, 'I think we need to talk.'

I slide off the chair onto my knees in front of her and grab her perfectly coiffed dark hair, pulling her face towards me so she's only inches away.

'Where is Tilly?' I spit the words at her.

Her eyes are wide with shock and she pushes me away,

but she isn't fast enough. I hold onto her more tightly and, as she recoils backwards, I'm left holding two large clumps of hair which are no longer attached to her head. Mrs Painter is shouting and someone's screaming. A high-pitched noise, like a wounded animal. A buzzer sounds and two men have their hands on me, attempting to restrain my thrashing limbs. Someone puts a needle in my arm and I rub the dark strands between my thumb and forefingers before I realise the noise is coming from me and it feels like I'm losing her all over again and then my vision darkens until I can no longer see anything at all.

THEN

Jack – *Five months after Tilly's birth*

The flat is a mess. Not just a few pieces of paper lying around on the kitchen counter type of mess, but the kind where I don't know where to start to clear first. A bundle of Tilly's clothes lie in the washing basket, with another load waiting to come out of the machine. I forgot to remove them last night. Dried up leftovers from the ready meal I ate are stuck to the plastic container and the bin needs emptying. I've run out of washing-up liquid and have to take the top off to dilute the tiny amount left at the bottom of the bottle. It squirts out too fast into the sink, leaving a few small bubbles and iridescent patterns that whirl amongst the grease. My stomach curdles as I put my hands in the water and pull out the mug Ali always drank from. I thought I'd put that away at the back of the cupboard.

Edward will be here at any minute and I'm not even dressed. Tilly's in her travel cot I've put up as a playpen in the sitting room as I don't like leaving her on the floor when the carpet needs hoovering. I pick her up and take her with me into our bedroom and put her on the bed, placing some pillows either side of her to ensure she doesn't roll off. I scrabble around trying to find some clean trousers amongst the clothes that are slung over the bottom of my bed. The front door bell buzzes as I hunt for my belt. He's early. I press the button on the intercom to let him in and put the front door on the latch as I put Tilly back in her playpen and fold up the blanket that's slipped off the sofa, tucking it back on the seat. He knocks on the door, even though it's already open, before he comes inside and stands awkwardly in the hall.

'Cup of tea?' I ask.

He nods and follows me into the kitchen, standing close to the wall, trying to keep himself out of the way whilst I take the milk carton out of the fridge. It's almost empty when I shake it, only a few drops left at the bottom. I make myself a strong black coffee, hoping it'll ease the throbbing in my head. It's a familiar routine when he visits every other weekend. I'd refused to see him at all after it happened until Em had persuaded me; she'd known how desperate he was to see Tilly. Our relationship now is fragile, an uneasy truce that's stitched together with gossamer threads that fray at the mention of Ali's name. I don't like talking about her. He tries, but I don't want to hear what he has to say. Coming here is a compromise for him; he gets to see Tilly, providing he doesn't mention his daughter.

He picks up the empty milk carton and goes to put it in the bin, hesitating as he notices the bottles in the recycling. I'd started having a glass every night since coming back from the hospital. The images of Tilly in intensive care had been etched permanently into my mind and alcohol had been the only thing that helped to numb the horror. Transparent tubes from various machines had been fed through the holes in the side of the perspex container where she'd lain, sedated. After a couple of weeks, I'd become accustomed to the bleeping noises the equipment made and hadn't jumped to press the alarm every time one of them let out a shrill tone. I hadn't been able to bring myself to touch her; she'd looked so fragile. I'd sat for days watching her tiny chest move up and down, wishing I'd been able to breathe for her. I hadn't wanted to go to sleep in case something happened. Having failed to save her the first time, I'd refused to leave her on her own again.

The consultant had said she'd been unbelievably lucky. He'd only heard of three other people who'd survived the fall from that bridge. The paramedic who'd brought them in had told me they wouldn't have stood a chance if there hadn't been a high tide and they hadn't been pulled out of the water so quickly by the crew of the boat they'd landed next to. Ali had taken the brunt of the force of impact. He'd thought Tilly's blanket had acted as a parachute, the windy conditions slowing their speed as they'd entered the water. Tilly had been put on a ventilator to support her breathing and a heat mat to raise her temperature back to normal. They hadn't been able to give a prognosis as to the long-term effects, but I'd been told to expect the possibility of brain damage. She'd stayed in hospital for five weeks, but when she'd finally been allowed home I'd carried on drinking.

One large glass a night had crept up to two or three. I rely on them to get any sleep at all, but they don't block out the nightmares that continue to haunt me. Tilly sealed inside a plastic coffin. Hospital tubes writhing like snakes around her, strangling her whilst I watch, helpless to do anything, unable to break into the thick sides of the box. Finding myself on the bridge, either stuck in a car watching them, or worse, climbing over the barrier to reach them, then falling myself. I always wake with a jolt the moment before I hit the water, my heart pounding, covered in a slick layer of sweaty fear. I roll over and look at Tilly lying in her cot beside me, consumed with guilt that I hadn't seen it coming.

I hand Edward a mug and he sips slowly, the liquid still too hot to drink.

'I'm sorry the flat's in a bit of a state,' I say. 'I've been so busy at work, I haven't had a chance to clear up properly. I didn't collect Tilly from the childminders until six-thirty last night and by the time I got back . . .' I let my explanation trail off. 'Do you want to sit down?'

He smiles. He's so scared of offending me that our conversation is stilted. I'm the one who always has to take the initiative. He puts his drink down on the coffee table and hovers over the travel cot, turning around to check I don't object to him picking her up. I don't speak, but he waits for my brief nod before he goes ahead. I wish our interaction was easier, but Ali's taken that away from us and I'm not sure how to get it back. Em says I need to give it time.

When we'd returned from travelling, Ali and I had stayed with him as we hadn't been able to afford to rent our own place. I hadn't known him that well before we'd moved in, but after a few weeks of living together we'd bonded over awkward encounters outside the bathroom in the mornings. We'd stayed up talking after Ali had gone to bed, a couple of empty bottles of beer on the table beside us. I'd regarded him as the father I'd never had but hadn't appreciated we only had that relationship because of Ali. Now she was gone, I felt I'd lost him, too.

We treat each other politely, almost as if we're strangers, our whole history together seemingly eradicated by what happened a few months ago. There's an ache in my chest when I watch him with Tilly. His mannerisms remind of me of things Ali used to do. Of what Tilly could have had if Ali had still been here. There are so many things I want to say to him, but I don't know where to start.

'We're going to meet Em and Harry in a bit,' I tell him. 'They've got tickets for a visit to Father Christmas. It's only at the local garden centre, it's not far.' The thought of spending all day in the flat, analysing every sentence before it leaves my mouth is unbearable. The conversation is already uncomfortable and he's only just arrived.

'That'll be nice,' he says, cuddling Tilly. She puts her arms round his neck and giggles when he pulls a face at her. I find it easier when Em's with us. She manages to find the right words. Her presence stops Ali sitting on the sofa next to me, watching me struggle to pretend she doesn't exist.

'Are you OK looking after Tilly in here for a minute?' I ask.

He nods.

When I come back, he's propped her up against a cushion as she stuffs the pages of a fabric book into her mouth.

'She's enjoying that,' he says.

I smile, swallowing what I really want to say. Yes, she is. But how can you look at her without being constantly reminded about what Ali tried to do? If she'd succeeded, Tilly wouldn't even be here. I tell myself I'm being unfair.

It's not his fault. He's done nothing wrong, but I want to find someone to blame. Someone to share the burden of guilt. Someone who's buffeted by the same waves of overwhelming sadness when I look at my daughter that leave me gasping for breath.

'I've tidied up a bit,' he says, pointing at a pile of papers on the table. 'Hope you don't mind.'

I nod, picking them up and a few pieces fall on the floor. We both lean down to retrieve them and a couple of newspaper cuttings slide out of an open envelope. Edward unfolds them, staring at the black and white print. I thought I'd put them away. I must have got them out of the drawer again last night. He's scanning the pages, his face creased.

'Don't read them, Edward.' I hold out my hand to take them.

'It's . . . it's about Ali,' he says, looking at one.

'Yes, they're just press reports.'

He doesn't pass them to me and continues scanning one of the carefully cut out articles. I wince. He looks up, frowning, and his voice quavers as he speaks.

'I don't understand.'

I lean over and take it out of his hand.

'It's just what they write, Edward. It's better to ignore it.'

I put it back on the pile of correspondence, where he continues to stare at it.

'Were you sent it?' he asks.

I could lie. I could tell him I'd cut it out. But I've lied to him enough already.

'Someone put it through my door. Anonymously. I should have just put it in the bin.' I don't tell him I've had many more like it. Stuck under the windscreen wipers on my car. Sent to my work. That I'd heard people whispering as I'd walked past in shops. Messages that had been left on my answerphone. My first childminder had told me she couldn't take Tilly anymore after she found out who I was.

Edward looks at me, not speaking, and slides his hand a few inches closer across the arm of the sofa towards mine. I can tell he doesn't know what to do. We've had no physical contact since Ali left. He'd always used to give me a hug when he arrived at the flat, but now he keeps his distance, any affection reserved for Tilly. Perhaps he thinks I'm too brittle, that I'll break if he touches me. Sometimes I think I will.

'I'm so sorry, Jack,' he says.

'It's fine.' I rub my forehead to try to ease my splitting headache.

Edward starts to speak. 'Your family are . . .' I look at him and he pauses, staring at his hands. 'I have regrets too, Jack. I wish—'

My mobile bleeps and I pounce on the interruption. I don't want to have this conversation. It's easier to keep him at a distance. I pick up my phone and read the message.

'Em's going to meet us in twenty minutes. I'll get Tilly's car seat if you can get her coat on? She needs to be wrapped up as it's chilly out there.'

I stand up and walk away from the sofa before he can say anything else.

The build-up to Christmas used to be my favourite time of year when I was younger. The lights, the chocolate advent calendar, the excitement. My dad had always been away at his annual work conference, so my mum and I had been able to decorate the tree together without him. We'd spent hours hanging up the delicate ornaments. I'd always saved my favourite red and silver glass bauble until last, unwrapping it from the safety of its tissue paper to put on one of the tallest branches. My mum had put the angel on the top, a tiny plastic one with a glitter halo. Then we'd opened the French doors at the back of the sitting room and turned all our house lights off so the tree had been the only thing lit up against the black sky. We'd stood in the cold darkness with mugs of hot Ribena, each of us making a wish. It had taken years for mine to come true.

We arrive at the grotto, which has been set up in the local garden centre a few minutes after eleven. Harry's holding Jessica whilst trying to stop Josh swinging himself round his legs. A tinny version of 'Jingle Bells' rings out every time the automatic entrance doors slide open. Em hugs Edward, who's pushing Tilly in her buggy. I envy them. I've never asked whether they talk about Ali. It's easier not to know.

'You're late.' Harry's breath puffs in clouds around him as he laughs. He enfolds Edward, clapping him on the back. 'Jack being a Sunday driver again, was he?'

We go in through the doors, handing the tickets over at the kiosk, where the person in the booth asks if we want to pay extra for a personalised photo and a cuddly toy. Harry shakes his head, complaining it's cost him a small fortune already.

I walk over to a display of giant animated teddy bears that are singing and moving in time with the music. I ignore them, my attention focussed on the families here. So many mothers holding hands with their children who are giggling with excitement as they watch the display. I should have expected it, but there's a physical pain in my chest, as if someone is wringing out my heart. Ali's absence couldn't be more visible. I swallow the lump in my throat. Harry must notice as he asks if I'm all right. I'm not sure why everyone says it, and what they think my response will be. I tell him I'm fine. One of my many standard answers.

There's a small booth selling coffee and I order a cup, waiting with Em in the queue. They don't sell proper food. I haven't had breakfast this morning and am beginning to feel a bit queasy. I pick up a couple of chocolate muffins for Edward and myself whilst I rub my temples.

'Headache?' Em asks.

I shrug. 'Kind of.'

Em looks down at her hands. 'You shouldn't drink when you're looking after her.'

'I only had a couple of glasses after she'd gone to bed,' I say. 'She sleeps straight through now.'

Em reaches out and puts her hand on my arm. 'What if she woke up, Jack? What if something happened to her and you needed to drive?'

I don't reply, savouring the aroma as the rush of caffeine cuts through the pain in my head.

'I'd get a cab if I thought I was over the limit. And something did happen to her,' I say. 'I'm already responsible for that.'

'Of course you're not. We've been through this.' We had. But despite her reassurances, and those of the counsellor,

I know it's true. They think I'm punishing myself for not seeing what was going to happen. They don't know the things I'd done had pushed Ali to it.

I wrap my hands round the cardboard mug to squeeze out the last of the heat.

'Why don't you go and see her?' Em asks.

I shiver. I can't tell Em it's because I'm scared. I can't bring myself to face her. I don't want to look into her eyes as she asks why I hit her. They'll take Tilly away from me and she's the only thing I have left.

'Edward says she doesn't remember what happened,' I reply. 'He thinks I should wait until she's better.'

Em opens her mouth to say something, sees the look on my face and then changes her mind. The giant teddy bears stop singing and a door opens behind them. We form a queue and are ushered a few at a time into the next room by a large elf.

'Not exactly aiming for realism, are they?' Harry mutters, looking at the elf. 'He's taller than I am.'

I walk next to Edward, letting him push the buggy through the open doors. We're directed in front of a bearded man, dressed in red, who keeps adjusting his hat to stop it falling over his face.

'Huddle together please!' Someone points a camera in our direction. We attempt to get ourselves, the children, Santa and the buggy into some kind of order. 'Smile!'

I grin, despite not feeling remotely like smiling, and wonder why I thought this would be a good idea. Another photo where I'll have to explain to Tilly why her mother isn't with us. You should be here, I think. You should be the one pushing Tilly in her buggy.

'Thank you, everyone.' The elf claps his hands. 'Now, if we can move on to let some other people in? Happy Christmas, folks.' He opens another door and ushers us out into the gift shop.

I take the pushchair from Edward to manoeuvre it through the narrow gap. The place is swarming with visitors.

Harry grabs Josh's hand and looks at him. 'Stay next to me, OK? Don't wander off.'

I glance over to where Edward is talking to Em. 'I'll meet you by the exit,' I say to Harry. I need to get out. Crowds make me uncomfortable. I push the buggy through the hordes of people, aiming to reach the doors without knocking anything over.

It catches my eye as I walk past the rows of Christmas cards. A black and white photo of the suspension bridge, snowflakes falling softly around it. I stop and lift it out of the rack. The room quietens. I stare at the massive chains that stretch between the two towers fixed to the road that runs below by snow-covered iron poles that gleam like colossal icicles. I glance at Tilly reclining in her buggy. Will she remember? Was she asleep? Did Ali let go of her before they hit the water? I have so many unanswered questions.

I drop the card into the hood of the buggy, overcome by a desire to look at it, to study where she'd done it. I've deliberately avoided going anywhere near the bridge since it happened.

I walk through the tills without paying. I don't want to admit to anyone, including myself, that I'm going to take the card home. I wait for someone to stop me, to ask what I'm doing with it so I'll be forced to put it back, but no one does.

I lower my shoulders in an attempt to ease my aching neck muscles. The counsellor had taught me some relaxation exercises, but I hadn't been doing them as much as he'd said I should. Sometimes I make a half-hearted effort last thing at night as I drift off to sleep, her face the last thing I see before me in the dark.

Em and Harry are waiting by the exit.

'Shall we go?' Em asks. 'We've bribed Josh with the promise of a biscuit in the car. Want to come back to ours for a cup of tea?'

I glance at Edward, who shakes his head. 'No, thanks, I should head home.'

'Are you sure?' I ask, relieved I don't have to spend any more time with him on my own. He nods. 'I can drop you at the station if you want?'

Harry tries to stop Josh from climbing on a stone fountain. 'You know you're both more than welcome?'

'No, honestly,' I tell him. 'Thanks for the offer though.'

Em wraps her arms round his neck and gives me a peck on both cheeks.

'I'll call you tomorrow,' she says to me as she bends down to kiss Tilly in the buggy. 'Bye, gorgeous.'

Edward and I walk to my car, encountering the usual fight with the seat belt to get it to fit around Tilly's seat. Over five months of practice and I still can't do it properly. I remember Ali's hands sliding it expertly into place the day Tilly came home, checking she was safe. The same hands that had held onto her as she'd jumped off the bridge.

The counsellor had tried to explain about the psychosis, but I'd let his words wash over me, not able to comprehend what he was telling me. I'd smiled when he'd finished talking and had pinned the leaflets he'd given me to my noticeboard when I'd got home. I'd caught glimpses of them when I'd brushed past them in the hall, reminders that pricked my conscience, adding to my guilt. After a few weeks I'd taken them down, putting them away in a drawer, where they still lay, unread. He'd said I shouldn't blame myself for not realising how ill she was. But he doesn't know — no one knows what I did and I'm carrying the knowledge like a cancer that's slowly eating away at me.

Edward looks at me as he opens the car door to get out when I pull into the station.

'I know you don't want to talk about her, Jack, but she's still Tilly's mother.'

A cold sweat prickles at the back of my neck.

I stare at him. 'What's happened? Has she remembered something?'

Edward shakes his head. 'Her psychologist says there's been no significant change in her condition. But I think you should consider going to see her. It might help her to remember.'

I turn away from him to look straight ahead out of the windscreen. 'I don't want to see her, Edward.'

He gets up out of his seat and turns back just before he shuts the door. 'Just have a think about it. What's best for Tilly.' He walks off into the ticket hall.

I drive home in silence, pulling up outside the flat without being able to remember how I got there.

I put Tilly in her travel cot and turn on her mobile so the toy animals swing round in a circle above her head. She's beginning to get more active, pushing herself up onto her hands and knees. It won't be long before she's crawling. Ali has missed all of it. I feel a perverse sense of satisfaction. The consultant's words echo in my head. There may be long-term damage. All Tilly's subsequent auditory and sight tests have come back normal and she's met all her developmental milestones, but the slightest jerk or quiver sends prickles of alarm through my head.

After I've made her tea and given her a bath, I settle her down for the night. I'd dragged her cot into my bedroom when she'd outgrown her Moses basket so she could sleep next to me. I hadn't wanted her anywhere near what had been written in that room, despite it being no longer visible. I worried the words would somehow slide out from under the paint and into her head, contaminating her. Once I'm sure she's asleep, I pour myself a large glass of red and pull the card out of the hood of her buggy. The bridge is such a vast structure, the river winding its way beneath until it disappears in the distance. Standing on the side, Ali would have been able to see for miles, she and Tilly insignificant compared to the enormity of the landscape. My eyes fill with tears when I think about how desperate she must have been. I miss her. I know Edward's right, I know I should go and see her.

Another glass slides down almost without me noticing. I don't want to see her. I'm frightened that if I do, she still won't remember me, or Tilly, and without her I am nothing. I couldn't bear that. But if she does remember, then she'll leave me. I'm haunted by the sound of my hand on her face. I slam my glass down harder than I mean to on the coffee table and the stem shatters. As I let go, it rolls off the table onto the carpet, a line of crimson liquid sinking into the pile behind it. I get some kitchen roll and dab ineffectively at the stain. It isn't going to come out.

The emotion that's been building up all day explodes in my head. Picking up one of the sofa cushions, I bury my face in it, letting out a scream that only fades when I have no breath left, knowing if Tilly wasn't asleep next door I'd be tempted not to take another.

NOW

Alison

Someone's sitting in an armchair, facing me, when I open my eyes. At first I don't recognise her as everything is blurry, but then her red jacket comes into focus. I try to get up off the couch, but my limbs are too heavy, my legs disconnected from my body.

'You've been sedated,' she says. 'That's why it's difficult to move. It'll wear off in a few minutes.'

'Whe . . . zz . . . Till . . . eee?' My mouth won't form the words I want to say.

She puts her hand on my wrist to feel for my pulse and I don't have the energy to pull away. I catch a glimpse of her painted nails. She tucks her dark hair behind her ear and I remember how it felt between my fingers. I marked you, I think. Like you marked me all those times your nails dug into my skin. You put needles in my arm. You don't think I can remember you hurting me, but I do.

She stands up. 'I'll get you some water . . .' I try to speak but she ignores me, ' . . . and then we'll talk.' She walks over to a small sink in the corner of the room, fills a jug and pours some of the contents into a plastic cup on the table.

I shake my head as she brings it towards my lips. I refuse to take anything from her. She's a monster in disguise. She knows something about my daughter and she won't tell me.

'Where—?' I ask, and she interrupts.

'You're in my office. I asked them to bring you up here. You can relax. I'll answer whatever you want to ask me.'

I reach for the cup she's holding, my arm an unwieldy lead weight, and swallow to get the saliva moving round my mouth. My hand starts to tremble and she takes the cup away before I spill it. Tears prick the back of my eyes, but I refuse to let myself cry in front of her.

'Where's Tilly?' I ask. It's the only thing I want to know.

Sarah sits down in the chair opposite me, opens a file and reaches for a pen off her desk.

'To answer that I'm going to have to ask you some questions. Agreed?'

I nod, making a supreme effort to move my legs off the end of the couch so I'm sitting upright. I want to face her as an equal.

'Where do you think you are?' she asks.

'In your office. You just told me that.'

'And where's my office?'

'On the fourth floor of the building I work in.'

'Right.' She makes a note in her file. 'In the same building as the library. Do you remember coming here before, Alison? To my office?'

I shake my head and she stares at me.

'You have been here,' she says. 'Many times. You've been coming here every week for the last six months since I took over your case.'

I have no idea what she's talking about. I look around. I've never been in this room before. I gaze at the small figure of a buddha she has on her desk and frown. It does seem familiar. Not that I'm going to tell her that. She notices me peering at it and I turn my head away.

'Do you recognise that?' she asks.

I shake my head and run my palm over the velvet fabric of the couch. The buddha reminds me of a larger one I used to have on a shelf. A long grey shelf. When I'd lived with Jack. We'd bought it on holiday in Sri Lanka. It had been supposed to be a good luck symbol to help us conceive. I shake my head to get rid of the unwanted memory.

'Can you remember why you come to see me?' Sarah asks.

'I don't come and see you,' I say. 'I met you for the first time a couple of weeks ago in the canteen.'

She clicks the end of her biro. 'You think that's the first time we met?'

'Yes,' I insist. As I say the words, I realise they're not true. I've always thought I knew her but could never remember where from.

Sarah doesn't contradict me but continues to click her biro. On and off. On and off. It's irritating.

'I just want to know where Tilly is.' I'm begging, but I don't care. I'll do anything to get her to tell me.

She clicks her biro again. 'Where do you live, Alison?' she asks.

I will my body to return to normal so I can get up and leave to find my daughter, but it won't move.

I stare at her. 'Near here. In a flat.' I'm not giving her my address even if she asks for it. 'Why do you have a letter from

Jack in your bag? What do you know about Tilly?' My head throbs from whatever she's drugged me with.

She clicks her pen again. 'Can you take me there?' she asks.

'Where?'

'To your flat. Can you take me?' She looks down at her file, scribbling something. I want to rip it out of her hands and force her to tell me what I want to know, but I can't. I don't even have the strength to move properly. I have to stay civil.

I frown. 'What, now?'

'Yes, now.' Before I have a chance to refuse, she adds, 'And then I promise we can talk about Tilly.' She slides her file into her bag and stands up. 'Do you think you can walk?'

I hesitate, then nod, pushing myself gingerly to my feet. I'm determined to do this if it means she'll tell me what I want to know.

She stands beside me, letting me put my hand on her shoulder and we make our way slowly down the corridor towards the lift, the blue carpet tiles the colour of deep water under my feet. She smiles at me encouragingly as the doors slide open. She doesn't seem to realise I'm only doing this to get the information I want.

'So, where do we go, Alison? How do you get home?'

I hesitate, then press the button for the ground floor. Sarah holds her pass in front of the control panel and the lift moves down smoothly. We stand in silence. I let go of her shoulder, my limbs starting to respond to my brain's instructions. My mind, which has been whirling with a multitude of thoughts, has gone quite still. It knows something I don't. I'm still standing in the shallows, squinting into the sun, oblivious to the wall of water advancing towards me as the tsunami approaches. Almost here. We step out of the lift.

'Where now?' she asks.

Directly in front of me is the main reception and the glass doors leading out to the car park beyond. A couple of staff stand behind the desk.

Sarah puts her hand on my arm and repeats her question. 'Where now, Alison?'

I ignore the light streaming through the exit ahead of me and turn towards an empty corridor in the opposite direction. We walk in silence, the carpet muffling the noise of our foot-steps. Sarah's leather bag swings rhythmically with each step. Are there more letters from Jack hidden in there? She's been deceiving me all this time. I'm only doing this to humour her. After she's told me where Tilly is, I'll never speak to her again. I haven't seen her every week; she's making it up, trying to confuse me. One couch feels very like another when you're sitting on it. We reach a white door. I stop and she hesitates beside me.

'This is it. This is my flat,' I say, holding up the pass hang-ing round my neck to the control panel by the door and hear the familiar beep as it clicks open. I'm home. My face burns even though I'm ice-cold.

'Would you like some water?' Sarah puts her bag down and turns on my kitchen tap. She puts the plastic cup down on the table as I sit on one of the chairs, my legs buckling beneath me. 'So, this is where you live,' she says. I nod, picking up the cup. 'It's not far from my office, is it? Can you think why you might have been coming to see me?'

I shake my head. Flashes of memories. My arms hurting.

'We talk,' she says, sitting down opposite me. 'We talk about what happened last year. Except normally I talk and you don't, because up until now you haven't been able to remember.' She stares at me, waiting for me to speak.

I drink some water. I want to keep drinking. I don't want to think about this.

'But I think you do now, don't you?' She moves my hand away from my head to stop me twisting my hair into tiny ringlets which I pull out and rub between my fingers. 'Do you remember now, Alison?' she asks.

Don't make me think about it. I grip the cup, tipping it up so the liquid runs into my mouth, down my throat, and across my face. I gulp and gulp but can't swallow fast enough. Now I remember. I'm drowning. I've lost Tilly and I'm drowning.

The water had been freezing. It had been like concrete when I'd hit the surface. It had hurt so much that I couldn't help letting go of her. Shooting pain had flared up my legs with an agony that took my breath away. For a moment, the pain had filled every crevice of my mind and every inch of my body. It had wiped out the voice, it had wiped out everything. I'd been consumed by the brightest, white-hot fire I could imagine. Every fibre of my being had wanted to surrender myself to it. It was the truth. I saw it now. The intensity was so great it had overwhelmed anything that came before. And then it had faded.

Water was above me. Below me. Surrounding me. I couldn't breathe. I couldn't see the surface. Every time I'd kicked, another shooting pain had fired down my legs. It had been easier to stay still. Let the water take over. I was so cold. I'd hoped Tilly wasn't cold. I'd shut my eyes as my hair had twisted around in front of my face. I was so cold, I was numb. A feeling of peace had lapped gently

286

through my head. This had been the only way. Finally, it was
quiet. My mind was completely empty and I'd drunk in the silence
as it had washed over me, wave after wave.

Sarah puts her hand on top of mine. 'Alison?' The empty
cup is on the table. 'You're all right. You're safe.'

'I . . . drowned.' I gasp for breath.

'You didn't drown. You're safe.'

'I was in the water,' I say.

Sarah nods. 'Yes. But you're safe now.'

'I jumped, didn't I?' I can't bring myself to look at her.

She doesn't let go of my hand. 'You did. But you're OK.'

I can't answer as it's not me I care about. Her body had
been so light in my arms. I'd thought I was saving her. And
now I'd give anything to take it back. I pull away from Sarah's grasp and put my hands over my ears. I cannot hear her
say the words.

'Alison,' she says, putting her hand onto my arm, 'Look at
me. You're OK.' She pauses. 'And Tilly is OK.'

I can't process the words as they don't make sense; it's like
she's speaking to me underwater. She has to repeat them, the
syllables filtering through my brain one at a time whilst she
looks at me. The sense of relief is so overwhelming, I start to
shake. I'm not sure I believe her, but for the moment I cling
to the words like an anchor. She's OK. Tilly is OK.

I start to cry and cover my face in a vain attempt to hide
my guilt. I am still a mother. I repeat the words over and over
again in my head, using them to block out everything else.

Sarah holds out several tissues and I take them and wipe
my eyes, holding the damp screwed-up bundle in front of
my mouth, inhaling through the paper to slow my breathing.

Sarah is staring at me, but all I can see is my baby. In her white Babygro. The ache to see her is more painful than anything I've ever felt, but it's an agony I'm happy to endure if it means she's still here.

'When . . .?' I mumble.

'This all happened over a year ago. You've been here ever since you left hospital.' A vague memory of a bed and plaster casts. 'You hurt yourself very badly when you landed in the water. You broke the bones in your feet, both your ankles and your pelvis, and you had severe internal bleeding. You were in hospital for three months and you didn't remember what you'd done. When you were released, they sent you here.' She looks at me, assessing whether I'm following what she's saying. 'It's a psychiatric unit.'

My whole reality shifts, and then settles itself. I stare at her as things fall into place inside my head.

'Where's Tilly?' I can barely say the words. That rush of love, the bond that I'd been waiting to feel after she was born spreads across my stomach, concentrated into something so powerful I realise I would do anything to protect her. Anything.

'She's safe. She's being looked after. You weren't capable of caring for her and she couldn't stay with you in here.'

I look at the floor. 'This isn't my flat, is it?' I say.

'Well, it's your private space. In the unit. Every patient has one. You've got a living area with a kitchenette where we're sitting now, a bedroom and bathroom, so it's similar to a flat.' I know she's only being kind. 'We specialise in encouraging patients to develop their independence so they can cope on their own when we feel they're ready to leave.'

I look at the black letters on the pass hanging round my neck. 'This isn't my name,' I say.

'We changed it to try and minimise the publicity. There was a lot of press interest in your case,' Sarah replies.

'And my job?' I ask.

'In the library?' I nod. 'Mrs Painter says you've been a role model for the other patients. She agreed to look after you when you were in there, Alison. She's had a lot going on in her life recently and I think having someone else around to talk to has really helped her.'

'So, I can leave if I want to?' I don't want to waste any more time. I need to see Tilly.

'Not at the moment,' Sarah replies. 'You were sectioned when you were admitted. I have to agree you're fit to go.'

'When can I see Tilly?' I demand.

'We need to make sure you're better first.'

'But I have to see her,' I say.

She leans back on the chair. 'Alison, we have to take things slowly. A lot of things have changed.' She speaks carefully. 'You've been at this unit for a year. I only started working on your case six months ago when your condition hadn't improved as much as we'd hoped.'

I look around the room, as if seeing it for the first time. Two cupboards on the wall above a counter next to a stainless-steel sink. A microwave. A small sofa. My plastic cups. A drawer of plastic cutlery. None of it actually mine. I put my hand on the table to steady myself.

'Are you OK?' Sarah asks.

'It's all plastic, isn't it?' I say. 'My knives and forks and cups. So I can't—'

Sarah interrupts. 'It's the same in every unit. It's not just yours.' She smiles. 'I'm so glad you're finally talking about this, Alison. Until a few weeks ago we all thought you were making good progress, but then I showed you something Jack had asked me to give to you. A silver bracelet. Do you remember?'

I shake my head, my thoughts fluttering, not able to settle.

'I think he'd hoped it would jog your memory, but I never would have shown it to you if I'd known it would provoke such an extreme reaction. We'd tried a similar approach before with a couple of things your father had brought in when you were first admitted. We'd asked him for anything you had a particular emotional attachment to. He gave us a postcard of Weston-super-Mare where he used to take you on holiday and a glove that he said you carried around with you when you were little. You didn't show any reaction to them, but when you saw the bracelet you became quite hysterical and shut down completely.'

I remember Jack fastening it round my wrist after we'd found out I was pregnant. The one tiny heart charm dangling from the chain.

'You refused to talk and wouldn't even acknowledge me anymore,' Sarah continues. 'The team agreed to suspend your therapy sessions until we considered you were in a fit state to resume them. I've been meeting you informally during your lunchtime over the last couple of weeks as the canteen seemed to be somewhere you felt safe. You began to talk to me when we were in there. The only other time you'd leave your room was to visit the library, so Mrs Painter agreed to take you under her wing and get you to do some jobs for her. You seem to enjoy it.'

'Why didn't you tell me you were a doctor?' I ask.

'When I first met you, I did tell you who I was, but in these last few weeks you've treated me like a stranger. It's as though we'd never met and I was concerned if I mentioned it again it would affect your recovery. All those involved with your treatment agreed you needed to remember things in your own time.'

'Now I have,' I say, 'it means I'm getting better, right?'

'It's a very positive sign, yes,' Sarah replies. 'But there's a way to go yet and we don't want to rush things.' She looks at me. 'I . . . I don't think you quite realise . . . how much has changed. Tilly's over a year old now. She's not a baby anymore.'

I know that. Of course, I know that. She isn't the same tiny bundle I . . . I start to hyperventilate.

'Take deep breaths,' Sarah says. 'In and out slowly. Out for a count of five.' Sarah holds my hands whilst she talks. 'Focus on me. Nothing else.'

I breathe with her and block out all thoughts of Tilly.

'Let's go back to my office,' she says. 'Do you want me to see if we're allowed outside for some fresh air?'

I shake my head. I don't want to go out. Not yet. I run my finger over my eyebrow and pull out a stray hair. I walk slowly with her to reception and look out through the glass doors to the car-park. It doesn't feel safe. I ignore the glances in my direction from the staff at the desk as Sarah summons the lift. She holds her pass up to the control panel as she presses the button for the fourth floor.

Now I understand why the lift wouldn't take me upstairs to her office. My pass doesn't allow me access. I don't tell her I went up the stairs at the back of the library and looked through the glass panels down the corridor but couldn't get in.

She sees me staring at the control panel.

'There are cameras on every floor,' she says. 'For security reasons.'

'You've been watching me?' My voice rises.

'We have to monitor all our patients.' She stares straight ahead. 'You've always been quite safe. We've kept a close eye on you.'

I'm silent. I'm not sure I believe her. We walk out of the lift and sit back down in her office.

She gets out a file in which I can see pages of illegible writing. 'These are your medical notes,' she says.

A whole book written about me. People have been studying me and I've had no idea. Everything I've thought for the past year has been a lie. I can't trust myself. I could be imagining this, too. I have to grip the arms of the chair to steady myself.

Sarah stares at me. 'You were given an antipsychotic drug called Haloperidol,' she says.

I see her nails round a syringe as it digs into my skin. Some things I do remember. I swallow.

'But I'd been reducing the dosage over the past couple of months until your recent episode as I wasn't sure if it was actually helping you and the side effects can be unpleasant.' She pauses. 'Things like weight gain, nausea and hallucinations can all be a result of the medication.'

She's been filling me full of something alien, turning my body into something unrecognisable. I don't know who I am anymore.

'It's been used successfully to treat post-partum psychosis in the past,' she says, 'but in my opinion, you were in a state of shock after what happened and this drug wasn't helping to treat your condition, so we've tried some sessions of hypnosis.'

Why is she skirting around the issue using words like *condition?* I wish she'd just come out and say it. I'm insane. I don't understand what's real and what's not and I tried to kill my child.

'Have you heard of post-partum psychosis, Alison?' I shake my head. 'It's a severe episode of mental illness following childbirth. In your case, we think having Tilly made you hear voices and see things that weren't real. Unfortunately, it wasn't picked up quickly enough. It's not as uncommon as you might think and if you're treated, patients can make a full recovery.'

Remember? I block out the small voice that rises from the ashes in my head. I don't know if I believe her.

'Why me?' I ask.

Sarah looks at me. 'The short answer to that is we don't know. Statistically, around one in a thousand women will suffer from this type of illness, but if there's a family history of the condition it can increase your risk of experiencing it.'

I stay very quiet. I remember touching my mother's face in the car in our garage. I'd never seen her so peaceful. She'd either been silent, refusing to leave her room, or full of an energy I couldn't keep up with, even as a child. I'd wondered why she'd seemed so still. I hadn't realised it was because she wasn't breathing. Now I wonder if she was suffering with something similar. Maybe no one even realised she was ill. The thought makes me swallow hard to stop myself from crying. I wish I could go back and tell her I understood. I'm aware Sarah's watching me and I don't want to talk about it. It would feel like a betrayal.

I look at the notes Sarah is holding. Pages of scribbled black writing. They seem familiar.

'Do you remember what you thought,' Sarah asks, 'after you had Tilly?'

I close my eyes and try searching back through the fog and then I hear it.

'There was a voice. I can't remember exactly what it said, but I had to do what it wanted.' I take a deep breath and wait for the memories to sharpen. 'It told me I had to get out of the flat. That Jack was going to hurt Tilly. He'd hurt me and he wanted to hurt Tilly.' I stop talking and put my hand up to my cheek.

'You haven't asked me about Jack,' Sarah says.

I open my eyes.

'I don't need to,' I tell her. 'I know he's been here. I've seen him.'

'Jack hasn't been here, Alison.'

I smile. 'He has. He's been leaving letters for me in my flat.'

'I'm afraid he hasn't.' She clicks the end of her pen.

'I've seen him in the library too.' I put my hand up to twist my hair, then put it down again as Sarah looks at me. She's lying.

'You *think* you've seen him, but he hasn't been in here.' She hesitates. 'Actually, that's not quite true. He did come here a few months ago. But he didn't see you. When you arrived, you insisted that you didn't want any contact with him. You told us he'd been violent towards you. I'm still not sure if that's true, but my primary duty is to ensure your safety, so I had to respect your wishes. Jack hasn't seen you. It's a secure unit here. You've seen the control panels on all the doors. No one comes in or out without the staff knowing about it.'

My heart begins to thump.

'So how come I've got letters from him? He must have delivered them. I found them . . . they didn't have any enve-lopes,' I say.

'I gave them to you,' she says. 'All except the one I kept in my bag that mentioned Tilly. I didn't want to give you that one until you remembered what had happened and I felt you were ready to read it.'

'You gave them to me?' I ask. 'When?'

'A couple of months ago in our therapy sessions. I thought they might prompt you into remembering what happened. Jack found out I was treating you and came here with them, and asked me if I'd give them to you. I couldn't confirm I knew who you were as that would have been a breach of patient confidentiality, but I read them, and together with your treatment team we made the decision that it might be helpful for you to have them. You refused to look at them, but you took them back to your room afterwards.'

I frown at her in disbelief. 'No, I didn't. Jack left them in my flat for me.'

Sarah hesitates whilst she looks at me. 'No one's been in your room, Alison. It's always locked and only you and the staff have a key. I think you took Jack's letters away with you, hid them, and when you had your recent episode you blanked out the fact I'd ever given them to you at all.'

'I saw Jack,' I say insistently, the words coming out louder than I expect. 'Running down the stairs. And in the library.'

'Hallucinating is one of the common symptoms of your illness as well as a side effect of the drugs you're taking,' she replies, clicking her biro. 'And you think you're seeing Jack rather than anyone else because there's so much that's unresolved between you. There are still so many things you want to say to him.'

Jack has been here. I know he has. He'd grabbed my arm, tucked my hair behind my ears and held my hand. His touch had been unmistakable.

He'd told me it wasn't my fault. But I know it was. I remember now. I remember being in the car with him and being terrified about him taking me to the doctor's, thinking they'd take Tilly away from me. I'd almost made him crash. I put my hand up to my cheek. I'd thought he was trying to hurt Tilly, to take her away from me when all he'd ever been trying to do was protect her. From me. I just hadn't been able to see it before. He must hate me. I have to tell him how sorry I am.

'I think . . .' Sarah pauses. 'I think you have to try and see things from Jack's point of view. He was so angry about what happened. To start with, he refused to see you. Then he changed his mind, but once he realised you'd requested there be no contact, he had a few . . . difficulties . . . in dealing with it.'

'What kind of difficulties?' I ask.

'He couldn't accept he wasn't allowed to see you. He was very . . . persistent.' She chooses her words carefully.

'What do you mean?'

'We had to send him a letter advising you'd asked not to see him, and that he shouldn't try to visit or contact you. He ignored it. I think he felt what happened was his fault. That something he'd done made you do what you did. He kept trying to phone me. He came here and tried to get into the building. Then he turned up at my house. Luckily my husband was there . . . but we had to call the police. I'm afraid Jack ran off as he was . . . very distressed.'

I interrupt her. 'I need to see him . . . explain . . . make him understand . . .'

'You can't see him, Alison. He's not here.'

'Can I ask him to come?'

'No,' Sarah replies.

'Why not?' I shout in frustration. 'I'm telling you I want to see him. Why can't he visit and bring Tilly?'

'Tilly isn't with Jack.'

Someone is pouring freezing cold water into my chest. 'Who's she with then?'

'She's safe.' Sarah doesn't look at me. 'She's with your father.'

'My father?'

Sarah hesitates. 'Your father's dealt with everything. You asked that he be considered your nearest relative. He's our point of contact in your case. He visited you when you were first admitted, but as you were unresponsive, we advised him to stay away until we could see an improvement. We update him regularly on your condition and he's the one funding your treatment. Tilly went to live with him after . . . when Jack wasn't able to look after her.'

I stare at her. 'So . . . Jack . . . when did I last see . . .?'

'The morning you jumped from the bridge. You haven't seen him since.' She glances at me, trying to work out what to say next. 'Alison,' she says gently, 'Jack isn't here anymore.'

THEN

Jack – *10 Months after Tilly's birth*

I have the same recurring nightmare every night now, aware I'm asleep but powerless to wake myself up to stop its inevitable conclusion. I'm on the bridge, watching helplessly from inside a car as she climbs over the metal barrier, one end of the blanket wrapped around Tilly, the other fluttering loosely in the wind. I tug at the door handle, but it slides through my fingers, refusing to open. Why is no one trying to stop her?

More cars pull over and a few people get out, congregating in a huddle near their vehicles, watching from a distance. She ignores their shouts. I pound my fists on the window. Please don't do it. I rip open the glovebox to see if there's something, anything, I can use to open the door. There's nothing.

She looks out over the river, one hand on the railing. My voice is hoarse and tears run down my face.

'I'm begging you,' I scream, my hands pounding on the glass. 'Please don't do it.' I catch sight of the golf umbrella on the back shelf of the car and grab it, shoving the pointed metal tip into the passenger window. At first there's a dull thump, but after slamming it a couple of times with all the force I can muster, the glass fractures, then shatters over my hands and the seat. I roar her name as the breeze hits my face and watch in horror as she lets go of the railing and falls forward, seemingly in slow motion, with Tilly's blanket trailing like a pair of deformed wings behind her.

'Jack!' Someone's calling me.

I try unsuccessfully to bury myself under the covers as the curtains are drawn back.

'Jack!'

I don't want to wake up. I have to get back, to stop her . . .

The duvet is thrown off roughly. My face feels puffy as I peer through the slits of half-open eyelids.

'Edward?' I croak. Ali's dad stands at the side of my bed.

'Get up.' He turns and walks out of the room.

I fight to disentangle myself from the bed linen. My head spins. I blink as I look at the clock. Ten o'clock. Shit. Shit. I grab my dressing gown off the back of the door and stagger into the sitting room. Edward is sitting on the sofa holding Tilly and her shoulders are shaking in the way they do when she's been crying for some time. He's rubbing her back.

'You didn't hear her.' His voice is cold.

'What the hell are you doing here?' I shout. 'How did you . . .?' I notice the breeze on my face before I see the pile of glass on the carpet. 'You broke in?' I ask, incredulous.

'Yes, I broke in. I had no choice. I'd been buzzing the intercom for ten minutes and no one answered so I came around the back and looked through the window to see *her*,' he gestures at Tilly, 'hysterical in her travel cot. I didn't even know if you were here.' He looks at me in disgust. 'How long has she been in there?'

I can't get my thoughts into any kind of order. I'd put her

down to sleep next to me in her cot last night. I remember that.

'D'you not know?' he demands.

'No . . . I do . . . I thought I'd put her . . .' I trail off. Had I? Or was that the night before? I'm not sure.

Edward looks at me, speaking deliberately slowly. 'You can't remember at all, can you? You don't know why your daughter's in a travel cot in your sitting room, in a soaking-wet nappy, crying her eyes out at ten o'clock in the morning. What are you doing, Jack? What if she'd managed to climb out?'

I rub my face and swallow down the bile that crawls up my throat. I try desperately to think what I did last night, but it's all a blur.

'I don't think at the moment you're fit to be a father.' He says these last words quietly, but they're sharp enough to cut through the fog of my hangover.

I put my head in my hands.

'You're not coping, Jack. I know what Ali did was unforgiveable,' Edward says, 'but she was ill. You'd know that if you went to see her.'

'I can't face her. You don't understand.' His eyes narrow in disbelief. I fight the urge to sit down, my head thumping.

'I do understand, actually, Jack,' he says. 'Ali was ill. What she did wasn't a deliberate decision. I should know, I speak from experience.' He lets the words sink in slowly through the haze in my head. Tilly turns her face out of Edward's shoulder to look at me.

'What are you talking about?' I ask. 'Did you know she wasn't well?'

He shakes his head. 'No. I'm talking about Ali's mother.'

I look at him holding Tilly and feel a stab of pity. He'd lost his wife in a car accident and now he's lost his daughter. I'd seen the tiny star Ali had got tattooed on her ankle to remember her.

'I'm sorry about your wife, Edward. But that's no comparison to what Ali did—'

He interrupts me. 'I found them.'

'Found who?'

'Ali and Elizabeth, my wife. I was the one who found them. I got home from work and saw a glove lying on the drive by the entrance to our garage. I recognised it as one of a pair I'd given to Ali for a Christmas present. They had this panda design on them and she'd taken them everywhere with her. I went to pick it up and realised it was stuck under the edge of the garage door, so I opened it. It was one of those big metal ones that you slide up and over on a frame. You know?' He barely glances in my direction, but I nod, watching his hands stroke Tilly's back in a continuous rhythm. 'And I nearly stepped on Ali's head. She was lying right behind it. On the floor. Unconscious.' His eyes focus firmly on our mantelpiece. 'Elizabeth was in the car. The engine was off when I arrived, but she'd filled the place with fumes. Perhaps she'd turned it off at the last minute. Regretted her decision. I don't know. They said lying down by the door saved Ali. The extra oxygen.'

I'm silent for a moment. 'How old was she?'

'Elizabeth? Thirty-three.'

'And Ali?'

'Eight. The doctors told me afterwards Elizabeth was

anaemic, so the fumes affected her more than Ali. My daughter was lucky. If you can call it that. She had to carry an
inhaler round for years, but other than that, physically she
recovered well. So, I do understand how you feel, Jack. I
understand every emotion you've been through. I pretended things were OK at home. Pretended I didn't have any
concerns about the way Elizabeth was behaving. I thought
everyone changed once they had a child. I was furious with
her for a while afterwards. For leaving us. For not talking
to me about how she'd felt. But it wasn't her fault. It was
mine. I should have realised she was ill. Back then, no one
admitted they had a problem. It wasn't something you talked
about. But if I was in your situation and someone offered
me the chance to see her again . . . I'd give anything for
that opportunity. And Ali would too, I know it. Tilly's got
that chance.'

'Why didn't you tell Ali what happened? When she was
older?' I ask.

'I didn't want her to hate her mother. Or me, for not being
able to stop it.'

'You should have told me,' I say.

'Why?' Edward smooths down Tilly's damp hair. 'Ali had
never shown any indication of . . . I didn't know something
like that could be hereditary. I did try to say something on the
phone after she hurt her hand. I thought something wasn't
right. That it wasn't an accident.' He looks at me. 'It wasn't,
was it?'

I shake my head.

'But you didn't tell me,' he adds.

'It was difficult,' I say. 'Ali . . . didn't want me to.' I can't tell him I hit her. The shame still crawls over my skin. He'll never forgive me if he finds out.

'Then perhaps you can understand why I didn't tell you about my wife. I didn't want you to think I was interfering when you'd just had a new baby. I kept telling myself Ali wasn't Elizabeth. After Ali was born, I never knew what I was coming home to, Elizabeth was so up and down. I think I missed the worst of it, being out at work all day. She'd tried to hide how bad things had got for her. After you told me about Ali's wrist, it made me wonder, and I thought if anything else happened I'd say something. But by then . . .'

We look at each other in silence.

'I need a cup of coffee,' I say. I go into the kitchen, where half-eaten plates of food are stacked up on the counter. My stomach protests at the smell. I fill the kettle with water and open the fridge. My fingers are trembling. I put the mugs on a tray and carry them back into the sitting room, slopping the contents of Edward's over the side as I put it down in front of him. 'Sorry, I'm a bit clumsy this morning,' I apologise.

He hesitates. 'You need help, Jack. Proper help.' I don't answer. 'You haven't even asked to hold her.' He glances down at Tilly, who, exhausted by all her crying, looks like she's drifting off to sleep. 'Em called me,' he says. 'She's worried about you. That's the reason I came over.'

'She hasn't said anything to me.'

He sips his coffee and hesitates before asking, 'Why don't you go and see Ali?'

I stare at him. 'Have you seen her recently?' I ask. I'm not sure if I want to know the answer. He holds Tilly a little tighter.

'No. I visited when she first went in, but she . . . she wasn't very responsive. She just lay on her bed and stared at the wall. I get an update from her psychiatrist every week, but they said it would be better to stay away until she's ready to see visitors. They've been working to reduce her medication.' He clears his throat, checking Tilly's still asleep.

'I can't face seeing her,' I admit.

'I understand.' He doesn't. 'But perhaps you could get through to her,' he continues. 'She'd never have hurt Tilly if she was well. You've been with her twelve years, Jack, you know your wife.'

I don't look at him. 'I'll think about it.'

Edward strokes Tilly's back. He looks embarrassed. 'I should probably have told you this before, but when she was in hospital, she said she didn't want to see you.'

I stare at him. 'What?'

'When she came out of intensive care, she kept saying she didn't want anything to do with you. That you'd hurt her.' I freeze, my expression blank. 'I didn't say anything to you at the time as I knew she was talking rubbish, but she wouldn't listen to me. You weren't there, you didn't see how confused she was. She didn't even remember who Tilly was. She said she didn't want you to contact her. Back then, I didn't feel I was in a position to disagree. But now I think you should. I think you could help.' He pulls a piece of paper out of his pocket and puts it on the coffee table. 'They've got a new doctor treating her . . . a Dr Henderson. These are her details. If you write to her, she might let you visit.'

'Why didn't you tell me that Ali didn't want to see me?' I ask.

'What was the point? Until now you've always refused to see her. You barely ever mention her. And I understand that. You have a right to be angry. I hoped after a while that Ali would come to terms with what actually happened and then you'd change your mind about visiting her. But from the updates I've had, it doesn't seem as though that's the case, so whatever they're doing in that place isn't working. I think you need to go and see her.'

I shake so much as I start to put down my mug, I have to hold onto it instead. I'm still deceiving him by not telling him what I did to Ali. Hitting his daughter. I dread him finding out.

He puts Tilly into her travel cot and tucks her blanket over her. 'Why don't you let me take her for a while,' he says.

I shiver. 'What?'

'Tilly. Let me take her, so you can get back on your feet. You look exhausted. You need to take a few weeks off work, clean this place up and sort out your drinking.'

I stare at him. I'm not giving up Tilly. She's all I have left.

'And you should go and see Ali,' he continues. 'They've changed her name at the Unit. Alison Reid, I think they're calling her. To avoid any publicity.'

I grit my teeth. 'I don't think that's a good idea,' I say.

'Look at her, Jack.' We both stare at Tilly in her travel cot. 'I'm sure her childminder is great, but she's not family. I'd be able to spend all day with her. Please.'

I'm about to refuse and then watch as she rolls over and screws up her nose in exactly the way Ali used to do. I need to think about what's best for her, not for me. Edward could give her the attention that I can't. What if Edward hadn't woken me up? What if Tilly had got out and hurt herself? He's right, I need to sort myself out. But I can't lose her. It would destroy me.

Edward looks at me. 'How about I take her for a couple of weeks. Just until you get things sorted out.'

My stomach turns over. 'I can't let you do that, Edward.'

He looks at me. 'What d'you think Ali would say, Jack? If she was here. Would she want you looking after her in the state you're in, or do you think she'd say she'd be better off staying with me for a while.'

I well up. 'That's unfair. She's not here to make that decision.'

Edward doesn't speak, watching Tilly as she lies on her back, her eyelashes feather-like against her cheek. The thought of not having her, not being able to hold her against me, to smell her, to lean over at night and watch her in her cot as her chest rises and falls, her eyes flickering under her lids as she dreams, is so painful I'm not sure I can bear it. I love her more than anything. And I have to do what's best for her. I swallow.

'Perhaps you could take her for a week or so. Just until I sort things out.' As I hear myself say the words, I experience a falling sensation, as if I've just given up the one thing that's keeping me connected to reality.

Edward smiles. 'It's the right decision, Jack. I can bring her over at the weekend if you want. I'm not far away. You can visit her whenever you like. It'll just give you some space.'

I have to stop myself snapping back with an unkind remark about not needing space, about Ali having left a void in my life that's so big I don't think anything can ever fill it.

Before I change my mind, I put some of Tilly's clothes, nappies and her teddy into a bag. Not too many things. I want to keep it minimal so he has to come back. I order a taxi to take them back to Edward's house. I don't trust myself to drive. I'm not sure if I'm still over the limit.

Tilly clings to my neck as I say goodbye and it takes all my willpower not to turn around and refuse to let her go. I put on a brave face, the one I've been wearing for the last nine months, and smile at her.

'Bye, gorgeous girl. I'll see you soon. Grandpa Edward will look after you. It's not for long. I'll see you at the weekend.' I breathe in the smell of her, planting kisses on her damp forehead. 'I love you, Tils. So much.'

I wave at the taxi until it disappears from view and go back into an empty flat I can't bear the sight of. I don't know who I am anymore; no longer a father or a husband. I am no one. Just a functioning body.

I hoover the glass off the living-room floor, nail a board over the window and clear up the worst of the mess before I sit down at our coffee table and pull out the photo of the two of us in Amalfi that I'd given the police ten months earlier. I study Ali's face. Her dimples. Back then I hadn't ever considered the possibility we might not end up together. Now I have to face the fact the woman in the photo is a stranger. We've fallen apart and I have no way to mend the broken pieces.

I pull off a couple of pages of cream writing paper from the pad in the drawer underneath the table, pick up a pen and begin to write.

Dear Dr Henderson,

I believe you look after my wife, Alison Reynolds. I wondered if
you would be prepared to meet me to discuss her situation. I can
be reached on my mobile – I've written the number below, but
I've also included details of my home phone, together with my
home and email address in case these are a more convenient way
for you to contact me.

Yours sincerely,

Mr Jack Reynolds

I seal the letter in an envelope and copy down the address
Edward has left me. I dig around in the bottom of the bowl
on the hall shelf to find a stamp. Pulling out a book of six, I
stick two on the front to be sure, put the letter in my pocket
and head out of the flat.

I need to see my wife.

NOW

Alison

I gaze down at myself wearing the one dark blue dress I have in my wardrobe. The colour emphasises how pale my skin is, the material hanging loosely round my waist. The tiny mirror in my bathroom isn't big enough to look at myself full-length, so I try to imagine what others will see. Sarah had agreed it was appropriate for a funeral. I didn't think it would fit, but in the two weeks since coming off the Haloperidol, my whole frame has shrunk.

I'd known instantly something was wrong when she'd avoided answering my questions. The carpet tiles in her office had rippled like waves as my eyes had welled up. She'd struggled to find the words to break the news, fishing them out of the pool of water one by one, hiding them amongst a flood of other comforting phrases to try to lessen the horror as they landed at my feet. Her hand hadn't left my arm as she'd sat facing me on the couch. She'd embraced me as I sat, rigid, trying to adjust to a new reality.

Sarah had focused on the practicalities of the situation, allowing me to shut everything else in a room which I crept back to when no one was looking. I'd peered round the door to glance at what I couldn't bring myself to think about before shutting it firmly and pretending it hadn't happened. Even with her help, it had taken a while to finalise all the arrangements as a post-mortem had been required by the coroner.

My hands shake as I put on my shoes. She's lent me a pair of small navy heels to match the dress and done her best to prepare me, but I'm still terrified. Of so many things, but mainly of leaving the unit. It's the first time I'll have been further than a few hundred feet outside the building. We've spent time walking round the grounds in some of our therapy sessions we've had since I remembered what happened, but I've never left the safety of the perimeter. I'm going to have to blend in amongst a crowd of strangers in a crematorium; he hadn't wanted a Church service. Sarah had tried to reassure me that everyone would be there for him, not for me. Most of them probably won't even recognise me, but I know some will. Some will be looking for me. Some will never understand, let alone forgive, what I've done. Even with her standing next to me, the thought of any confrontation paralyses me to the point where I know I'll be incapable of the simplest action of putting one foot in front of the other.

Jack's mum had tried to call me after Sarah had broken the news. I'd refused to speak to her. I couldn't face it. I didn't want to hear her sympathy. To have her tell me to cherish the memories. I can't deal with that right now.

I run my fingers over my eyebrows. At the moment they're beginning to feel more like a thick line. Sarah says it's an outward sign that I'm healing inwardly. I know they won't stay like this. My habit is too ingrained to break. She said the funeral will be cathartic though. That facing the reality of the situation might help the grieving process. So far, I haven't even cried. I'd only agreed to go to the service on the condition that she came with me. We'd decided I'd go to the crematorium and nowhere else; come in last, stand at the back and leave first.

There's a knock at the door. It's time. She doesn't need to get my permission to enter as her pass lets her straight in, but she's started giving me a small amount of independence to get me used to the idea of leaving the unit and returning to some kind of normality, eventually.

'Ready?' She's dressed as immaculately as ever. 'I brought a bag I thought you might like to take with you.'

I clutch it nervously. At least it gives me something to do with my hands.

'Let's go then.' She doesn't give me any time to hesitate so I can back out of the situation. No mention of where we're going and what I'm going to face. I wonder if she has any sedatives hidden in her bag along with her tissues and purse.

We pass Mrs Painter on our way out. Sarah must have told her where we're going as she stops when she sees me, coming over to put her hand on my arm. Her fingers are bare, the paper-thin skin almost translucent. I notice she's changed her hairstyle. Sarah told me she's seen her meeting one of the caretakers for lunch in the canteen. She smiles at me and her eyes well with tears as she clears her throat.

'Sometimes I've realised the only thing we can do is let things go,' she says as she gives my arm a gentle squeeze. 'I'll see you tomorrow, Alison.' I nod in reply. I've kept working in the library with her. I enjoy it. It gives me something to do between my therapy sessions.

We head past the reception area and across the car park, my feet slipping as I'm not used to walking in heels, particularly on the wet ground. Sarah shuts the passenger door behind me as I slide into the seat. It's strange to sit in a car for the first time in over a year. I shudder, remembering the last time I was in one. My breath turns the glass window opaque and I have a sudden urge to draw something. My finger makes a squeaking sound as I write an 'A' and a 'T' in the condensation. We're both still here.

Sarah fastens her seat belt and swivels the dial to turn the heating up. She looks across at me. 'Just breathe slowly,' she says.

I grip the strap on the bag as she pulls off.

'If I go this way, we're going to go over the bridge. I know we talked about it, but are you still OK with that? We can always go a different route if you want.'

I shake my head. 'It's fine.' I'm not sure it will be, but better to get it over with. I've pictured it so many times in my head in the last couple of weeks, I'm curious to see whether the reality is any different. We drive down roads that I begin to recognise. Rectangular Georgian buildings, large symmetrical windows looking out over the street.

Sarah glances at me. 'Deep breaths, Ali. Your bag won't come undone.'

I don't realise I'm fiddling with the clasp. I put my hand back in my lap. She hasn't turned the radio on; I assume she's keeping the car quiet so she can hear if I start to hyperventilate. I spot the towers as she turns towards them at the end of the road. The huge stone blocks rise up out of the landscape. I expect a surge of panic, or terror, of something. But there is nothing. I am numb.

Sarah keeps glancing across at me as she drives between the wide barriers. There's a line of traffic, so we have to slow down; I keep my eyes glued to the brake lights of the vehicle in front. I still feel nothing. And then we're in the middle of the bridge. The queue of cars comes to a halt, waiting for the traffic lights at the far end to change.

I look out of my window. I'd stood a few metres away from this spot, so close I can almost touch it. I remember walking there. Holding her. Making sure her blanket had been tucked around her to keep her warm from the wind. Cars stopped. Someone shouting. It's as if I'm remembering a different person, a different life. I have no sense of the desperation I must have felt to stand on the side of this structure and step off.

'You OK, Alison?' Sarah asks.

I daren't look down, I keep my eyes fixed on where the river disappears into the horizon. I nod.

'The crematorium isn't much further. We're going to be early, but we can always wait in the car.'

We drive under the tower and off the other end of the bridge. It's only a road; stone and metal. It doesn't possess any of the power I'd attributed to it in my nightmares.

The crematorium car park is packed. Sarah has to drive round three times to find a space, so by the time we've stopped, the service is due to start. I take a deep breath as I open the door. It's cold outside after the warmth of the car and I shiver, adjusting my grip on my handbag. Sarah's waiting for me and, though every part of me screams not to go any further, I know I need to do this. To put him to rest.

We head inside the building, already full of mourners. There's an Order of Service on every seat and I pick one up as we sit down at the back.

Sarah smiles, her hand on my arm. 'He was a popular man,' she says, as she gazes round the room.

My head is full of images of him. Holding my hand. Smiling at me when I told him I was pregnant. Stroking Tilly's face. I try to swallow the lump that rises in my throat but can't manage it. We'd been through so much.

Sarah pushes a tissue into my hand as the music starts. 'Unforgettable' by Nat King Cole. One of his favourites. I try to focus on the Order of Service and take deep breaths. The words swim before my eyes and despite Sarah's hand on my arm, I wonder if I'm going to be able to make it through this.

Someone edges along the pew so they're standing next to me.

'Is it OK if I sit here?' they whisper and I nod my head, not taking my eyes off the Order of Service. There's a feeling of something solid, something comforting in their presence. Like coming home after a long time away. I daren't look at them. I'm not sure if I'm imagining things. The vicar stands up at the front of the room and there's silence apart from the rustle of paper and tissues as the music finishes.

'Welcome, everyone. We have come here today to remember before God, our brother Edward Alfred Locke, and give thanks for his life. To commend him to God our merciful redeemer and commit his body to be cremated and comfort one another in our grief. Let us pray.'

I look up at the photos of my dad that are positioned on top of the coffin and beside where the vicar is speaking.

At least we'd had the opportunity to talk when he visited me at the unit. My first visitor. At least he'd been able to tell me how much he loved having Tilly with him, how much she enjoyed hearing stories about me, and how much she was looking forward to meeting me again. At least he'd been there for her over the past couple of months when Jack had disappeared, unable to cope. He hadn't felt any pain; it had been a heart attack. Not something anyone could have predicted. He'd been visiting Em with Tilly and I was glad he'd been surrounded by people who loved him, that he hadn't been alone. I just wish I'd had a chance to say goodbye. To thank him properly not only for looking after my daughter but also for doing his best to protect me in the aftermath of Mum's death, despite his own grief. I didn't need to tell him I loved him; he knew that. Though perhaps not enough.

As we bend our heads to pray, the person standing next to me passes me a piece of paper. I take it without looking and put it on top of my Order of Service and read it as the vicar's voice echoes round the hushed room.

Ali,
I am so, so sorry about your dad. I've missed you. Can we talk afterwards?
Jack

I tuck the paper inside the Order of Service and reach out my hand, feeling his fingers beneath my own. Although I'm sure I recognise his familiar touch, a part of me wonders if he's actually real, and I nod in reply without looking at him, not able to process the emotions that threaten to overwhelm me. We stand together, our heads bowed, and on the other side of me I feel the rough skin of my dad's cheek press against mine as he kisses me goodbye.

I keep my eyes firmly fixed on the vicar at the front of the church for the entire service, other than a couple of occasions when I risk a glance at Sarah, who I can see is also staring straight ahead. As the chords of the last hymn fade, the congregation rises to its feet and I allow myself to look at the man standing beside me. It is him. A slimmer version of the man I last saw over a year ago. He smiles at me, the creases next to his eyes deeper than I remember.

'Hi, Ali.' It's a familiar greeting, but there's a warmth to his tone. I don't sense any anger or bitterness, but it's so long since I heard his voice I wonder if I've misread the nuances that I was once certain of.

'Hello, Jack,' I reply.

We file out first, past the deep red velvet curtains that hang across the windows in the grey entrance hall, and he doesn't let go of my hand. Or perhaps I'm not giving him the chance.

Sarah smiles at me as I look back at her, and I watch as she starts a conversation with the person behind her to give me some space.

'Are you going to the wake?' he asks.

I shake my head. 'I can't face . . . No.'

He nods. 'I'm so sorry I disappeared.'

I open my mouth to speak, but he interrupts me before I can get out the words.

'Please, Ali. I need to explain. I didn't desert Tilly. I just had to get away for a while. Your dad was already looking after her whilst I sorted myself out. I'd never have left her otherwise. I thought I'd only be away for a couple of weeks, but it ended up being longer.'

'Why didn't you tell anyone where you were?' I ask. I feel the pressure on my hand tighten ever so slightly.

'I just needed some space to think things through. I wasn't allowed to see you and I ended up drinking far too much and being cautioned by the police after I crashed our car. I couldn't face speaking to your dad. I haven't even spoken to my mum. I left a message on her answerphone to let her know I was OK. She kept trying to call me, but I never answered and I turned my phone off.'

We continue to walk a short way down the gravel path towards the entrance to the car park, away from the other mourners. The cold air bites at my cheeks, but I concentrate on the warmth of my hand in his.

'I gave Dr Henderson your silver bracelet before I left,' he says. 'Did she give it to you?' I nod. 'And I wrote you some letters.'

'I know,' I say. 'I read them.'

He stops walking, turning to face me, taking my other hand in his. I don't normally like people touching me, but I've missed this. I wish I could shrink my whole body and curl up in his palm instead of standing on the tarmac with every part of me exposed.

'I'm so sorry, Ali. I should have realised you weren't well and done something more quickly. Asked for help. I thought you were trying to leave me and all I wanted to do was make you stay. I thought we could sort everything out on our own. I know what happened wasn't your fault . . .'

I cut across him. 'It was. It was my fault. I should have told you how I felt. What I thought I heard. But I was convinced I was protecting Tilly. I never meant to hurt her.'

'I know that. I know how much you wanted to be a mother.'

Tears which had been absent throughout the funeral service slide down my cheeks leaving me unable to speak.

'I contacted Em a couple of days ago, just to let her know where I was,' he says, 'and she told me about your dad. I had no idea she'd been looking after Tilly since he passed away or that you'd got so much better over the past few weeks. If I had, I'd have come straight back. I just needed some time away after the accident. I was a mess, Ali. I'm still a mess. I know I want us to be a family again, but I have to tell you something first. We need to start with a clean slate, and if I don't tell you now, I'll get too scared and I won't do it at all.' His hands shake beneath mine and I know what he's going to say before the words leave his mouth. He looks down at the ground. 'Before our last round of IVF,' he says, 'you know I took some money out of our savings and gave it to my dad. I only did it because he'd threatened to get back in contact with Mum and I didn't feel I had a choice. It meant we didn't have enough for the IVF and I didn't know how to explain that to you, so I lied. I told you I didn't get a bonus. I should have told you the truth, I'm so sorry.'

I stare at him and let go of one of his hands as I put my fingers over his lips. 'You don't have to do this, Jack.'

He can't meet my eyes. 'But I need to explain.'

I shake my head. 'I don't want to hear the details. It's in

the past. I just need to know you still love me and you want this to work.'

'I've always loved you, Ali,' he says, looking up at me. 'I've never stopped.'

I stare over his shoulder, aware of the figures in black that are moving towards us, their gaze fixed on us, and I shudder. It feels like they're judging me, walking in solemn pairs to pronounce their sentence. There's nothing they could say that would make me feel more guilty than I already do. Sarah follows them slowly down the path, stopping to talk to other guests to delay her arrival. I don't deserve Jack's forgiveness. Seeing him makes me realise I almost destroyed him as well as our daughter and I'm not sure how we can live with that. I don't want to leave, but I know I have to go back to the unit.

Jack puts his arm round my shoulder as he sees Sarah approach and pulls me towards him. 'I'm here for you. We'll be OK, Ali. You, me and Tilly. We'll work it out.' I put my arms round his waist and bury my head in his shoulder, desperate to believe what he's telling me is true.

AFTER

Alison

The house isn't large. If you measure the floor space, it's probably smaller than our old flat. But I love it. The floorboards creak, the front door doesn't shut properly when it rains, but from the moment I walked inside I knew I belonged here. Not the part of me that worries about paint colours and large bowls full of decorative rattan balls, but the real core of me. The one with all the flaws.

The move had been Jack's suggestion. Away from the town where what I'd done was embedded in the architecture itself, a constant reminder each time we drove over the bridge. He'd been the one to suggest the family name change too. He'd known without it we'd have to live in the shadow of what I did, and neither of us is strong enough yet to cope with that. People have accepted us as another new family in the village, and although we haven't deliberately lied about what had happened, we haven't chosen to reveal it either. One day maybe.

I look out of one of the small leaded windows to where Tilly's playing in the garden with Jack; kicking the leaves he's swept into a pile and trying to climb onto the plastic swing we'd bought second-hand a few months ago for her third birthday after it had been advertised in the local post office window. If you ignore the fact that there's a small bald patch by my ear which I try to cover with my short, bobbed, dark hair, we're a picture of domestic bliss. But I'm not asking for perfection; no family has that.

There had been a letter waiting for me with my dad's things when I'd got out of the unit, with the rest of my redirected post. It had been from Jack's father. I'd read the first couple of sentences and then thrown it away without looking at the rest. I didn't tell Jack. He's had enough to deal with and I don't want to give the man I've never met the opportunity to hurt his son any further.

The sound of crying comes through the speaker on the baby monitor. I walk upstairs and pick him up out of his Moses basket. Archie Edward Reid. Four weeks old today. He's an unexpected addition to our family. No IVF. No injections. Not planned at all. I hadn't even realised I was pregnant until I was over three months gone. Jack had been terrified. I'd seen it in his eyes when I'd finally told him. The pools of brown liquid reflecting the fear I tried to bury beneath my smile. I hadn't told him I'd spent the previous week considering whether to go ahead with the pregnancy at all. After the initial shock, we'd devised a battle plan. I'd read more articles than I thought possible and we'd armed ourselves with helpline numbers and spoken to Sarah who organised an on-call psychiatrist. And waited with a feeling of dread that grew in size each month along with the baby.

Archie had arrived in a calm, darkened room at four in the morning. I'd handed him straight to Jack and had refused to hold him until the psychiatrist came down to the ward to reassure me I was fine. I'd lain with him in my arms in bed and had listened for the voice. All I could hear had been other mothers with their babies. Feeding, crying, talking. I thought it had left me in peace.

For the first few days after he was born, I overanalysed every thought that came into my head. Was that me? The true me? Were the doubts that crept around in my mind part of being a mother or were they something more sinister? The first stirrings of an attempt to take control? I was conscious of having constant company. No one had taken their eyes off me for more than a few minutes. The midwife had insisted on helping me bathe him, studying my reactions when he'd cried. Jack had been allowed to stay past normal visiting hours; I'd discovered him huddled in the corridor with the psychiatrist on more than one occasion, stepping apart quickly when they saw me, pretending it was a casual chance encounter.

Hours turned into days and we'd come home. Most of the time there's silence in my head. Sometimes when he doesn't think I'm looking, I catch Jack watching me. Studying the way I hang out the washing. Listening to what I say to Archie and paying more attention to me than a husband normally gives to his wife. But if that's the price I must pay for what I did then I can live with it, it's nothing compared to my remorse.

I haven't told him I've heard the odd whisper when Archie and I are alone. There's nothing to tell. At the moment it's just a sense that someone's breathing quietly in my ear, watching me. Not speaking. Not yet. I haven't had the urge to fill a notebook, write on a wall, or anything so much worse.

Archie snuggles into my neck and I carry him downstairs and outside.

Jack looks up when he sees me coming. 'Is the monster awake?' he asks.

'I think so. We've probably got a ten-minute window before he starts screaming for food.'

Jack smiles. 'Em called. They're coming over next weekend.'

I nod. 'It'll be nice to see her. I know you get to see Harry every day at work, but I haven't seen Em for ages.' I blow a raspberry onto Archie's cheek. 'It was good of your mum to pop in today. She's brilliant with Archie.'

He pushes the swing higher. 'I've got my hands full with this one. She's going to the moon today, apparently.'

I look up as Tilly flies through the air, laughing, her head bent backwards and legs stretched out, small plaits trailing in her wake. There will always be moments when the balloon of guilt in my chest expands so much it squeezes all the air out of me and I have to fight to take a breath. But I've learned that these moments are temporary, that things will adjust to a normality I can live with. Tilly is still very much a Daddy's girl but, there are times now when she comes to me first for comfort rather than Jack, so it feels like we're beginning to build a bond. I know it will take time but I'm working on it.

I twist my hair out of Archie's grasp and he squirms.

'Photo, Daddy. I go so high now, I a big girl.'

I smile. Jack pulls out his phone.

'You're right, Tils, you're very grown up. I'll get one when you're right at the top.'

She squeals as she kicks her legs and Jack catches the moment as she rises up towards the sharp winter sun; a flying angel silhouetted against the brightness.

'One of us?' He advances towards me. I don't like my photo being taken anymore, but I let him put his arms around me and he holds the camera above us.

'Wait. Me too, Daddy, me too.'

Jack lifts Tilly out of the swing and carries her over.

'Smile,' he says.

I smile. Archie grimaces. I look at the screen. I think I hear something whisper in my head, but I look at Archie, then at Jack, and it's gone before I can work out what it said, leaving me wondering if I ever heard it at all.

Jack presses the button and we peer at the image of ourselves, frozen in time.

The five of us and the start of something new.

Acknowledgements

This book is dedicated to my daughters, Charlotte and Liberty, because being their mum is both the hardest and the best thing that I do. At the grand old ages of thirteen and eleven they have been my most ardent supporters since I started writing 'All In Her Head' and I'm so grateful for their unending confidence in my abilities, especially during the many times when I didn't have any myself.

So many people are needed to make a book successful.

Huge, huge thanks to my amazing agent, Sophie Lambert, who had faith in this novel from a very early draft, who gave me the best advice on how to make it a million times better and has encouraged me every step of the way.

A big thank you also to my editors Harriet Bourton and Francesca Pathak and the whole team at Orion. As a debut novelist I couldn't have asked to work with a nicer group of people who have all been so generous with their extensive expertise.

To 'the girls', Anna, Ceril, Els, Lynn and Nanna, who I have been friends with for over twenty years and know how much I wanted this. A massive thank you for being there through the best and worst times. Love you all lots. Big thanks also go to other close friends who have all cheered me on through the rejections to get to this point – Zoe, Claire, Charlotte, Kate and Nicole, whose support in so many different ways - from telling me I could do this, to helping with school lift shares, is very much appreciated. Also, to all my Twitter writing friends who have been a great source of encouragement through what can sometimes be lonely times - particularly @LauraPAuthor, @lisforlia and @stupidgirl45.

To Amanda Reynolds who mentored me and has now become a hugely valued friend and confidante. Winning her competition truly changed my life and I will be forever grateful to have had the opportunity to learn from her experience.

To all my family - particularly my parents, who instilled in me a passion for reading and a love of books from an early age. They were in Australia when I told them I had a book deal (and I'm not sure if they actually believed me) and I'd like to thank them for everything they have done for me, and continue to do.

To my grandmother, Lily, who sadly died before she knew about this novel, but the legacy she left me in her will enabled me to sign up for a course at Curtis Brown Creative which confirmed just how much I wanted to write this book (as well as how much I had to learn!). Thank you to Anna, Jack and Katie at CBC for all their help.

And finally, above all, to my husband, Martin. Who knows life is short and encouraged me to take a risk. Without his support I never would have followed my dreams and written this at all. I love you. Always.

Credits

Nikki Smith and Orion Fiction would like to thank everyone at Orion who worked on the publication of *All In Her Head* in the UK.

Editorial
Harriet Bourton
Francesca Pathak
Lucy Frederick

Copy editor
Jade Craddock

Proof reader
Linda Joyce

Audio
Paul Stark
Amber Bates

Production
Hannah Cox

Contracts
Anne Goddard
Paul Bulos
Jake Alderson

Design
Debbie Holmes
Joanna Ridley
Nick May

Editorial Management
Charlie Panayiotou
Jane Hughes
Alice Davis

Publicity
Francesca Pearce

Finance
Jasdip Nandra
Afeera Ahmed
Elizabeth Beaumont
Sue Baker

Operations
Jo Jacobs
Sharon Willis
Lisa Pryde
Lucy Brem

Marketing
Katie Moss
Jennifer Hope

Sales
Jennifer Wilson
Esther Waters
Victoria Laws
Rachael Hum
Ellie Kyrke-Smith
Frances Doyle
Georgina Cutler

Reading Group Questions

- What do you think of the book's title? How does it relate to the story?

- Who was the most sympathetic character, and why?

- The book switches around between past and present. How did you find this whilst reading? Did it enhance the story?

- Which scene has stuck with you the most? Or were there any sentences that particularly stood out for you?

- Did you guess that Alison wasn't in fact working in a library before that was specifically revealed? Did that spoil the story for you?

- The story is narrated by both a female and male protagonist. Why do you think the author decided to tell the story in this way?

- The book tackles emotional and psychological issues and themes and reveals important things about the characters at suspenseful moments. What makes a good plot twist? Did this book surprise you with the revelations it uncovered?

- The book explores the darkest corners of a mother's mind. In the UK, approximately 1 in 10 women suffer from post-natal depression after giving birth and 1 in 1,000 suffer from post-partum psychosis. Do you think mental health issues regarding motherhood are discussed enough in today's society?

You'll be gripped by the twists and turns of
Nikki Smith's new emotionally charged thriller

LOOK WHAT YOU MADE ME DO

Sisters Jo and Caroline have had a
difficult relationship growing up.

When their father dies, his will raises more
questions than answers.

It's clear he's been hiding something.

But Jo and Caroline have secrets too.

And theirs might turn out to be even more lethal . . .

**Because everyone knows that a
perfect family has the most to hide.**

*Coming in hardback and eBook in April 2021
– available to pre-order now!*

Read on for an exclusive sneak peek . . .

Prologue – July 2018

Paul notices it first. I'm too busy darting from one room to another trying to find her, anxiety expanding in my chest like a balloon, making it hard to breathe. She isn't in the kitchen or the lounge. Or behind the sofa in the snug, although with the various toys lying discarded on the floor and felt-tip pens and colouring books littering every surface, I have to look twice to double check. I run upstairs, two at a time, my heart pumping, and throw open her bedroom door. The room is empty. Dropping down on my hands and knees, I peer under her bed.

'Livvi?' My voice wavers and I clear my throat.

There's no answer and nothing to see on the cream carpet apart from a thin layer of dust, the grey fluff forming thick circles round the bottom of each wooden leg, as if attracted by a magnet. I stand up and wince, biting my lip as a burning pain shoots through my toe. I've stubbed it on the edge of her chest of drawers. Cursing, I hobble into Grace's room, pulling open her white painted wardrobe doors covered in half-torn Disney *Frozen* stickers that she's tried to peel off now she's outgrown them. The rows of clothes hang motionless, no pairs of small legs protruding underneath.

'Livvi? It's Mummy,' I shout into the silence, trying to ignore the throbbing in my foot. 'You need to come out if you're hiding. I promise I won't be cross.'

I listen intently, praying for the sound of a creaking floorboard, a muffled giggle, footsteps scuttling across the carpet. Nothing.

Our bedroom is at the other end of the hall where our duck-egg blue throw lies undisturbed on top of the duvet, in exactly the same position I'd left it this morning. There's no sign of any obvious tell-tale lumps that I pretend not to spot during one of our games of hide-and-seek. Oh God, where is she? Our wardrobe is locked. The bathroom's empty. I wince as I swallow the metallic taste where I've bitten the inside of my cheek, running back down the stairs to the kitchen.

'She's not upstairs. I've searched everywhere,' I say.

Paul glances over my shoulder whilst I'm speaking, staring out through the patio doors across our lawn. He's not listening to me. I grab his arm to get his attention, wondering if he can feel the same ice-cold fingers that are squeezing my lungs, the same weight that has sunk to the bottom of my stomach like an anchor, preventing me from moving.

'What are you looking at?' I ask, trying not to shout. 'We've already looked outside.'

I can't keep the edge of hysteria out of my voice as I pull on the sleeve of his shirt, urging him to do something, anything, to find her. He shakes my hand off roughly, pushing me aside as he twists the door handle and realises it's locked, his gaze still fixed on the bottom of the garden.

'What? What is it?' I screw up my eyes against the brightness and blink away the tears that blur my vision. 'She's not out there, Paul.' Two swings dangle limply beneath a metal frame and the trampoline is empty, the canvas mat stretched tight, waiting expectantly for the next jumper.

'Get out of the way,' he yells. I stagger backwards, shocked by his unexpected aggression. 'Are you blind, Jo?' He jabs his finger repeatedly towards the end of the garden as he struggles to get the key off its hook on the wall and into the lock. I can't see what he's pointing at. 'There!' he shouts. 'Look!' I can hear the panic in his voice as he fights to open the door.

At first all I can discern through the faint patterns of small handprints smeared on the pane of glass is his office at the end of the garden, the timber structure silhouetted against the evening sun. He finally manages to turn the key before I notice the faint haze around the bottom of the building that is spreading slowly across the grass. It drifts in swirls and the smell hits me the moment Paul flings open the patio door. Smoke.

'Have you searched in there?' He glances at me and I don't need to answer. He sprints across the lawn, screaming her name, as I sink down onto the tiled floor, unable to move as I watch the flames appear. Their red and orange tongues are initially hesitant, contemplating the taste, but once they realise it's a meal to be savoured, they rise up and devour the whole building in a matter of minutes.

***

Find out what happens next when
Look What You Made Me Do
publishes in hardback and eBook – pre-order now!